Rook

STEPHEN G. EOANNOU

For Nick and Elena, partners in crime.

Author's Note

On November 4, 2012, *The Buffalo News* ran the article "The strange, true story of a Buffalo bank robber-turned crime novelist" by Charity Vogel. It was a Sunday and I read the article standing in my kitchen. By the time I was finished, I knew I wanted to write about Al. I thought he was a fascinating combination of contradictions. Plus, he was a Buffalo guy. *Rook* grew that day from an idea to a novella, and then from a novella to three linked novellas, and finally to a novel. That evolution could not have taken place without the help of others.

I relied on newspaper articles, both local and national, for details of Al's life in the early 1960's. None of that would have been possible without the help of the very patient Grosvenor Room librarians at The Buffalo Central Library, who had to show me how to use the microfiche machine every damn time. In my defense, I *did* write your instructions down. I just forget to bring them with me.

"Gunshots In Another Room: The Forgotten Life of Dan J. Marlowe" by Charles Kelly further fleshed out my understanding of Al. It also introduced me to Marlowe and his own writing and I'm grateful for that as well.

Details about weapons, evidence, and leads were all culled from Al's FBI file obtained under the Freedom of Information Act.

Although this is based on a true story, it's a work of fiction, nonetheless. Timelines have been adjusted to fit the narrative structure and the characters –Al, Lolly, Bobby—are all how imagined them or wished them to be. Scenes, dialog, hopes, and dreams are all, of course, my own invention. This cast of characters has lived with me since that first day I read about them on that Sunday morning back in 2012. I'll miss spending time with them going forward, even Bobby.

I need to thank all my early readers, especially my Balcrank sisters: Carla Damron, Dartinia Hull, Beth Uznis Johnson, Holly Martyn, and Ashley Warlick. You are all better writers than I and I'm blessed to be in your lives. Thanks to Jim Walke for all his input and coming up with the title. You were right; mine was pretentious. And thanks to Andrew Gifford, who told me very late at night in a very dark bar to stop being a coward and write the damn book.

Finally, I'd like to thank the entire team at Unsolicited Press for giving *Rook* a good home and bringing Al and Lolly's story to life. For that I am grateful. A special thanks to my editor, Gage Greenspan. You made this a better book and I apologize *for constantly using italics incorrectly.*

—SGE

The human element, the human flaw and the human nobility—those are the reasons that chess matches are won or lost.

—Viktor Korchnoi, Chess Grandmaster

Chess is ruthless: you've got to be prepared to kill people.

—Nigel Short, Chess Grandmaster

Part 1:

Gambit

Crime…was always like a chess game for cash prizes.
—Al Nussbaum

Chapter 1

A gentle snow, the first that year, had begun to fall. Flakes landed on the windshield, each crystal distinct and plain to see, before the wipers cleared the glass. Snow accumulated on the bare trees that lined Kings Highway but melted as soon as it touched the sidewalk in front of the Lafayette National Bank. A police radio, one that Al had rigged to the station wagon's dash, crackled with the dispatcher's broken voice. The call was for a disturbance far from where he was parked, so he continued humming a nameless tune. His right hand rested on the .45 next to him.

The wind picked up and early morning holiday shoppers hunched to the snow. They pulled scarves tighter across throats and buried gloved hands deep in overcoat pockets. They hurried in and out of stores, and Al wondered if his wife, Lolly, was Christmas shopping back home. He could see her walking down Buffalo's Main Street, pushing Alison bundled in the pram as she went from store-to-store—L.L. Berger, Hengerer's, maybe stopping at Adam, Meldrum, and Anderson's to watch mechanical elves, twirling skaters, and waltzing Victorian couples in the front window. She loved those displays, and they had been going every Christmas since high school to look at them.

He was parked across from the bank in front of the GIP Luncheonette; a Salvation Army Santa stood bell ringing nearby. "Charity Drive 1961" was painted across his donation kettle, the words flanked by holly sprigs. His eyes and cheeks were red, and he stared at the fogged windows of Flo's Turf Club on the corner. Al was certain there was nothing Santa wanted more than to walk through that door, sit at the bar, and drink Four Roses until all the crumpled dollars in his kettle were gone. He wondered if Santa had noticed the station wagon.

A blue Oldsmobile pulled in front of the bank exactly at nine-thirty. Bobby got out of the driver's side, a tan raincoat slung over his arm. He pulled the brown slouch hat down on his forehead and glanced up and down the street but not at the station wagon. At the same time, Curry slipped from the passenger's side. His matching tan raincoat contrasted with his dark skin and red corduroy cap. He crossed in front of the Oldsmobile and slid behind the wheel. The fake mustache Al had applied that morning with theatrical glue looked real enough, at least from across the street. The stolen Olds crept to the corner and then turned left on Utica Avenue towards the side entrance of the bank as Al knew it would. Kings Highway became a chessboard, and he studied it, seeing three moves ahead and knowing where pieces would slide and when.

He knew other things, too.

He knew that Bobby, still standing in front of the bank in the falling snow and awaiting his signal, carried a Thompson submachine gun under his raincoat, had a live hand grenade in each pocket, and a two-way radio clipped to his belt. The wire to the earpiece ran under his sweater, out his collar, and was concealed by the scarf wound around his neck.

Al picked up the military-grade walkie-talkie from his lap and pressed the button. "Street clear. Green light."

Bobby slid on a pair of Ray-Bans, pulled his hat even lower to his brow, and then sauntered to the bank's main entrance. Curry, carrying an army duffle bag, made his way toward the Utica Avenue door. Al leaned back in his seat and continued humming.

Bobby strode into the bank. Al watched the street but was envisioning what was happening inside. He pictured Bobby letting the raincoat fall, revealing the Tommy gun, then pushing open the double-glass doors leading into the bank with his shoulder. He'd yell, "This is a hold up! I don't want no trouble, just the money," exactly as Al had made him practice. The sight of that machine gun would drain courage from anyone thinking about being a hero. Everything inside a person stops—their thinking, their ability to run or scream, their bravery—when that black barrel is pointed at them. They're left with a pounding heart and a pair of struggling lungs trying to find air. That's why Al had Bobby bring the Thompson.

Curry would glide through the Utica entrance then, not saying a word, a .22 in one hand and the duffle bag in the other. He'd jump the counter and hustle from teller-to-teller, cleaning out cash drawers. Bobby would cover whoever was in the bank with the machine gun, moving the muzzle from side-to-side, person-to-person, face-to-face. Al was counting on at least fifty grand, a nice early Christmas present for them all.

Then he heard it.

Four bursts, muffled by thick walls, closed doors, and the distance to his parked car, but he had heard four bursts nonetheless. Thompsons are loud. The reports bouncing off marble floors and high ceilings must have sounded like artillery rounds to those standing in line waiting to withdraw their Christmas Club money.

He hoped he'd heard wrong, that it was his imagination or a backfiring bus over on Utica, but the Salvation Santa had stopped bell ringing and his gaze had shifted from Flo's to the bank. He had heard it too.

Damn you, Bobby. You were just supposed to point the gun at them.

He cranked the window down and leaned out, straining to hear more gunshots. Snowflakes landed on his cheek, melting to cold tears. He didn't, thank God, hear the Thompson again. Maybe Bobby had fired rounds into the ceiling to scare people, the plaster dust drifting to the bank floor like powdery snow, but he didn't believe that. Bobby had changed over the last few months, empowered by the string of bank robberies they had pulled. He had become more unpredictable and difficult to control.

The bank's door opened and a man—not Curry or Bobby—ran out and sprinted up Kings Highway. How he got past Bobby mystified Al. Even with one good eye Bobby should have seen him. Maybe Bobby had some dark desire to have a shootout with the police, firing the Tommy gun from his hip like in an old Cagney movie. Maybe he thought it was romantic to go down in a hail of bullets and bleed out on the sidewalk, his blood turning the melting snow pink.

Top of the world, Ma.

I never should have given him the Thompson, Al thought.

"One got out," he said, into the walkie-talkie, his voice calm, professional. "Watch your time."

Santa started ringing his bell again. He must have thought the noise was a backfiring bus, or maybe he didn't care. Al upped the volume on the police scanner, looked down the street for more trouble, and worried that the escaped man would be a good citizen and report the crime.

And he did.

He could've run home and locked the door, happy to still be alive. All he had to do was hug his wife and keep his mouth shut. He could've been one of those guys you read about in the papers who step over bleeding women or drive past smoldering wrecks because they don't want to get involved, but he wasn't one of those guys.

A patrol officer was running toward the bank with his service revolver drawn. How that good citizen found a Brooklyn cop so fast also mystified Al. Pedestrians scampered out of his way, some ducking into stores when they saw the gun gripped in his hand. The bell ringing stopped again.

That good citizen, the one not afraid to get involved, must have told the officer that the robber inside the bank had a submachine gun and had already shot one, two, maybe four people. Any man in his right mind wouldn't charge into a situation like that. He'd do the smart thing and cover the door and wait for other cops to show. That would be Al's plan. He had always thought of the police as a city army. Why not wait for reinforcements? But this beat cop was running hard, arms and legs pumping, and yelling for people to take cover. Al knew he wouldn't wait for reinforcements.

"You got company," he said into the walkie-talkie. "A cop. Front door."

This time he expected to hear the Tommy gun blast when the cop entered the bank, and he did. A burst sent the officer flying backwards through the vestibule's double doors in an explosion of shattering glass. That's when Al could see six moves ahead like Mikhail Botvinnik, the Soviet chess champion he'd been reading about. Old J. Edgar Hoover, already trying to figure out who had pulled those other bank jobs up and down the East Coast, would make them his top priority. He'd resurrect Eliot Ness to identify them and then hunt them down if he could. The police radio crackled to life then—an All-Units call about the bank robbery, about shots fired. Patrol cars, one-by-one, responded that they were heading to The Lafayette National Bank, 4930 Kings Highway, Brooklyn, right across from where Al was parked.

He held the walkie-talkie to his mouth again. "Time to go. The cavalry is on its way."

He put the station wagon in gear and eased away from the curb toward the rendezvous spot he had picked out weeks ago. Sirens grew louder from all directions, but he didn't panic and drove under the speed limit with both hands on the wheel. Anyone who noticed would assume he was a cautious family man, which he was when he wasn't robbing banks. Bobby and Curry should've exited via the Utica door by now and should be running toward the Oldsmobile, the duffle bag bulging with cash in Curry's hand. A black-and-white police car whizzed by the station wagon toward the bank. The cruiser grew smaller in Al's rearview mirror.

He drove six more blocks before pulling up to the curb in front of a boarded-up collision shop. He got out of the car and affixed signs reading "N&W Services," his import/export company back in Buffalo, to the rear-side windows. He hoped they'd make the station wagon blend in even more, just another company car on the New York streets. The wind had died, and the snow flitted down in fat flakes; some clung to his eyelashes and sweater. He slid back behind the wheel and saw Curry walking around one corner of the abandoned garage gripping the army bag, the fake mustache gone. Bobby ambled around the other side. Both took their time to get to the station wagon, as they had rehearsed. Bobby stopped once to tie his shoe, laying his Thompson on the wet ground.

Curry crawled in the back and curled on the seat, pulling a blanket over him in case the police were already looking for two white suspects and a Negro traveling together. Bobby climbed in next to Al, who nosed the station wagon away from the curb towards Manhattan before Bobby had closed the door all the way.

"What the hell happened?" Al asked. "There wasn't supposed to be shooting."

Bobby swiveled his head, but his right eye, made of glass, never moved. It stared at Al off-center, like there was something dangling from his cheekbone that had caught his attention. Al looked away. The dead eye always unsettled him.

"The guard thought he was Wyatt Earp, a real gunslinger. He thought he could outdraw someone with a machine gun pointed at him. He tried pulling his gun from his holster with me aiming the Tommy right at him. Who the fuck does that?"

"A dead man," Curry said, from under the blanket.

Bobby lit a cigarette, the smoke making his good eye squint; his hand shook. "Damn right a dead man."

"The machine gun didn't scare him?"

"Christ, Al. Not everything goes according to your fucking plan. Maybe if you went inside the bank once in a while instead of hiding in your station wagon you'd know that."

A patrol car pulled in front of them and no one spoke. Al needed to be careful about what he said next. Bobby's body was alive with adrenalin and whatever imbalanced chemicals his system produced. He started to squirm and rub his arms, and Al imagined him peeling off his skin layer-by-layer, revealing whatever festered at his core. His dead eye pointed slightly east the whole time, but his other eye was moving back and forth. The first time Al had seen him grow fidgety and his good eye race was in Chillicothe, where Al was serving a sentence for gun-possession. Marella, a loudmouth Italian, had been giving Bobby a hard time about his eye ever since he had transferred into their cellblock. He called him Dead Eye and One Eye when he saw him. The last time he called him that the three of them were alone in the laundry. Bobby grew squirmy and jittery and his good eye started shooting back and forth. Al remembered how the pressure in the room had changed. The weight of the air had pushed down on his head and shoulders, compressing his spine. If a barometer had hung on the wall, the mercury would have shot through the top, gushing red like a severed artery. Then Bobby had the loudmouth on the ground. He sat on his chest. One hand held him by the jaw to keep his head still. He squeezed Marella's cheeks until his mouth formed a painful opening. The other hand dug at his left eyeball with a bent spoon that he had sharpened to a spade. Bobby worked at the muscles and optic nerve that held the eye in place like he was shucking an oyster. Marella screamed and tried to buck Bobby off, but Bobby was determined. That left eyeball—*oculus sinister*—was dangling by the time Al dragged Bobby away and pushed him out the door.

The air in the station wagon felt heavy like it had in the laundry room, so Al drove with his mouth shut. He wanted to keep his eyes.

"Get away from that cop car," Bobby said.

Al ignored him.

"Lose him," he said, louder.

"We're perfect right here," Al said. "We're safe. He's not looking behind him. We'll follow him right out of Brooklyn, and he won't even know it. He's our very own police escort. Play it cool."

Bobby took a deep drag, ashing the cigarette, and calmed a bit. He sank farther into the seat.

"What about the cop? The one that ran into the bank," Al asked. "He's dead too?"

"He was still moving last I seen," Bobby said, never taking his good eye off the police car. "I think I shot him in the badge."

"Really?"

"I wasn't aiming. The badge got in the way. Another slug hit him in the leg. The other bullets missed him, I think. His lucky day."

Something inside Al dropped a bit. He had hoped that Bobby had shot the badge on purpose, but he should have known better. The season of miracles only lives in Christmas carols and department store windows. He didn't say any of this to Bobby. Instead, he said, "Lucky bastard," and Bobby grunted in agreement. Al didn't ask him what it felt like to shoot a man.

They drove another mile and then the police cruiser they'd been following peeled away with the flash and wail of lights and siren. Even though it was racing from them, the sight and sound of the police car in pursuit made Al's stomach drop even further. Sometimes he heard that sound and saw those revolving lights in his dreams. He kept heading towards the Brooklyn Bridge, though, driving the speed limit and monitoring the police radio. They had already found the abandoned Oldsmobile.

"Killing that guard, shooting the cop, changes everything," Al said, following signs towards the bridge and keeping any challenge out of his voice. He stated it as a fact, no different than if he'd said it was snowing harder or that the roads were growing slick.

"What do you mean?" Curry asked, still hiding under the blanket.

"They'll be coming for us," he answered. "The cops, the Feds, everyone. We'll be running soon."

"Christ, Al, this was our fifth job. They were going to come after us anyway, sooner or later," Bobby said, folding his arms across his chest and rocking back and forth. "Let 'em come."

"A man died, maybe two. If they catch us, we could get the electric chair," Al said, already seeing how this would end.

Nobody said anything to that, not even Bobby.

Chapter 2

Lolly would have decorated the apartment for Christmas right after Halloween if Al had let her. Throughout the year, she would buy decorations and ornaments at church bazaars and rummage sales—Father Christmases with wizened faces, porcelain reindeer with raised forelegs, singing angels, their mouths perfect ovals in heavenly song. She wrapped them in tissue, then newspaper to protect them from chipping, and stored them in sturdy cartons in the attic, the contents of each box written on the outside flap in black marker. She had already collected more decorations than she could display in their second-story flat, something Al would often point out when she brought home another nativity set or length of garland. She would smile and kiss him to silence, keeping it secret that she was stockpiling the ornaments for when they owned their own home and had many more rooms and doorways and windows to decorate.

She had decided to have their entire apartment, including the Christmas tree, decorated before Al returned from his business trip that night to surprise him. She had spent the morning carrying down ornament boxes and going through them, deciding which decorations she would use this season and which she'd re-wrap for another year, and wondering if this would be the last Christmas they'd spend living above her parents.

It was possible.

Al had been working so hard and traveling so much these last six months. Surely, they'd have enough for a down payment on a house soon. Sitting amongst the opened decoration boxes on the living room floor, she stopped unwrapping a wooden magus, Melchior, the one who had brought gold to the Christ child, and tried to imagine their own home. This was not the first time she had played this game. Lying in bed alone, waiting for Al to return from a trip or Alison to wake for her bottle, her mind would drift to different Buffalo neighborhoods—Parkside by the zoo, sprawling North Buffalo, the Delaware District with its mansions and mini-mansions—and she'd try to picture where they would live and raise a growing family. Sometimes when they were driving in the station wagon and Al was explaining something about chess or electronics, she'd turn toward the passing houses, his voice a drone, and hope to spot that perfect house that would make him pull to the curb so they could walk through their future together.

She was partial to multi-colored Victorians—rose clapboards, green details in the portico, tan sashes and railings. Rising turrets intrigued her; she had never been in a round room and wanted to close her eyes and walk around one, her fingertips never leaving the wall. Victorians meant Richmond Avenue, Linwood, West Ferry. She looked down at the partially unwrapped Melchior; they would need his gold to afford a place on those streets. She wondered how much Al had saved. When she had asked, he had always answered, "Not enough, but we're getting there." She was determined to sit down with him and finally go over their finances and see how close they really were to moving out of her parents' duplex.

She finished unwrapping Melchior and set him on the coffee table next to Caspar and Balthazar and the framed picture of Lolly and Al on their wedding day. It was not their formal wedding portrait but rather a small black and white photo with scalloped edges that her father, Stan, had taken. Lolly is seated next to Al and smiling, her wedding dress billowing around her. Al is grinning at the lens, looking boyish and innocent, wearing the traditional Polish groom's hat that was placed on his head as part of the *oczepiny* ceremony in the hope that the marriage will be full of happiness and laughter. Behind them her mother Sylvie, unaware or ignoring the camera, frowns and fusses with the back of her gown. Lolly thought how nice the photograph would look on a mantle someday.

There was one house she always drove by when she had the station wagon. It was in the Delaware District on Lafayette Avenue but was not as ornate as a Queen Anne. There was something about the house, though, its solidness or warmth, that drew her to it. While the Richmond Avenue Victorians were beautiful and lavish, the mauve house on Lafayette seemed more obtainable even though she had no idea how much a home like that would cost. It was built later than the Victorians, 1915 or so, she guessed. She would park across the street and could imagine Alison playing on the wide front porch behind the balustrades, Al cutting the lush lawn in his Ray-Bans, and herself standing on the long driveway, a baby—a boy?—in her arms, taking in the entire summer scene.

The cigarette smell announced her mother before Lolly heard heels clicking up the backstairs to her apartment. Her stomach clenched as if slender, invisible fingers had wrapped around it and squeezed. She didn't want to fight with her mother on the day she was decorating for Christmas, the day Al was coming home, a day that held such promise. She wouldn't let her mother bait her into an argument, she thought as she rose and crossed the small living room to the kitchen and her mother arrived at the top of the stairs cradling the baby.

"Princess Alison needs a nap," Sylvie said, her voice raspy and dry, the Pall Mall bobbing between her lips when she spoke. Some ash fell onto her sweater, and she shifted the baby to one arm to brush it away.

Sylvie was tall and filled the doorway. She'd been called statuesque for as long as Lolly could remember and stood taller than Al when she wore heels. She had kept her figure over the years. Good genes, she always said, but Sylvie was one of those women who lit a cigarette instead of picking up a fork. Small lines creased her cheeks and fissured from the corners of her mouth. Without makeup, her skin looked gray and contrasted with her dyed copper hair, a color that reminded Al of stripped detonation wire.

"I'll take her," Lolly said with outstretched arms. Alison, nearly asleep, rubbed her eye with a scrunched fist.

Sylvie passed the baby and looked over her shoulder to the living room. "Did you carry all those boxes down from the attic yourself?"

"Yes, mother. I'm not pregnant anymore."

She strolled towards the baby's room holding Alison on her shoulder, humming a lullaby in her ear as she rubbed small circles on her back. Sylvie followed. The apartment was quiet except for her humming and Alison was asleep before they reached her crib. Lolly laid her down and covered her with a pink blanket with dancing white elephants that had been hers when she was a child. The two women stood next to each other, almost touching, and watched the baby sleep. Sylvie blew cigarette smoke away from the crib.

"You shouldn't smoke in here," she whispered, and motioned her mother to follow her.

"And you shouldn't be carrying heavy boxes from the attic."

She left the door ajar in case Alison cried or whimpered in her sleep. With luck, she would nap for an hour, maybe longer. Al always told her that a lot could be accomplished in an hour, that fortunes can sometimes be made in less than sixty minutes.

"The boxes are filled with ornaments and decorations, Mother. Tinsel, for God's sake. They're not heavy at all. Do you want coffee? There's some left."

The two women went into the kitchen. Sylvie sat at the table and pulled a glass ashtray from Atlantic City towards her, a souvenir from one of Al's recent business trips. Lolly poured coffee into a cup decorated with hand-painted poinsettia leaves, placed it on a matching saucer, and then took the few steps to the kitchen table. A gingerbread house cookie jar with windows painted a soft yellow to suggest warm light, perhaps from candles or a fireplace, was set in the middle of the table. Tomorrow Lolly would start baking and fill the jar with Al's favorites—sprinkled press cookies, anise rounds, and Polish *pierniczki* shaped into hearts.

"You're not having any?" Sylvie asked, as Lolly set the cup and saucer in front of her.

She shook her head and sat in Al's chair opposite her. "I want to see if Dad will take me to get a Christmas tree."

Sylvie raised the cup to her thin lips, blew the steam away, and looked at her daughter over the rim. "Your husband should take you to get a tree, like he should've lugged all those boxes down."

"I want to surprise him, Mother. I want the whole place to be decorated when he comes home tonight."

Sylvie took a sip of coffee and then set it down on the saucer, a smudge of lipstick pink on the rim. "Are you sure he's coming home tonight?"

Lolly blinked several times before answering. "Why wouldn't he?"

Sylvie raised and lowered a single shoulder and then reached for her cigarette. "Don't be naïve. You know why men don't come home to their wives and babies."

"He's on a business trip, Mother. He's with Bobby, for god sakes. Not another woman."

"Bobby," Sylvie snorted, and smoke escaped her mouth. "That's reassuring."

Lolly looked at her hands. They sparkled silver from one of the old ornaments she had handled, the glitter having fallen off with each touch. She tried to keep calm, reminding herself not to argue. "Bobby is all right."

"All right? There's nothing about that boy that's all right, especially what he's doing with Al."

"And what's he doing with Al, Mother? What exactly are they doing?"

"I don't know *exactly*. What I do know is that neither of them are any good, and when you put them together they're worse, like chemicals that shouldn't mix."

Lolly leaned across the table. "Well, I know *exactly* what they're doing. They're on a buying trip in New York for their company and Al *will* be home tonight."

"He's buying so close to Christmas? Honey, this is the time of year he should be *selling*. This is when companies make money, not spend it."

"He's buying next year's models," Lolly said, her voice wavering at the end.

"Sure, he is," Sylvie said, and took another drag off the Pall Mall, her coffee forgotten and cooling. "All I know is that one of these days he'll go on a business trip and he won't come back."

"Don't say that, Mother," she said. "Please don't say that."

"It's true. I know it in my bones. I don't know if he's going to end up dead or back in prison or disappear, but I know one of these days he won't be coming home."

"Why do you hate him? He's only been good to me and Alison. You've never given him a chance."

"I knew he was trouble the first time he knocked on the door downstairs to take you to that East High dance. Maybe if he went to jail when he stole that car in high school it would've straightened him out. I don't know how his father got him out of that one, God rest his soul."

"Are you still bringing that up? He stole that car ten years ago when he was a teenager. It was a prank. A dare. He took it for a joyride, that's all."

"Then what about the trouble he got into for selling guns? Was that a prank too? He went to prison for that, didn't he? That's what killed his parents. Broken hearts not heart attacks."

"He *did* go to jail and *that's* what straightened him out. Look what a good father he is. Look how well his company is doing."

"Is that where he's getting all his money? From his company?"

"Where else would he get it from, Mother?"

Sylvie stubbed out the Pall Mall in the Atlantic City ashtray with quick jabs and studied her daughter, squinting through the lingering cigarette haze. Her eyes were hard, black stones. "How," she asked, "did I raise such a stupid daughter?"

Lolly pushed herself up from the table. "You're ridiculous. I can't even talk to you anymore. Is Dad home?"

"Of course, he's home," Sylvie said, picking up her coffee cup. "Good men are always home with their families."

*****

Lolly hurried down the front steps to Stan's idling Chrysler. It had been snowing for over an hour and the grass was covered white. The season's first snow rallied her Christmas spirit after her mother's visit, and she tried to put their argument behind her. Warm air seeped from the car as she opened the door.

"Hurry," Stan said, an unlit pipe between his teeth, "before you let out the heat."

She slammed the door closed and leaned over to kiss her father's cheek before settling into the Chrysler.

Sylvie always complained that Stan kept his car too hot and would yell at him to turn down the heater, that it was making everyone sick, but Lolly had liked his cozy cars since she was a little girl. It had always been so easy to drowse off, even on short rides to her grandmother's house or home from church; the tires murmuring on the road and Sinatra or Perry Como crooning on the radio were vague sounds that sometimes worked their way into her dreams.

"Isn't it too early to buy a tree?" he asked, as he backed the car out of the driveway onto Bailey Avenue. "It might lose all its needles before Christmas."

"It will be fine, Dad. I want to surprise Al."

"He'll be surprised when he wakes up Christmas morning to a bare tree."

She closed her eyes and breathed in the air that smelled of Stan's cherry tobacco. She felt like a child again: safe and snug, not caring where they were going or when they'd arrive. Sylvie's accusations about Al running guns or stealing cars or doing *something* seemed like a long-ago, imagined conversation.

"What's wrong?" Stan asked.

Her eyes opened. "Nothing. I was resting. Carrying all those boxes tired me more than I thought."

"That's not it. Something's wrong. I can see those two little lines between your eyebrows. They come out when you're upset."

She rubbed her forehead with fingertips, searching for small wrinkles and creases. "Everything is fine."

He looked at his daughter before turning his eyes back to the road. He gripped the wheel in the ten and two o'clock position and checked his mirrors often. "Those lines were showing when you came down to my apartment and asked for a ride. Were you and your mother fighting again?"

She looked out the window. Bailey Avenue was lined with shops and storefronts; there were no passing Victorians or Colonials or Tudors for making wishes or daydreams. "Fighting? Not really."

"That means yes," he said, and took the dead pipe from his mouth and set it in the ashtray. "What about? Al?"

"What else?"

"Your mother wants the best for you. You know that."

"Al's the best for me."

He braked for a red light, leaving plenty of room between the Chrysler and the bumper ahead of him. He had always been one of those men who looked older than his years. A lifetime of hard work and disappointment had prematurely aged him. His hair had grayed in high school and his shoulders were rounded, worn down by the heavy lifting he had done in damp warehouses throughout the city. Al said Stan's shoulders hunched because Sylvie was always on his back.

"I like Al. You know that, honey," he said. "I tell everybody that he's always the smartest guy in the room. It doesn't matter what room or who's in it. Al is at least a step, maybe two, ahead of the rest of us."

She reached out and rubbed his shoulder through his winter coat. "I think that too, Daddy."

The light changed and the car ahead of him didn't move. Stan tapped the horn. "Al can be a success at whatever he sets his mind to. Chess, electronics, you name it. Your mom's worried that he's setting his mind to the wrong things with that Bobby character."

Lolly felt those slender fingers grasp her stomach again; she thought she'd left them behind with her mother. "Oh, not you too, Dad. Not today," she said, and knew she and Al had to move out soon. They would buy a small starter home in North Buffalo, and she would keep dreaming of that mauve house on Lafayette Avenue. Or they could move into another apartment far from her parents' accusations. It would take them longer to save for a dream house, but Lolly was becoming more convinced it would be worth it. She knew Al couldn't wait to get away from Sylvie.

The car in front of them finally drove off, and Stan barely pressed the accelerator, reluctant to move forward. He cleared his throat. "I ran into my friend Haggerty yesterday. You remember him, don't you? The cop I went to high school with? The big Irishman?"

She nodded, thinking that her mother had been right about one thing: the Chrysler was too hot. She unbuttoned her coat.

"I told him about Al and Bobby…"

"Why would you *do* that?"

"Listen, will you? He asked about you and Al and the baby in a friendly way, the same way I had asked about his wife and son. I told him you were all fine and that Al and his partner Bobby were doing great in their electronics business. And then Haggerty asked me something funny."

"What?" she asked, holding her stomach, trying to loosen that invisible grip.

"He asked if Bobby was an ex-con like Al."

"Why would he ask such a thing?"

"Haggerty saw them the other day. They were in that restaurant on Genesee Street. The Greek's place. They were huddled in a booth together and Al was doing all the talking. Haggerty said Bobby was listening and nodding, but he could tell right away that Bobby had served time. He had that jumpy, nervous look to him."

"It's his glass eye. It makes him look different," Lolly mumbled, but she knew what Haggerty had meant. She had seen Bobby when his head would move from side-to-side and his good eye would scan the room, reminding her of a dog who had been beaten too much.

"Maybe it was his eye," Stan said.

He turned into the Clinton-Bailey Farmer's Market and nosed the Chrysler into a parking space. He frowned, backed the car out and then pulled in straighter.

"Wait. What did you say when your friend asked if Bobby had been in prison?" she asked.

Stan switched off the engine. "I said I didn't know, that I didn't think so. I've known Haggerty a long time, honey, but I've lived long enough to know that you don't tell cops any more than you have to."

"It's good you didn't say anything," she said, but didn't know why it was good. A voice, maybe the voice that belonged to those invisible fingers, was telling her that they didn't need the police looking into Al's business, even if he wasn't doing anything wrong.

"Here's the thing, honey," Stan said, reaching for his pipe. He pulled out a match, lit it, then touched the flame to the bowl and puffed the cherry tobacco to life. He waved the match and dropped it in the ashtray. "Haggerty knows that Al had been in prison in Ohio. Hell, everyone in the neighborhood knows that. It's no secret. But Haggerty said if Bobby was an ex-con, too, Al may be violating his parole by associating with a known felon. He could go back to jail for something like that, Lolly. Was Bobby in prison?"

She nodded. The heat in the car oppressive.

"For what?"

"I don't know. Something about a car."

"Jesus, Lolly. Grand theft?"

She didn't answer. She was sweating and her stomach ached. She pushed open the door, stepped into the cold and falling snow, and ran into rows of Virginia pines, Blue spruces, and Douglas firs. She wished she were disappearing into a real forest, far from Buffalo, and not into aisles of cut trees impaled on spikes, the sap oozing from fresh wounds.

Chapter 3

Al dropped Curry off and watched him blend into the crowd. He hoped he stayed blended, another passing face on the subway or sidewalk that the police wouldn't notice. New York City, Curry's hometown, was a good place to hide, but Al and Bobby would continue to Buffalo to count and split the money before going their separate ways. Bobby would head downstate with his girlfriend, Jackie Rose, give Curry his cut, and then go on to Atlantic City. Al would stay home, resuming his quiet life as husband, father, and businessman for as long as he could. He knew he'd be running soon; the shootings had guaranteed that. He hoped he could at least spend Christmas with Lolly and the baby before he had to disappear.

He was fighting midtown traffic when Bobby fell into a talking jag. This wasn't new, but the jags were coming more frequently and lasted longer. Sometimes it seemed every thought that swirled in his brain had to be blurted. Al wondered what prompted that tidal of words. Bobby's brain would start firing or misfiring and the words would come in a torrent. As they sat in traffic, Bobby talked about cars.

"The new Impala, the '62. That's a hell of a car. A good car for me, you know? One the cops won't notice, but not a goddamn old lady car like this piece of shit. I'm thinking Super Sport, the SS. Convertible, man. Two-door. Blood red. Fire red. Candy apple, baby. Can you see me driving that? I can. Top down, wind blowing through Jackie Rose's blond hair. Damn, I'm getting hard picturing it. And under the hood? All business, brother. Eight cylinders. Turbo fired V8. A pair of Carter four-barrels. 409 horsepower! *409!* Bye, bye, Mr. Policeman. Those are my taillights you're looking at. You won't put me in no goddam electric chair because you can't catch me."

Did he really think no one would notice a good-looking blonde hanging out of a cherry red convertible? That was his idea of blending in? Before Al could point out that particular weakness in his automotive plan, Bobby sucked in a short breath, and as quickly as shifting from first to second gear he switched from babbling about engine torque and compression ratios to their old argument.

"You got to grow a pair, Al. Hiding in your granny car while me and Curry do all the work is bullshit. *We're* taking all the risks. *We're* the ones getting shot at. What kind of man are you? What kind of bank robber doesn't go *inside* the fucking bank? This ain't no game. This ain't playing cops and robbers in the backyard. You planned it? Bullshit. Eyes on the street? Bullshit. Watching for cops? Bullshit. You getting the same cut as me and Curry? Bullshit. Bullshit. Bullshit."

Al gripped the wheel tighter. When they had started working jobs together, Bobby never talked to him this way. A single glance would have stopped him in mid-sentence, and he'd lower his good eye, unable to look at him. But Bobby had grown more unstable and argumentative over the last month and rants against Al were coming almost daily now.

"An even cut ain't right. You know it. I know it. Curry knows it. Why do you even bring a gun to the robbery? In case you get a parking ticket? You going to shoot a meter maid? A jay walker? A crossing guard? Guns are dangerous, Al. Better be careful. You might shoot yourself in the leg. In the foot. Could shoot your toe clean off while me and Curry do all the work. It happens. All the time. Every day. Bam! There goes a toe."

There was no arguing with Bobby when he babbled. Al ground his teeth until his jaw ached, wondering how long it would be until Bobby's mind snapped or until he had to cut him loose and get another partner, one he could control like he had once controlled him. He kept his mouth shut and waited for another topic to ooze from Bobby's brain. It didn't take long for him to switch from second to third gear. This time he had it in for Roger Maris.

"Who the *fuck* is Roger Maris? Who is he? Some kid? Some nobody? He thinks he's better than Babe Ruth? Thinks he's better than Mickey Mantle? Nobody is better than Mickey Mantle. Sixty-one home runs? A fluke. A goddamn fluke. Never again will he hit that many. He won't even get close. Fifteen, maybe. Twenty tops. Christ, he'll be lucky if he makes the team next year. He'll be back in the minors playing in Bumblefuck, Iowa. He'll be out of baseball in eighteen months. End up as some goddamn waiter or bartender lighting my cigar and calling me Mr. Wilcoxson. Roger Maris? *Fuck* Roger Maris."

Al didn't know what he had against Roger Maris.

There were other rants, other gears shifted: JFK ("The fucking Pope's boy."); Jackie Rose ("A good girl. Such a good, good girl."); and the FBI ("They'll never take us alive, Al.").

His words washed over Al, who held the steering wheel like he was holding the side of a raft. He wanted to hang on and not let the waves take him under. He was a patient man and knew what always followed this flood of punctuation-defying sentences. Bobby's words slowed, then slurred and then, thankfully, stopped. His head dropped, his chin touched his chest, and he began to snore. Only then did Al relax his grip, allowing the blood to flow back into his whitened knuckles.

It was quiet enough to think.

*****

Traffic had thinned once they'd left the city. Skyscrapers and concrete were replaced by barren farm fields and low-hanging sky that seemed to meet in the horizon, giving Al the impression that he was enclosed in a world devoid of color. He drove towards home, towards Lolly. Her face rose before him on the other side of the windshield. Blue eyes flecked with gray points brightened and danced the way they did when she saw him walking through the door or when she looked at their Alison. He had always known that one day he might be forced to look in those blue-gray eyes and tell her about the banks and how he had to disappear for a while. Soon he would be forced to have the conversation he had rehearsed but dreaded speaking every memorized syllable to her.

He pushed away her image, unable to reimagine that conversation or the pain that would seep into those eyes, pain that he would cause. Instead, he needed to think about what needed to be done. Suitcases would have to be packed, one filled with clothes and one filled with books and guns. He'd keep them in the back of the station wagon, so he'd be ready when the time came. He glanced in the rearview mirror and saw Curry's blanket covering the duffle bag on the back seat. His cut of the money wouldn't be going into his import/export business or used to buy and resell weapons, or for a house as he had planned. He'd need cash for the road and money to leave behind for Lolly and the baby. He'd have to keep the gas tank filled in the station wagon.

A horn blared.

The station wagon, like his thoughts, had drifted and he was straddling the broken white line that separated the two northbound lanes. He jerked the wheel and a two-toned green Bonneville with Michigan plates passed him, the driver waving his middle finger as he sped by. Al had enough firepower with him to blow the driver and his fancy Pontiac all the way back to Detroit if he'd wanted to, but he waved and mouthed "Merry Christmas." *He's lucky Bobby isn't driving*, he thought.

It struck him then that he'd been straddling more than traffic lanes. For eighteen months, since Lolly and he had married, he had been living in two worlds: one at home with her and the baby and one on the road robbing banks with Bobby. He had always known that he couldn't go on living in those two worlds forever, that someday it would all end. His plan was never to go on until he was killed or captured or forced to run. He wanted to get enough money hidden away so he wouldn't have to worry about paying bills and enough to get his business of importing radio equipment, binoculars, and walkie-talkies off the ground and prospering. He wanted to buy a nice house in a good neighborhood and move out of the apartment above his in-laws. Then he'd walk away from Bobby and Curry and this life, but he knew that he would miss it. He liked planning the jobs, fooling the cops, getting away with it all. He liked the free money. But Bobby had been right about one thing.

Not everything goes according to his fucking plan.

*****

"I'm hungry," Bobby said, startling Al.

Bobby had that prison habit of waking immediately—no grogginess, no wondering where you are, no being caught in that filmy world where your mind and muscles hesitate, a hesitation that could lose you an eye. Bobby woke like they were still in Chillicothe.

"I'm hungry," he said again.

"Okay." Al realized he was hungry too.

They were halfway home but still had Lake Ontario and Lake Erie ahead of them. The lakes weren't frozen yet and cold winds blowing across warmer water could suck up moisture, freeze it, then drop heavy snow bands without warning; the skies in the distance were already darkening, the snow falling harder. *That's all I need is to be trapped on the highway with a psychopath and a bag of stolen money during a blizzard*, Al thought. That scenario reminded him of the magazines he liked to read: *Black Mask, Ellery Queen, Front Page Detective.* All those stories had a twist at the end, one you didn't see coming, at least the good ones did. He hated guessing the ending partway through the plot. When that happened, he'd never read anything by that author again. *If you got one damn job to do, do it right*, he thought.

"There's a town up here," Bobby said. "Next exit."

Al pulled off into a town that probably would have died ten years ago if New York State hadn't put a highway on its doorstep. Their eating choices were slim, but Al knew when Bobby said he was hungry, he meant that he was thirsty too, so he parked in front of a little bar and grille on the corner. The faded blue awning over the door sagged with snow like the whole thing was about to collapse. Written on the awning in old English type was the bar's name—Founding Fathers'. The place smelled damp, but it was comfortable enough with an ancient potbelly stove burning in the corner. A middle-aged couple sat at a table eating their sandwiches and not talking to each other. The man must've been an athlete once—a football player or wrestler. His neck was still thick and his shoulders wide, but everything else had drooped: his cheeks, his chin, his belly. The wife had aged better and wore her hair short and styled like the new first lady; Bobby grinned at her until she looked away.

They sat at the end of the bar closest to the front window so Al could keep an eye on the station wagon and the money blanketed on the back seat. There wasn't a bartender or waitress in sight.

"What the hell kind of place is this?" Bobby asked. "I feel like I'm back in fucking school."

Hung on the walls were different sized presidential portraits and posters of Washington, Jefferson, and Lincoln. There were others too: Teddy Roosevelt wearing his round Windsor eyeglasses; a few of President Grant, his thin lips pressed together and unsmiling; several of FDR with a cigarette holder tight between his teeth. Some Al didn't recognize. Chester Arthur? James Polk? Who the hell knows what Rutherford B. Hayes looked like? Al spotted a small painting of Grover Cleveland, an adopted Buffalonian in one corner, but not any of Millard Fillmore, a true Buffalonian, but probably the most forgettable president ever to hold office. Evidently Founding Fathers' had forgotten him, too, because there wasn't a picture of him hanging anywhere.

"I guess the owner likes presidents," Al answered. Through the window, the station wagon slowly whitened as the snow continued to fall. No one came near it.

"This place gives me the fucking creeps. All those dead guys staring at me. I'd like to spray them all with the Tommy gun. And where the hell's the bartender? I'm going to jump the bar and serve myself in a minute."

Al ignored Bobby and took in the place. Mixed in with presidential portraits were campaign posters and buttons— "Back Ike For Peace, Progress and Posterity," "This Home For Hoover," "My Guy Is Adlai." Hung from the ceiling were faded U.S. flags of all different sizes and varying amounts of stars. Some of the flags were frayed and torn, possibly survivors of long-ago battles but more likely they had hung in the rafters for so long the pub's dampness had rotted the cloth. "Don't Tread on Me" hung in the middle; Al liked that one the best. Behind the bar, propped among bourbon and scotch bottles, stood a small chalkboard with the handwritten menu—the soup of the day, sandwiches, the Blue Plate Special, and the message "Trivia Tuesday" at the bottom.

The door from the kitchen swung open and a flush-faced Irishman came out wearing an apron tied around his wide waist with his name—Fat Mike—embroidered across the front. A red bowtie choked his jowly neck and a straw skimmer with a red, white, and blue ribbon encircling the crown was perched back on his head. His nose was mapped with broken blood vessels. He reminded Al of everyone's annoying uncle, the one who pulled quarters from your ear. Bobby stiffened on the stool next to him. He didn't like his looks either.

"Gentlemen, forgive me. I didn't know you were here. What can I get you?"

"Boilermaker and a fried bologna sandwich," Bobby said, his voice low and mean like he wanted to reach across the bar and choke him with his bowtie.

Fat Mike wasn't stupid. He made a living at sizing up people, reading faces, knowing when they had too much or not enough. Al was sure Fat Mike could feel the hate rolling from Bobby in waves. He jerked his attention to Al, setting his fleshy cheeks and jowls in motion. Or maybe that dead eye had unsettled him, and he had to look away as fast as he could.

"And you?" he asked Al.

"Two cheeseburgers and a Coca-Cola."

Fat Mike nodded and started pouring the draft. Bobby stared at him. The bartender snuck quick looks at him then would drop his gaze. He licked his thick lips and swallowed hard. His bowtie bobbed. Al could tell Bobby's stare was affecting him. He over-poured the beer and foam ran down the mug's side. Bobby sat back on the stool, pleased with himself. He had always thought his glass eye held magical power and could make people squirm when it bore down on them. He was certain it gave him an edge, a super strength, like the heroes in his comic books. The few times Al and Bobby had played chess in prison, Bobby hardly studied the board; he kept staring at Al, trying to make him nervous with that lifeless socket so he'd make a regrettable move. He could've stared at Al until Christ came off the cross and it wouldn't have mattered. Al was certain he could beat Bobby even if he'd had his own eyes spooned from his head and left dangling.

"What's 'Trivia Tuesday?'" Al asked, as Fat Mike placed the drinks in front of them. Bobby grunted next to him.

Mike wiped his pudgy hands on the front of his apron like he couldn't get them dry enough. He wouldn't look at Bobby at all. "It's a little game I play with my customers. I ask them questions about the presidents, and they try to guess the right answers. There are no prizes or anything. It's for fun or a free beer or two. My regulars enjoy it."

"Ask me one," Al said.

"It ain't Tuesday," Bobby said, his voice loud enough that the middle-aged couple glanced over. "It's Friday."

Mike took a step back from the bar, getting out of Bobby's lunging range. His face paled, making those spidery red lines on his nose more pronounced. "I don't mind."

"*I* mind," Bobby said.

"It's okay. Go ahead," Al said. "Ask away."

Fat Mike glanced at Bobby then back at Al. "All right," he said, wiping his hands on his apron again. "This one stumped everyone last week: Who was the only U.S. President to earn a Ph.D.? Not an honorary one, mind you. One he went to school for."

Al sipped his Coke. His customers must be slow. *Woodrow Wilson*, he thought. "That's a tough one, mister. I don't know. One of the Roosevelts maybe?"

Mike's eyes brightened, the color returning to his face, pleased he had stumped another customer. "Nope! Not a Roosevelt. Woodrow Wilson."

Al slapped the bar. "Woodrow Wilson! I didn't even think of him."

Fat Mike nodded, his cheeks and jowls shifting in waves. "Everyone always forgets about Wilson."

"Ask me another," Al said.

"What about our food?" Bobby asked. "My bologna sandwich gonna cook itself?"

Mike pressed his lips together in a kind of a smile, took a step toward the kitchen, but he couldn't help himself. He blurted the next question before Bobby could spit another word. "Besides Wilson, who were the other U.S. Presidents widowed in office?"

Al sipped his Coke again and ran through the chronological list of presidents in his head as Bobby smoldered next to him; Al swore he could feel the heat radiating from him. He knew the answer was John Tyler and Benjamin Harrison but instead he shrugged, smiled his best little boy smile, and told Fat Mike that he had stumped him again.

"John Tyler and Benjamin Harrison," Fat Mike said. "Many people get confused and say Andrew Jackson, but he wasn't president when his wife died. Only president-*elect*. He wasn't sworn in yet."

"Is that a fact?" Al said

"Get my food," Bobby said, through clenched teeth.

Mike hurried through the kitchen door, turning before it swung behind him, and smiled at Al.

Bobby leaned into Al until their shoulders touched. "Cut the crap," he hissed in his ear, the whiskey fresh on his breath.

"What?" He wouldn't have minded if Mike asked him another question.

"If the cops follow us here, don't you think that fat bartender will remember the guy who sat at the bar and couldn't answer any of his goddamn questions?"

"No, I think he'll remember the one-eyed prick who acted like he'd kill him over a goddamn bologna sandwich."

Bobby was ropey strong from working the fields in California where he grew up, and all his muscles seemed to tighten under his clothes. Even the muscles in his cheeks started working, throbbing in and out as he clenched his jaw. Al worried that he might snap right then, smash his beer mug against the bar, and go after him with the jagged end. He had never worried about Bobby turning on him before but lately that fear was washing over him more often. Al felt the reassuring weight of the .45 tucked in his waistband; he fought the urge to reach back and touch it.

Bobby's good eye, though, was dead steady.

"Stop talking to him," Bobby said. "Stop talking, period." He swung off the stool and sulked to the jukebox.

He fed coins into the old Wurlitzer with pulsing neon tubes. The songs came on one after the other: "Tossin' and Turnin'," "Bye Bye Love", "Runaway." He leaned against the wall tapping his foot to The Everly Brothers and Del Shannon, smoking one cigarette after the other until he was hazed in blue smoke. Only when Fat Mike brought their food did he return to the bar. He and Al ate without speaking, both of them hunched with an arm curled around their plates, protecting what was theirs, eating like they were back in prison already.

Chapter 4

Lolly had decided to walk home from the market despite Stan's argument that it was too cold, too snowy, and that the sidewalks were icing. She had left him tying the tree she had selected to the roof of his car and had set out in the storm, wishing she'd worn a heavier coat. As she bent to the wind, the snow swirling around her, she conceded that her father had been right. It was too cold and the sidewalks were glassing over, but walking was much better than being locked in the too-warm Chrysler and forced to hear his concerns about Al.

She was through with all that.

The only other people walking were children, maybe in the second or third grade, heading home from school, delighting at the season's first snowfall. Their laughter fogged the air as they made snowballs—the wet snow perfect for packing—and threw them at each other, oblivious to the cold and wind. The only visible effects of the dropping temperature on them were their flaming cheeks and ears. She imagined Alison at their age making angels in fresh snow, or Al running up and down Lafayette Avenue pulling her in a little yellow sled as she squealed 'Faster'.

Lolly grew chilled after a few blocks. She held her coat closed at her throat and hurried as fast as the slippery sidewalks allowed. In the distance, she saw Bailey Avenue Books, a shop owned by her friend Maeve, and trudged there. She needed to stop in anyway, she told herself, and browse for one of Al's Christmas presents. He would read anything set in front of him—novels, machinery manuals, history books. He had an eclectic library he kept in barrister bookcases he'd made out of scavenged mahogany and glass from old storm windows. The shelves held titles such as *The History of Firearms, The Complete Book of Locksmithing*, and pulp fiction novels about bank robbers and men on the run. She wanted to buy him something nice, perhaps leatherbound, a book that he would cherish, maybe even a few Moleskine notebooks and an expensive European pen. He joked that he read so much that he should become a writer.

The bookshop was in a small, red brick building that had once been a library; Stan had taken her there as a child, holding her small hand the entire way. The city had decided that the library was too old, too small, and not needed. The building was closed and put on the market, but no one made an offer. After a year of being shuttered, the city determined there was no reuse for a sixty-year-old structure with leaded glass windows and brass light fixtures. The mayor's office thought the neighborhood would be better served if it was razed and paved as a parking lot. Maeve had stepped in then and bought the building at a good price. Al had wondered where she, a single Irish woman in her forties who had grown up in the city's old First Ward, a woman who worked as a sales clerk at a stationary store, had gotten the money to buy a building and start a business. Lolly thought she had inherited it. Al wasn't so sure.

The bell above the door tinkled when she entered the shop. Maeve was bent over, giftwrapping books for two customers who waited at the front counter. She looked up, a wisp of red hair falling across her face dusted with faint freckles, and smiled at Lolly, revealing a dimpled left cheek.

"I had to get out of the cold. It's awful out there," Lolly said, brushing snow from her sleeves.

"I'm glad you did. There's hot cider on the table," Maeve said, before bending back to her wrapping.

The store smelled of dried rosehip and old paper, and Lolly was glad to be inside. She pulled off her gloves and unbuttoned her coat in front of a display of this week's best sellers: *Franny and Zooey, The Agony and the Ecstasy, To Kill a Mockingbird.* Lolly wondered if Al would enjoy any of them, deciding, finally, that there wasn't enough action in any of these novels for his liking. She wandered down an aisle and heard Maeve's low and indistinct voice from the front of the store, and then a trill of laughter from the two women at the counter that bounced to the old library's high coffered ceiling and down again. Maeve's cat Fergus, a white Persian with a long flowing coat, rubbed against her ankles. She bent down and rubbed him behind the ears until he purred; he trotted away when she straightened. The bell above the door jangled again, and she wondered if the women at the counter had left with their wrapped gifts or if a new customer had entered.

An artbook on Vermeer, front-facing on the shelf, caught her attention. She paged through it, unfamiliar with the Dutch master's work but found herself drawn to the paintings of domestic life and the women he rendered in rich colors.

Her favorite, *Officer With a Laughing Girl*, reminded her of Al and herself seated at their own kitchen table. The cavalier sat erect in his chair, his arm bent, fist to hip, looking like nothing was impossible for him. She could see his back and shoulder muscles beneath his blood red coat and the power they contained. The woman was smiling, charmed by some story the soldier was telling, the way Al always charmed her with the anecdotes he brought back from his business trips. She was certain Al would see the painting differently than she, commenting on neither the woman nor the soldier courting her, but instead focusing on the map that hung on the wall. He was fascinated by maps and collected them, studying them for hours, tracing his finger along the different colored roads and routes, sometimes stopping and tapping his nail against the paper. He had an entire drawer filled with street maps, not just of Buffalo but of other places—Rochester, Washington, D.C., Brooklyn.

She returned the book to the shelf, realizing that she would enjoy it more than Al, and continued browsing. Lolly wandered down another aisle and saw a woman, not much older than she, holding a thin volume of poetry. She wore a black lambswool coat; light from the brass ceiling fixtures reflected off her silver-flecked buttons. Lolly watched, stunned, as the woman eased the book into her purse. She snapped her leather handbag shut and looked up to see Lolly staring at her with darkening eyes.

"Put it back," Lolly said, her voice harsh and cutting, like Sylvie's when she fought with Al.

The woman did not move.

"Put it back," she repeated, louder.

"You didn't see anything," the woman said, and started to move past her.

Lolly grabbed her sleeve, her grip sinking through the soft wool until it encircled the woman's bicep. "This is my friend's store. Put it back."

"Let go of me!" the woman said and tried to jerk free.

She tightened her grip, her anger fueling her strength. How dare she steal from Maeve? How dare her mother accuse Al of stealing? And her father too? She squeezed harder, hoping the woman bruised.

"You're hurting me. Let go."

"Lolly?" Maeve asked, walking toward them, confusion and worry shadowing her face. "What's going on?"

"Please," the woman said, her eyes glinting. "My arm."

As quickly as it had come, Lolly's anger drained and she released her. The woman opened her purse, her chin quivering, and handed Maeve a copy of Robert Burns' sonnets. She hurried toward the exit, a single tear trailing down her cheek. Lolly watched her until the door opened, the bell rang, and the woman disappeared into the driving snow.

Maeve glanced at her, a small, surprised smile revealing her dimple. "Well, Lolly. Who thought you'd make such a fine detective? I should hire you for store security."

Lolly did not answer.

"Poor girl. You're shaking," Maeve said. "Come with me. I think you need something to calm you, something stronger than hot cider with a cinnamon stick."

She followed Maeve to her office behind the counter; the other customers had left, and they were alone in the store.

"Have a seat," Maeve said, nodding to an upholstered wooden rocking chair that was occupied by Fergus. "Mind the cat, though. Push him to the ground. He thinks he's in charge, like most males do."

"Thank you," Lolly said, and picked Fergus up but held him on her lap when she sat down.

Maeve spooned instant coffee into two mugs then reached for the small pot simmering on the electric hotplate.

"I'm sorry," Lolly said.

"Whatever for?"

"I overreacted. I should have called for you."

"Nonsense," Maeve said, pouring hot water into the cups. "You handled it exactly the way a Bailey Avenue girl should have. She won't be coming back here, that's for sure. And that's fine. Let her steal poetry from somebody else."

Maeve stirred the coffee, then opened her desk drawer and brought out a bottle of Jameson. "It's the good stuff from Dublin. Not that Protestant swill from Belfast." She held it up to show the label and Lolly nodded. Maeve poured.

"I was having a bad day," Lolly said. "I was cold and frustrated and angry and took it out on her."

Maeve handed her a cup and Fergus jumped down and slinked under the desk. "Well, I'm glad you did. To hell with her and all the thieving cheats out there."

The two women touched coffee mugs and then sipped. Lolly winced at the first taste. "Strong," she said.

Maeve sat behind her desk piled with books and invoices and angled the chair towards her. "Supposed to be. Calms your nerves and puts an end to whatever's worrying you. Enough about that shoplifter. She's not worth our breath. We need to discuss important matters like how that little girl of yours is doing."

Lolly sat back in the rocker. "She's an angel. And growing so fast. I swear her face changes every day."

"You need to bundle that little pumpkin up and bring her down here to see her Auntie Maeve," Maeve said as Fergus jumped on her lap. "She'll make this one jealous."

"I will. I promise. Before Christmas for sure."

Maeve sipped her coffee. "And how's Al? I haven't seen him for a while. He's usually in here nosing through one book or another, but not recently."

"He's fine. Working hard and traveling a lot. He's in New York this week on business. Hopefully he'll get home tonight, but I'm not sure with this weather."

"New York?" Maeve said, smiling, dimpling. "Maybe he's doing something else in New York besides business."

"What do you mean?" Lolly asked and felt those invisible fingers envelope her again.

"I mean, maybe he's doing a little Christmas shopping for his bride. What do you think, Lolly girl? Where do you think Al is? Saks? Tiffany's? What's going to be in your stocking this year?"

She laughed, relieved, and then took a long sip of coffee. "If he's anywhere, he's at FAO Schwarz buying toys for Alison."

"Daddies and their girls. God bless them," Maeve said, raising her mug.

"I don't know about that. My father used to get so mad at me at this time of year when I was growing up."

"Stan? I've never even heard him raise his voice a single time."

"He'd get furious because I'd hunt all over for my presents, and when I'd find them I'd unwrap them, see what they were, and then rewrap them again. But I'd never quite rewrap them perfectly, or the paper would tear, and he would know and get so angry, saying I was ruining Christmas for him."

"So, you've gone from a sneak to catching shoplifters. Maybe there's hope for you yet."

The bell above the door rang.

Maeve took a quick sip of coffee before setting the mug on her desk. "Duty calls," she said, shooing Fergus off her lap and then standing. "Take your time. Finish your coffee."

Maeve patted Lolly's shoulder as she left to wait on her customers. Lolly relaxed, sank deeper in the rocker, feeling the whiskey spread through her. She imagined a small gift box wrapped in fine paper, the kind that might hold a cocktail ring or a pair of diamond studs, under her tree. Then she imagined a longer, thinner box tied with curled ribbons protruding from her Christmas stocking and wondered if it held a gold watch or bracelet. Perhaps a larger square box the perfect size for holding a string of pearls would be waiting for her on the coffee table Christmas morning.

She began rocking as the wind outside howled, rattling the old library's leaded windows.

****

Lolly balanced on a kitchen chair, reaching to string colored lights at the top of the tree. It was hard to get close and place them where she wanted. She had picked a six-foot Douglas Fir, nearly five inches taller than Al, that was full and bushy and filled the front living room corner. She leaned into the tree, the branches pushing back, until she managed to attach one end of the string near the top branch. She tossed the remaining length around the fir, then hopped down from the chair to climb up a small wooden step ladder on the other side to pull the lights around.

She had never hung lights before. That had always been Stan's job when she was growing up; last year, their first Christmas as a married couple, it had become Al's. Lolly had always stood watching as her father or husband had alternated from chair to ladder then back again, encircling the tree with red, green, and blue bulbs, testing each strand with an extension cord not only to ensure that they worked but also for Lolly to check that they were spaced and draped properly on the boughs. She would bite her bottom lip, pressing so hard it would blanch, as she directed her father or husband to raise or lower the lights until they were perfect. This year, after Stan had carried the tree up to the apartment and stood it in the stand, she had told him that she would hang the lights herself this year. His face had sagged, the disappointment clear in his eyes, but Lolly didn't care. She didn't want any more lectures about Al. Stan managed a thin smile and told her to call if she needed help. She didn't say anything—she didn't even thank him—but had locked and chained the door as soon as he went down the back stairs to his apartment.

A new Christmas record—*Favorite Christmas Carols from The Voice of Firestone*—played on the hi-fi. Al had brought it home after buying new snow tires for the station wagon before this latest New York City trip. Risë Stevens was singing "What Child Is This?," her voice clear and strong, hovering somewhere between soprano and contralto. The album cover, a red bow and ribbon on blue wrapping paper, laid on the couch, its cellophane wrapping balled next to it. A glass of Chablis, half empty, waited for her on the end table. She told herself that she'd better eat soon, or the whiskey and wine would put her to sleep long before Al got home.

As she looped the lights around the treetop, she thought how nice it would be if there were a fireplace in the apartment, filling the living room with the rich smell of burning hardwood. She had needed a roaring fire after her walk home from Maeve's. Her toes had numbed soon after she had left the bookstore, and when she got home, she'd stomped her feet to get feeling back, hoping the stomping disturbed her mother in her apartment below. If only she could have stood in front of a crackling fire, the flames dancing between logs, and warmed herself. She knew the house on Lafayette had two chimneys, one on the west side closest to Elmwood Avenue and one in the center of the house. She wondered how many fireplaces were inside as Brian Sullivan began singing "O Come, All Ye Faithful."

She hopped back on the kitchen chair to pull the lights around and wished Al were there to help her, to share the wine, to tease that she was being too particular about placing ornaments. She would squeal and pretend to resist when he wrestled her under the mistletoe. His business trips had been occurring more frequently and lasted so much longer than when they'd first been married; she was beginning to feel like a single parent. In the days leading up to a trip, he would grow quiet and still, sitting at the kitchen table for hours without moving. His body became a mute shell, and she'd wonder where his thoughts had taken him. She would ask, sometimes two or three times before he'd raise his head, what he was thinking and he would always answer, "Details," or "Planning," or "Getting ready." He would then rest his chin back in his palm and go back to whatever business strategy he was trying to formulate. She would move quietly around the apartment and keep Alison hushed so as not to disturb him.

She plugged the first string of lights into the extension cord, picked up her wine glass, and then stepped back to appraise her work. The lights on the left side needed to be raised. A single blue one blinked on and off and she frowned; she didn't care for blinking lights and never had them on her tree. She wondered where this one had come from. Then she smiled.

Al.

It had to be Al.

It would be just like him to plan a joke a year in advance. She could picture him screwing in the blinking bulb before putting the lights away for the year so she could stand here eleven months later and be teased. He must have imagined her expression—surprise? annoyance?—when she'd first see it flashing and laughed as he carried the light box to the attic. She sipped the Chablis and decided not to replace it. Every time it flashed, she would think of him and how she had married the most playful man in the city.

She set her glass down on the holly and ivy coaster and adjusted the lights. When she was pleased with the spacing and evenness, she started the second string. The Firestone Chorus was now singing a holiday medley—"A Virgin Unspotted/God Rest You Merry, Gentlemen/Deck the Hall." As she climbed on the chair, a gold Santa Claus key gleamed on the coffee table, reflecting the tree lights. Santa's face was carved on the key's bow, each beard and mustache curl exact and pronounced. They had bought it last year when she was pregnant from Pitt Petri on Delaware Avenue, a shop that carried merchandise too expensive for a young couple with a baby on the way. She and Al had seen it as part of the window display as they strolled by, their arms linked as they leaned into each other. She had to explain to him that the key was said to be magical and used by Santa to get into houses and apartments like theirs that didn't have a chimney. He had insisted they buy it, despite her protest about the price, saying that no kid of theirs was going to miss out on presents from Santa because they didn't have a damn key. At the counter, as the salesgirl wrote up their order, Lolly was amazed at the thick roll of bills he pulled from his pocket. He had explained that he'd sold all the transistor radios they had in stock to a downstate outfit and that they were flush, at least for now. Then he laughed and said he wished he had a magic key when he was in Chillicothe.

She pulled another light string from the box, untangled it, and then frowned. The key reminded her of Bobby. He had come over one night after dinner, uninvited and unannounced, carrying a wooden crate filled with clock parts, wire, locks, and keys of all sizes, some loose, some on rings, and a rusty set that a jailer might carry. Bobby had said he'd found the box at the curb put out for trash, and she couldn't understand why he and Al seemed so excited by this find. The two had hurried off to the garage to go through their discovered treasure. Once the lights were untangled, she climbed back on the kitchen chair, connected it to the first string and tossed the second set around the tree like a lariat. "O Little Town of Bethlehem" drifted from the hi-fi, and she wondered for the thousandth time what it was about that junk box that had intrigued Al. Why did he need wire and clock parts?

After she had circled the tree with lights and made sure they were placed precisely, Lolly took a break from decorating and checked on Alison, asleep in her crib, her bottom raised in the air. She was a good sleeper and wouldn't stir until it was time for her eleven o'clock bottle. Al would be home by then and would feed her. He'd sit on the rocking chair he had scrounged from someplace, the one he had repaired and refinished for the baby's room. He'd hold Alison in the crook of his left arm and the bottle in his right hand as Lolly watched from the doorway, certain her parents were dead wrong about him.

As she walked to the kitchen to get something to eat, she smiled when she saw today's date, the date of Al's return, circled in red on the wall calendar. She looked out the window and worried about the roads and visibility and the weather in New York City. She was glad that Al had bought new snow tires for the station wagon but even they wouldn't help if the roads were icy. If he didn't make it home tonight, it would be because of the storm and not any of the reasons her mother imagined.

Chapter 5

It was after seven when they arrived in Buffalo and pulled in front of Bobby's Olympic Avenue apartment. The sky had cleared and was filled with distant stars. The temperature had dropped after the sun had set as they neared Lake Ontario; their breath steamed the air when they stepped from the station wagon. Bobby trudged up the front walk, cursing the cold. Al grabbed the duffle bag from the backseat and followed. The ankle-deep snow seeped into his shoes and soaked his socks, but he didn't mind. The weight of the bag pleased him.

Bobby lived on the top floor of an old house cut into four apartments. His landlord, an old Polish man who had survived Treblinka, lived in the bottom unit, the serial number tattooed on his forearm visible when he wore short sleeves. The door to his flat opened as they climbed the porch steps, and the old man stuck out his head.

"You were supposed to shovel," he said to Bobby, his Warsaw accent still thick. "That was part of the deal for less rent. That you shovel."

"I was out of town," Bobby growled, never slowing and never looking at the old man.

"My wife almost fell on those steps."

"Good," Bobby muttered, loud enough for Al to hear.

"You shovel. It was part of the deal."

Bobby unlocked the door and ascended the stairs to his apartment without saying another word. Al nodded to the old man and followed. Jackie Rose waited on the landing, and Bobby took the stairs two at a time to get to her. He scooped her in his arms, lifted her off the ground, and began kissing her neck and burying his face in her blonde hair. She squealed as he carried her into the apartment, her legs wrapped around his waist. From downstairs, the landlord yelled for Bobby to come back and shovel the walk.

There wasn't much furniture in the place: a table with a few chairs, a sagging green couch with dropped springs, and a new RCA Victor color TV that Bobby had bought with stolen money. He always rambled about the brightness of the High-Fidelity tube and the richness of the walnut veneer. Even the shows broadcasted in black and white looked better, he said.

Al entered and took a few strides to cross the small apartment to the dining room. He pushed aside Jackie Rose's magazines—*Hollywood Tattler, Movie Teen Illustrated, Uncensored Movie Gossip*—from the table to clear a space for the duffle bag. She was nineteen, ten years younger than Bobby, and wore her bleached hair swirled and piled high like the magazine movie stars. She wanted to look closer to Bobby's age, but Bobby was an old twenty-nine, prematurely aged from prison and years of picking fruit under the unrelenting California sun. Lines checkered his neck and webbed from the corner of his mouth. His hair was receding worse than Al's which left him with the broad, furrowed forehead of a much older-looking man. And, of course, there was that eye.

Bobby didn't like the fancy hairstyles and makeup Jackie wore; he preferred her looking young and scrubbed clean.

Jackie Rose, still wrapped in Bobby's arms, looked at Al over Bobby's shoulder as he nuzzled her neck, her feet back on the ground. "How'd it go, Al?"

Al unzipped the duffle bag and dumped the money on the table into a smear of green. "We had some trouble."

"What kind of trouble?"

"Nothing to worry about, baby girl. I took care of it," Bobby said, walking her backwards to the couch. When her legs hit the couch's side, she fell back on the cushions, pulling Bobby on top of her. The springs complained and sagged farther to the floor.

Al sat at the table and counted the money as Bobby and Jackie Rose necked on the couch like teenagers, Bobby's hand busy under her soft sweater. He stacked the bills in even piles. Curry had done well. There were no sequential serial numbers. He had grabbed money only from cash drawers as Al had instructed.

"Thirty-two grand," he called to Bobby after he'd counted and recounted their haul. "Check it."

Bobby rolled off Jackie Rose in an instant, leaving her disheveled on the couch with her pink lipstick smeared and her dyed hair mussed. Her sweater was pushed up revealing soft-looking skin above her jeans. She stared at Al for a few heartbeats before pulling it down.

"Thirty-two?" Bobby asked, walking towards the dining room.

"I was hoping for fifty."

"Curry dropped a bunch."

"What?" Al asked, rising from the chair so Bobby could take his place at the table. "Where?"

"Heading to the door. He panicked a bit after I shot that cop and was moving fast and trying to shove money in the bag at the same time. He must have dropped ten grand. He didn't have time to pick it up."

"Goddamnit," Al said.

"Bobby, you shot a cop?" Jackie Rose asked, walking into the dining room.

"It's okay. He lived."

"We think he lived," Al corrected.

Bobby started counting the money, the furrows in his forehead deepening as he concentrated. This was going to take a while.

"Do you have something to drink, Jackie?" Al asked. "A Coca-Cola or something?"

"Sure, Al," she said, and flashed a movie star smile that he bet she practiced in the bathroom mirror while holding one of her magazines close to her face.

"Grab me a beer too, will ya, baby girl?" Bobby asked, losing count and starting over.

Jackie rubbed Al's shoulder as she made her way to the kitchen.

"Don't be pissed at Curry," Bobby said.

Al ran his hand across his chin; whiskers whispered against skin. "He left money behind."

"If you could do better, go inside the bank yourself next time," Bobby said, still counting the first stack of bills.

Al let it pass. The last thing he wanted was Bobby to start yelling about the proper way they should rob banks. His voice would bounce off walls and through the floor to his landlord, another good citizen, who would call the cops as fast as his old Polish fingers could dial.

The boiler in the basement rumbled to life and the gray radiators throughout the apartment started pinging and tapping like they were calling to each other. They made the lone sounds in the room until Jackie Rose came back with the drinks. She slid a bottle of Genesee Cream Ale in front of Bobby.

"We're out of Coke," she said, and handed Al an Orange Crush and another magazine smile.

Al drank that bottle and two more before Bobby agreed that there was thirty-two thousand dollars stacked on the table. He wasn't sure if Bobby had actually counted to that number or if he had given up and agreed with him to end it. Bobby grabbed his beer and stood, letting Al take his place in the chair again. Al divided the money into thirds.

Bobby took a long pull on his beer, draining it, and then gestured toward Al with the empty bottle. "Look, baby girl. The second robbery of the day."

"Don't start, Bobby," Al said, bent to the money, making sure he was splitting their take correctly. "I've had enough of your shit today."

Jackie Rose melded to his side. "What do you mean, Bobby? What second robbery?"

"Me and Curry do all the work and take all the risks, but Al gets an even split. That's the biggest crime right there."

"Fuck you, Bobby," Al said. His hands trembled as he pushed the money into three piles.

"You just sit in your goddamn car."

Al stood. Bobby was two inches taller, but Al was twenty pounds heavier and still had the .45 tucked in his waistband. "I'm going to tell you one last time," he said, keeping his voice low so the landlord wouldn't hear. "I pick the banks. I case them. I come up with the plan, the escape route, the guns. I watch the street, listen to the scanner, and drive the getaway car. I'm the one who can count the goddamn money right the first time. All you have to do is look scary, yell real loud, and wave a gun around. Oh, and not kill anybody, but you forgot about that today, didn't you, Einstein? You had to kill that guard, didn't you?"

Bobby took a step forward, but Jackie Rose held him back. He stuck his face close and Al avoided looking at that eye. "This little girl can listen to a goddamn radio and drive a goddamn car. It takes a man to do what I do."

"Did you ever pull one job before you met me without getting caught?" he asked and began ticking off Bobby's rap sheet. "Grand theft auto? Caught. Burglary? Caught. Assault and battery? Caught."

He stared at Jackie Rose. "Statutory rape? Caught...twice."

She turned away from Al. With the makeup washed off and without the Hollywood hairstyle, Jackie looked years younger.

"You were busted for everything, Bobby," Al said, turning back to him. "You couldn't plan shit and get away with it. Now you got more money than you ever had, so don't tell me a kid like her can replace me."

Bobby's good eye wasn't shifting around, so Al breathed a little easier. Sometimes he had to stand up to Bobby to keep him in line, but it was risky. Al clenched and unclenched his hands to give them something to do.

"Split the money and get the fuck out," Bobby said.

"Fine." Al sat back down and tried to keep from shaking.

"Let's have another beer, Bobby," Jackie Rose said, pulling him towards the kitchen by the arm. "I'm thirsty."

"Okay," Bobby said, letting her lead him away. "But then you got to pack."

"We're leaving?"

"First thing in the morning."

"For how long?"

"For good."

Al's head snapped up. "You're running already?"

"Yeah, smart guy. You think I'm gonna wait until the Feds kick in my door like you?"

Al didn't say anything. He wasn't ready to run. Not yet.

"Sooner or later the Feds are going to figure out it's us and come charging in here waving arrest warrants and machine guns. You should run too. Don't stick around here. Use your brain."

"There's Lolly to think about. And Alison."

"If you love her and the kid so goddamn much, take them with you now before it's too late."

"It's too risky. They may get hurt."

"Then be a man and leave them. Hell, they're better off without you."

Al sat back in the chair, wondering if that was true.

Outside, metal scraped against concrete as Bobby's landlord shoveled the heavy snow.

*****

Al pulled into his driveway, shut off the engine, and stared at his house. A wreath hung on their front door; the bow's twin red tails fluttered in the night breeze. A floodlight, spiked in the lawn, lit up the doorway. Snow covered the lights on the bushes, the blues and greens casting a muted glow. A single plastic candle with a clear bulb burned in each of the front windows of their second-floor apartment. His in-laws' flat on the lower floor was dark, giving the impression that the decorating was half-done.

He sat behind the wheel, afraid to step out of the station wagon, imagining a dozen pairs of headlights snapping to life, a bullhorn voice telling him to raise his hands, and the winter air filled with the sound of weapons being locked and loaded. Lolly would be above him, watching it all from an upper window, the Christmas candle showing the horror on her face as they led him away or shot him dead where he stood.

But when he opened the car door, no spotlights captured him, no voices called, no weapons were aimed at his chest. He grabbed a smaller duffle bag containing his take from the robbery, slid the .45 inside it, then made his way up the front walk after zipping the bag closed. He shuffled his feet like he wore leg irons, being careful not to lose his footing on the ice.

Garland was wound around the railing that led up to their flat. He climbed the stairs, avoiding the squeaky riser on the fifth step; the baby had started sleeping through the night. The garland had come undone at the top and was hanging. He stopped and reattached it. On the door leading into their apartment hung an evergreen spray. The entire stairway smelled of pine.

The only lights in the apartment came from the window candles, the decorated Christmas tree in the corner, and the flickering black and white television. Lolly was curled on the couch, asleep under an afghan her Aunt Helen had crocheted. She had fallen asleep reading the paper; the real estate section lay on top of her. Al slid the duffle bag into the hall closet, pushing it far back behind the hanging coats and fishing equipment that he hadn't used in years and then stepped into the living room. He'd move the money to a safer place tomorrow, maybe several places, dividing the money and stashing it in various spots around town so he could have access to cash in every part of the city.

He stopped and admired the Christmas tree, hoping Lolly hadn't lugged it through the snow and horsed it up the stairs by herself. From each bough hung hand-painted ornaments from Poland that had belonged to her grandmother: mica-glass bulbs covered with white snowflakes, colored stripes, or flowers, the petals mere paint daubs. There were others: fat Santas, golden-haired angels, and bells. Silver tinsel, hung strand-by-strand, dangled from every branch. A metal star covered in spun glass topped the tree and brushed the ceiling.

"Al?"

Lolly stretched on the couch then opened her arms to him, her lips curling into a smile. She straightened her legs to make room and the newspaper fell to the floor; an ad circled in red landed face down. He went to her and her soft arms pulled him down tight, her face warm from sleep when he pressed his cheek against hers. He smelled her perfume, something new she had bought called Interlude. He closed his eyes and breathed her in, his first easy breath all day.

"How was your meeting?"

"Almost everything went according to plan," he answered, and shoved aside the image of the cop exploding through double glass doors. He wondered if he had lived.

"Do you like the tree?"

"It's perfect."

"There's a blinking blue bulb near the top."

"Really? You hate blinkers. I wonder how it got there."

"I wonder," she said, and kissed him, biting his lip, and they both laughed.

He brushed the hair off her forehead then let his fingers trail down her cheek. "You didn't drag the tree home by yourself, did you?"

"No, Dad helped. Mother watched the baby while I decorated."

"How is our little girl?"

"Cranky. She wouldn't eat for Mother."

"Probably afraid of her."

Lolly slapped his back. "Be nice. It's almost Christmas."

"It is, isn't it? I need to finish shopping."

"Not tomorrow. At least not in the morning. I have plans for you."

"What kind of plans?"

"Secret plans."

"Those are the best kind, but I have my own plans for you tonight," he said, and kissed her long and slow like he had all the time in the world.

****

Lolly slept with her head on Al's chest, her dark hair cool against his skin. A ceiling crack, one he'd been meaning to plaster for months, stretched above their bed. It was shaped like New York State's western boundary, sloping down from its most northern point, then beaking out at Lake Ontario before snaking west, then south, indenting where Buffalo hugged the shore. He had been staring at the crack for hours, unable to sleep, placing imaginary circles to mark border towns—Ogdensburg, Oswego, Niagara Falls. Lolly's breathing and the ticking of the Big Ben alarm clock on the nightstand, its hands glowing pale green, filled the room. He hadn't slept this poorly since his early days at Chillicothe, when every noise, real or imagined, would startle him awake. He stroked Lolly's bare shoulder and listened for heavy boots thudding up the stairs, the front door splintering, and his name being called by harsh voices. He imagined revolving red and blue lights playing against neighboring houses and seeping through bedroom curtains, summoning families to watch his arrest like a real-life episode of *Dragnet*. The baby would wail, her screams mixing with Lolly's. His mother-in-law would stand in the downstairs doorway, holding her robe closed to keep out the cold, and not looking surprised at all as she lit another cigarette.

The problem was Al's mind. He couldn't stop it from working. Once he pushed the paranoia away, his brain would try to make plans and come up with the next moves he should make. He didn't have it all worked out, but he knew running didn't mean drifting from town-to-town, constantly moving where gas station attendants and bartenders like Fat Mike might remember him. Running meant that the old Al would disappear, and he would become someone else with a new look, a new identity, a new life. He would blend in with the others, just as his station wagon had blended with Brooklyn traffic. None of those small towns on his cracked ceiling map would do. He needed to disappear into a crowded city like New York, or Philly, or Boston and become someone else. Then the thought of never holding Lolly again or not being able to watch his baby grow would grab him and something inside him would collapse, like the floors of an imploding building pancaking each other until there was nothing left but rubble.

He hadn't cried since Chillicothe.

He stayed in bed until he heard the newsboy toss the paper on the front porch. He pulled away from Lolly; she rolled from him without a murmur. Their clothes were strewn where they had shed them, forming a trail from hallway to bed. He had to step over them to reach the closet. The door squeaked when he opened it and reached for his robe; Lolly's breathing remained deep and even. He checked the baby and she too was lost in sleep, but he knew that wouldn't last long. She'd be crying for the day's first bottle soon.

He padded his way down the chilly steps to the porch; the fifth riser protested when he forgot to step over it. The sun hadn't risen yet, and the morning was as dark and cold as the previous night. The newspaper had landed on the snowy porch, and he wiped it clean with his robe, then hurried to the kitchen. He made coffee in the percolator as quietly as he could, then sat at the kitchen table smoking. He read the *Courier Express* while waiting for the water to boil. It's almost four hundred miles from Brooklyn to Buffalo, but he thought there might be a small piece on the robbery tucked somewhere in the back between the Christmas ads for Sattler's Department Store and Kleinhan's Men's Shop. And he was right. A brief paragraph appeared in the "Around the State" section between an article on a power outage in Poughkeepsie and a tractor trailer crash in Utica. The murdered guard was named Henry Kraus and was pronounced dead at the scene of gunshot wounds to the chest; he was fifty-two years old. Officer Salvatore Accardi was also shot in the chest but survived when the bullet struck the patrolman's badge. The bank robbers' identities were unknown; they still remained at large, armed, and extremely dangerous. The article only mentioned two gunmen and nothing about a second car and a second driver. Bobby, the pawn, always said Al didn't go inside the banks because he's afraid, *but he's wrong*, Al thought. *I'm not afraid, and I'm not stupid, either.*

The coffee perked on the stove, and he lit another cigarette, forgetting that he had one burning in the Atlantic City ashtray at his elbow. He read and reread the story a few times, wondering if the Feds had lied to the reporter and if they already knew their identities, if they knew about his station wagon, if they were on their way. He imagined their dark sedans blocking off side streets around his apartment, choking off escape routes, and agents approaching the house from all directions.

What bothered him most was learning the family names—Kraus and Accardi; they were no longer 'Guard' and 'Cop' to him. He felt relieved that the article was short, and no photographs accompanied it. He didn't want to see Accardi, young and handsome, in his police academy graduation picture or Kraus and his wife beaming in their anniversary photo. He didn't want to know that Kraus was a war hero and had been decorated for his action in the Pacific or that Accardi had become a father a few months earlier. Learning that Accardi had survived the shooting was enough, not that it mattered much. *They can only strap me in the goddamn chair once*, he thought.

The baby howled in her room.

****

He let Lolly sleep late. He fed the baby, changed her, and dressed her in a soft, green outfit covered with snowflakes. They sat on the couch watching Saturday morning television—*The Shari Lewis Show, Mighty Mouse Playhouse*, and *Sky King*, where bank robbers and other criminals were hunted from the clouds; Schuyler "Sky" King always caught the crooks in the nick of time. At least he didn't shoot them dead in front of their wives. He could hear Lolly in their bedroom, opening and closing dresser drawers and the closet door squeaking a dozen times. The radio played on their nightstand, the words and melody a mumble to him sitting in the living room until a Christmas carol would come on. She'd then turn up the volume and sing loud enough for him to hear.

He caught a glimpse of her hurrying to the bathroom and then the sound of the shower running. He'd have liked to have joined her, but Alison sat on his lap, hypnotized by flashing images of flying mice and planes, happiest when she heard Lamb Chop's high voice, and she was wide, wide awake. He sat on the couch with his baby in his arms, picturing his wife in the shower, her skin pinking from hot water then turning soapy white as she lathered her body, her hands moving in small, slow circles over her breasts, stomach, and thighs.

Her shower didn't last as long as his imagination wanted. The water was shut off before he knew it and a few minutes later she was again in the hallway, hurrying to their bedroom wrapped in a gold towel. She paused for a moment, making sure he was looking, then dropped the towel before laughing and darting into their bedroom, leaving him grinning at the closed bedroom door like a kid who'd been given an early Christmas gift.

When Lolly came out, she was dressed in her best blue suit, the color matching her eyes and her brown hair brushed into place. She smiled at her husband with her whole face: her eyes brightened, her dimples deepened, her lips curled.

"Where are you off to looking so pretty?" he asked.

She entered the living room and kissed his lips then the top of the baby's head. "I told you that I had plans for you this morning. You better get ready or we'll be late."

"Where are we going?" he asked, handing her the baby.

"It's a secret plan, remember? Go shave and make sure you wear a tie. We'll drop the baby off at Mother's."

"She's not going with us?"

"Who? Mother?"

"Good God, no. The baby."

Lolly laughed. "No, you're stuck with me this morning. Go get ready."

He stood and kissed his girls one last time.

*****

He stared in the bathroom mirror, partially steamed from Lolly's shower. If it wasn't for his receding hairline, he'd look younger than twenty-seven. He still kept his hair army tight, and that made his face appear lean, youthful. His shoulders and neck were thick from his prison routine of pushups, chin-ups, and dips that he'd kept up since being paroled. Some prison habits are good and they're all hard to break. He could be mistaken for a University of Buffalo fullback or maybe one of the coaches.

He studied the tattooed snake that curled around a dagger on his right arm. The knife pointed upward at an angle, its handle colored gold, matching the snake's underbelly. The dagger's point glinted sharp and dripped blood the same color red as the snake's extended tongue. Even the green scales somehow looked menacing. He'd gotten the tattoo in the army after enlisting straight out of high school; he thought it would make him appear dangerous. Lolly liked it, though, and would trace the intertwined snake with her fingernail from its rattled tail to its slit black eyes when they lay in bed.

The tattoo had been documented in Chillicothe along with his hair and eye color, the birthmark on his neck, his appendix scar, his height and weight. He could dye his brown hair and wear lifts in his shoes to make him appear taller, but the tattoo would have to come off. He didn't need some good citizen, one who'd seen his inevitable wanted poster and description at the post office, to recognize the dagger when he stepped out of the shower at a Boston YMCA or in some shared bathroom in a Philadelphia boarding house.

He had come to this conclusion days before he and Bobby drove to Brooklyn and had made an appointment before they had left to have it burned off. Making that decision should have been a warning to him, a premonition that the Lafayette National Bank job was doomed, but he'd missed it. Some moves you don't see coming, no matter how long you study the chessboard.

"Are you done yet, Al?" Lolly asked, through the bathroom door.

"Done? I haven't even started," he answered, lathering his face with his shaving brush.

"Well, hurry. We've got places to go!"

He shaved faster than usual for her, nicking skin twice at the jawline. He dressed in a gray suit and maroon striped tie, almost forgetting to pull the tissue from the cuts before heading down the backstairs to his in-laws'.

Sylvie waited for them in her kitchen that smelled of the fried kielbasa she made each morning for Stan. Today the odor seemed stronger, more overpowering, and it grabbed Al as soon as he entered the apartment. The greasy pan sat congealed on the stove.

Her breakfast dishes—a cup of black coffee and an ashtray—were the only things left on the kitchen table. The coffee steam and cigarette smoke curled together and rose to the ceiling.

"There's my big girl," she said, her voice dry and grating. She took Alison from Lolly's arms and kissed the baby's cheeks, her forehead, her nose. Alison giggled and gurgled as her grandmother tickled her neck and made cooing sounds in her ear. Al didn't doubt that she loved her daughter and granddaughter, but when his mother-in-law's gaze landed on him, her face grew taut like the skin had been pulled.

"So, you're back from your trip," she said, disappointed, he imagined, that he hadn't died in a fiery crash somewhere between here and Albany. "You've taken so many lately. Where did you go last time? Syracuse?"

"Rochester. An over-nighter."

He thought of the Rochester job, a big haul, second to the M&T Bank they had robbed on the other side of Buffalo last January. His plan had worked like a machine with all the gears turning in time.

"You were only gone overnight?" she asked, setting her jaw. "I thought you had disappeared longer than that. You're always vanishing. A real Houdini. I told Lolly, one of these days you'll disappear for good."

"Where's Stan?" he asked, looking away from his mother-in-law.

She waved her hand in the general direction of the street. "Shopping, I think. Probably at the Broadway Market to pick up a few things."

He placed his hand on the small of Lolly's back and guided her toward the front door. "Tell him I'll be down later to finish our chess game."

71

Sylvie frowned at the prospect of seeing him twice in one day; she reached for her smoldering cigarette.

Al wanted to get away from her and her sausage-smelling kitchen as fast as he could. He knew later, when he came down alone to play chess with his father-in-law, she would go into her bedroom and close the door without uttering a word.

There was no trace of Christmas in Sylvie's apartment—no tree in the corner, no mistletoe hung in the doorway, no poinsettias on the table.

"Love the decorations, Sylvie," he called, over his shoulder as he followed Lolly out the door. "Even better than last year's."

*****

Al's first cold breath startled him and hurt his chest when he stepped outside. The blue sky contrasted with the white that blanketed the lawns and roofs and clung to the branches and power lines. Sunlight glared off the snow and he tapped his coat pockets for his sunglasses.

"What a perfect day," Lolly said as he held the passenger side door open for her, her face already rouged by the winter air. "I knew today was going to be perfect."

He put on a pair of aviator Ray-Bans, the same kind Bobby had worn during the Brooklyn robbery, and hurried around to the driver's side, glancing up and down the street, trying to spot unmarked cars and surveillance vans.

"Where are we heading?" he asked, sliding in and slamming the door.

He should've started the car earlier to have it warm for Lolly; the cold seeped through his suit pants from the vinyl seat. He wondered what time Bobby and Jackie Rose had left this morning and if he had already ditched his old car. He bet the heater in a new Impala blew hot air right away.

"West," she said. "Cut over to Delavan."

He shifted the car in reverse and backed out the driveway. Lolly reached to turn on the radio, then stopped. "What's that, Al?" she asked, her gloved hand frozen inches from the police scanner that he had forgotten to dismount last night.

"A police radio," he answered without hesitating and eased the station wagon down their snow-covered street. "Brand new model I'm thinking about adding to the line. I tested it on my trip yesterday. Works pretty good, not too staticky like some of them," he said, not a single word a lie.

"Oh," she said, looking out the window at nothing. All her excitement about their morning together disappeared. She shifted farther away from him, and he could feel her slipping away. He imagined her leaving her body and her true, best part was somehow passing through the car door and floating away on invisible currents, carried here and there, never returning to his side, like her mother was reeling her home.

"Listen," he said. He flipped on the radio and the usual dispatcher and patrol car chatter crackled. "Sounds pretty good, don't you think?" he asked, dreading any mention of the station wagon. He checked his mirrors.

"What kind of person would buy that?" she asked. He swore her voice was coming from outside the window.

"The manufacturer's rep said there's a whole market for them—retired cops, reporters, tow truck drivers. Even nosey neighbors like your mother," he said. He didn't add bank robbers to the list, but she laughed and everything was okay again. She was back by his side.

He lowered the volume but kept it loud enough to hear if the dispatcher gave his license plate number or description. "So, Delavan Avenue, huh? What's on Delavan? We didn't have to get dressed up to go Christmas shopping. And there's no fancy places over there for brunch."

She shook her head, smiling. "No, not shopping. Not brunch either."

"I know. We're going to a photographer. Get a nice portrait taken as a Christmas present for your mother. We'll put it in a gold frame, and she can keep it on her nightstand so my smiling face is the last thing she sees at night and the first thing she sees in the morning."

"Oh, she would love that," Lolly said, laughing.

He drove another ten minutes, leaving the east side for the Delaware District. He tried guessing their destination: the zoo, the circus, the movies, a visit with Santa. Lolly delighted in saying no to each one.

"Turn left on Delaware."

He checked his mirrors again, surprised there still wasn't a tail. Was the FBI that inept? Did he really have to run? Maybe he could stay. Was he still a step ahead?

"Don't go around the traffic circle," Lolly instructed. "Veer right on Lafayette."

"Are we going to the Park Lane?" he asked, nodding towards the expensive restaurant on Gates Circle across from Millard Fillmore Hospital, but Lolly shook her head.

Al wondered if an oil painting of Millard Fillmore hung in the hospital lobby and if it would be difficult to steal. He imagined the look on Fat Mike's fat face if he came to work one day and found a framed portrait of the thirteenth president propped under Founding Fathers' faded blue awning and a note that read "You forgot one."

"Go slow," she said, after he drove past the restaurant. "I love these old houses."

No other cars came off the traffic circle behind him; the police radio chirped about a two-car accident on Humboldt Parkway, far from them.

She was leaning forward, peering out the window at the homes. The avenue was wide and tree-lined with oaks and maples that formed a canopy of leaves in the summer, shading the street and the wide front lawns. In the fall, the canopy was afire with reds, oranges, and yellows. In December's grip, there were only bare limbs stretching from either side of the street and lacing together.

The homes—some Victorians but most built later—were three stories high and had wide, balustraded front porches. Lincolns and Cadillacs were parked in driveways, and Al imagined the owners of the cars and grand houses were doctors and surgeons who worked at the hospital on the corner and belonged to the Saturn or Buffalo Club, or had their boats moored at the Porter Avenue yacht club. He wondered if any had accounts in the M&T Bank they'd knocked off last January and if any of their money was now folded in his pocket.

"There," Lolly said. "That one. 676. Pull over."

She pointed to the mauve house on the passenger side. Al's stomach tightened when he saw the for sale sign stuck in the middle of the snowy front lawn.

"Lolly, what are we doing here?" he asked as he parked in front of the house.

"Look at it," she said.

Hedges lined both sides of the walk leading to the front porch, and a waist-high wrought-iron fence separated the lawn from the neighbor's driveway. A pine tree near the corner of the house reached the copper gutters, the downspouts a bluish-green patina. The tree cast a long shadow across the snow. No other cars pulled behind them.

"We can't afford this, Lol," he said. "It's huge. It's a mini-mansion."

Lolly faced him, her eyes wide and blue with possibility. "Oh, I know that, Al. But I've loved this house ever since I was a little girl. I don't know why this one and not the others. Maybe it was the color. I've been driving by this house and dreaming about it for years. I've always wanted to see the inside and when I saw it listed in the paper last night, I knew this might be my only chance. Can we go in, Al? Please? We have an appointment, but if you don't want to…"

She let the sentence trail, unfinished. He looked into her face, the face he had loved since high school, the face he tried to imagine in his Chillicothe cell every time he had closed his eyes, the face he knew he might never see again.

"Sure, we can go in," he said, his voice strained, his words strangled. "It'll be fun."

Lolly squealed and pecked his lips before opening the door and darting from the car. He followed, checking both directions, his eyes shooting towards Elmwood Avenue and then back to Delaware; a milk delivery truck made its way towards him, and he watched it until it turned the corner.

She stood on the shoveled sidewalk staring up at the dormers. He stopped beside her, pulling her close. She trembled against him, but he didn't know if it was from the cold or from excitement.

"Look at it, Al," she said. "Look at it."

"I am. It's big."

The front door opened and a slender man in a gray flannel suit stood in the doorway. "You must be the Nussbaums."

"We are," Lolly answered. "We're early. I hope that's all right."

"It's fine. My first appointment cancelled. Evidently they received more snow south of here than we did."

"They always do," Lolly said, her words sing-song, melodic, like she was speaking the refrain from some Christmas Carol she had heard on the radio.

Al followed, the tightening in his stomach turning to nausea. The front walk was shoveled to the pavement, but he moved as if the snow had accumulated to his hips. The realtor looked past him to the station wagon and frowned.

"I'm William Morrison," the realtor said, extending his hand. "Welcome to your new home."

Lolly sucked in her breath and shook his hand; Al bet that was his signature line, one he spoke to every young couple hungry to find a home and start a new life. He climbed the front steps and William flashed his salesman smile. *It didn't matter if they were hustling new Impalas or turn-of-the-century homes,* Al thought. *They all smiled the same damn smile—too wide, too toothy, too eager.*

Al smiled back.

"Al Nussbaum," he said, and shook his hand. William's grip was harder than it needed to be; guys like that always tried too hard.

He was definitely a William, not a regular-guy Bill or friendly Billy. Everything about him was as formal as his first name—his black hair was Brylcreamed into place, bisected by a razor part; his suit was tailored with a handkerchief folded into fingers and tucked in his breast pocket; his wingtips were polished to mirrors. He wouldn't have lasted five minutes in Chillicothe.

"Please, come in." He stepped aside so they could enter.

"Oh, Al," Lolly said, and his nausea deepened. "What kind of wood is this?" she asked William, taking off her gloves and touching the golden, shoulder-high wainscoting that lined the front hallway. Her fingertips brushed over the wood's medullary rays and wavy grain patterns the same way they traced Al's tattooed snake and dagger.

"It's quarter-sawn oak," he answered. "The wallpaper above it is hand-painted and original to the house, dating to 1915."

Lolly touched the wallpaper as well, as if she wouldn't believe any of this were real unless she felt it herself.

"As you can see," William said, squeezing by and leading the way into the foyer, "the same quarter-sawn oak was used on the grand staircase as well as on the Doric columns separating the foyer from the parlor."

She tugged off her wet boots, took a few stockinged steps into the foyer, and then stopped, taking in all she saw: the gleaming hardwood floors, the landing's leaded glass windows, the crystal chandeliers suspended from the ceiling. Al could see her breathing through her winter coat. He stepped out of his shoes and padded next to her. The gilded foyer mirror captured his reflection. His shoulders were rounded even more than Stan's, weighed down by the sadness that was replacing his nausea. He tried to straighten. Lolly took his hand.

"Mahogany was used in the living room," William said. "You can see the workmanship in the way the wainscoting is curved in the corners and the intricacies of the carved mantle."

The fireplace opening had to be three feet wide and almost as high; a fire crackled and popped inside. William caught Al staring at the flames. "The house was so chilly when I came here this morning, I thought a fire would be nice, give you a sense of the cozy evenings you could have here."

Lolly squeezed Al's hand then let go. She drifted towards the fireplace, the chimney drawing her in like smoke. Al bet the realtor would've had that fireplace loaded with logs and roaring even if he was showing him the house on the Fourth of July.

"It's beautiful," she said, reaching out to touch the mantle.

"The builders were especially clever with these pocket doors," William said, pointing to the sliding doors that separated the living room from the parlor. "The same beautiful red mahogany is used on this side, but step into the parlor, Mrs. Nussbaum."

Said the spider to the fly, Al thought.

William offered his hand and Lolly took it, letting him pull her into the parlor. "See?" he asked. "That side is mahogany, but this side is the same quarter-sawn oak to match the columns and the baseboards. Isn't that magnificent?"

"Oh, Al. You have to see this."

And he did. He stood next to her, close enough to smell her perfume and hear her breathing as they both felt the pocket door's smooth wood.

"Wouldn't this parlor be perfect for the Christmas tree?" she asked.

"It sure would," he answered, but he couldn't picture it. He couldn't picture any of it. Something beyond sadness, something thick and dark slugged through him until his veins ran black and he felt full and heavy.

He couldn't picture them living anywhere. Not after Brooklyn.

"Oh, if these walls could talk, Al! What secrets they must have!"

He looked at the plaster walls as Lolly went to touch the dining room's carved mantle, a fire burning in that fireplace too. He tried to push the despair into some dark corner inside him. Lolly was right: these walls must hold secrets. As William described the enunciator system, the call bells located throughout the house used to summon the servants to the correct room, Al tried to guess where the wall safe was hidden. Surely a house this big must have at least one. Did the original owner have it up high, behind the pretty lady's portrait above the dining room mantle? Or did he have the safe upstairs in the master bedroom, the access panel hidden in the closet? Perhaps it was down in the basement set inside the foundation, or behind a section of that quarter-sawn oak in the foyer. He imagined the safe filled with stacks of forgotten money, dusty family jewelry, gold and silver bars, all waiting to be his, and he felt better.

"You would be the second family to live here," William said. "Jacob Hackenheimer was the original owner and builder of the house. He was president and part owner of the Kurtzman Piano Company. Their factory was located on Niagara Street, I believe. Wouldn't a baby grand look perfect in the living room right where the wall curves? You could tuck it right in. Or maybe in the parlor, framed by the columns so it's the first thing your guests see when they arrive."

"I'd put it in the living room," Lolly decided, as if this were a decision that had to be made. "Right in the curve where you suggested. In the parlor I'd put upholstered chairs and a round table, maybe a loveseat. No! Not a round table. A chessboard table for you, Al!"

Al managed something of a smile.

"One of those fancy chessboards where the squares are made from exotic woods and the chess pieces are carved ivory. But, of course," Lolly continued, "the chessboard and chairs would have to be cleared out for the Christmas tree during this time of year."

"Of course," William agreed. "Perfect."

"How high are the ceilings?" Lolly asked.

"Nine feet," the realtor answered, and all three looked up towards them. "The parlor is a bit wider than that, so you could get a big tree."

"We could get a huge tree! I could use all my ornaments. Maybe we could cut it down too, Al. We could get all bundled up and drive out to the country and pick out the perfect one. You know my dad would help. We could tie it to the roof of the station wagon. Alison would love that! It could be a new family tradition. So much better than going to the Clinton-Bailey Market for a tree."

Al said nothing. What would be their new family tradition? Visiting him in prison? Visiting his grave?

Lolly looked into the living room where the wainscoting curved. "Alison could take piano lessons. Wouldn't that be wonderful? Maybe I'd take them too. I've always wanted to learn."

"Let me show you the rest of the house," William said. "We'll go up the backstairs that the servants used, and then we'll come down the grand staircase when we're finished. Can you imagine—what's your daughter's name? Alison?—walking down those stairs on her way to the prom or—dare I say?—on her wedding day?"

"Wedding day!" Lolly laughed. "We're really getting ahead of ourselves. She can't even walk yet."

"Time goes fast," William said. "Her wedding day will be here before you know it."

The realtor lead Lolly to the servant's stairs lined with yellow pine. Al wanted to hit him hard in the face, spreading his nose and blackening his eyes. Time doesn't go fast. It goes slow in prison, especially if you're somehow spared the electric chair and have to live out the rest of your years in a windowless cell made of concrete and bars.

There were three bedrooms on the second floor. "Four if you want to close the master suite's pocket door," William said, sliding the door shut and cutting the room in two. "You don't have to use the side with the fireplace as a sitting room. It all depends on how many more babies you plan to have."

Lolly looked over her shoulder at Al, who trailed behind, and her eyes danced like she wanted to start expanding their family that very second.

"This second bedroom also has a fireplace and smaller sitting room," William said, letting Lolly lead them. "If you choose to make this your bedroom, you could use the sitting room as a nursery until the baby gets older. That way her crib will be close during the night. Alison would be steps away."

"Wouldn't that be convenient, Al? Especially with the next one when I'm nursing again?"

"Very," he said, stepping into the closet and inspecting the walls, tapping with fingertips for the built-in safe. When he stepped out, both William and Lolly were staring at him. "Lots of closet space for you, Lol," he said. "For your dresses."

After touring the third bedroom and the two full baths, William led them up the backstairs. "The third floor has three additional rooms, a half bath, and of course storage."

"It's not all attic space?" Lolly asked.

"Not at all. The larger room at the front of the house was originally the billiard room," William said, letting Lolly and Al go first before following. "Of course, with a growing family like yours it could be used as a playroom or less formal family room."

"Oh, the space, Al! We're so cramped in that apartment," she said, taking in the former billiard room that ran the width of the house and looked out on Lafayette Avenue. "And it's only going to get worse when Alison gets bigger."

Al nodded. It was going to get worse.

"The two smaller rooms were used by the servants back when the Hackenheimers lived here. Both are about the same size. This first room was originally the sewing room and the back room was the live-in maid's bedroom. Of course, you can make these into offices or additional bedrooms if you wish. Or—and this is just a thought—this whole third floor could be used as an apartment. Do either of you have elderly parents who might someday move in with you?"

"Al's parents are deceased, but what do you think, honey? Should we ask my mother to come live with us?"

Al formed a gun with his forefinger and thumb, held it to his temple, and pulled an imaginary trigger.

She laughed then eyed William, the laughter fading, her jaw setting hard. "The house certainly is gorgeous and well-maintained, but what about the mechanicals? And the roof?"

"I have a typed sheet with all that information in the kitchen. This way." He and Lolly chatted about electrical upgrades, the condition of the gutters, and insulation thickness as they went downstairs. Al trailed behind, tapping walls, pushing moldings, still searching for hidden gold.

They inspected the basement, the heated garage with a turntable for spinning the car so it pointed toward the street *Perfect for getaways*, Al thought, then left William waving on the front porch. Lolly's breath formed clouds in the cold air that reminded Al of the dialog balloons in Bobby's comic books.

"My God, what a house! Wasn't that something?"

"It sure was," he said, checking the street, his eyes darting left, then right, and then scanning the parked cars that lined the curb.

"I was so scared when we walked in, Al. I was shaking."

"Scared? Why were you scared?" he asked, opening the door for her and squinting at the houses across the street, searching the windows on the first and second floor for federal agents pointing cameras, binoculars, rifles.

"Oh, I know it's silly, but I've been imagining the inside of that house for years and I was afraid I'd be disappointed. But I never imagined it would be so grand. That woodwork! My God!"

He tasted bile and closed her car door. When he slid in next to her and fired the ignition, she started talking again.

"And it's given me so many ideas, Al," she said.

"Ideas? For what?" he asked, putting the car in gear.

"For our house, when we start looking. I mean *really* looking."

His stomach percolated. "What kind of ideas?"

"Well, I definitely want a front porch. A big one where we can put rocking chairs and sit out after dinner and wave to neighbors."

He spotted a black and white Buffalo police car in his rearview mirror and the percolating in his stomach increased to a hard boil.

"And a fireplace! We don't need one in every room like that house but at least one in the living room. And not a fake one either. A real one so you can build real fires for us."

"Sure," he said, watching the cruiser get closer as his stomach rolled.

"And I would love a kitchen pantry. I adored the glass cabinets in there and all that storage space!"

He stopped at the corner and waited for traffic to clear so he could make a right-hand turn. Sweat beaded above his eyebrows. The cop had pulled right behind him. He couldn't try to outrun him, not with Lolly in the car.

"And we must have a backyard for Alison. She'll be walking and running before we know it."

He hung a right, watching his rearview mirror and waiting for the siren to shrill, the lights to flash.

The cop turned left, and Al made a noise, part sigh, part moan.

"What is it?"

He tasted something sour in his throat. "Nothing, Lol. Just the idea of her walking so soon."

She laid her head on his shoulder. "When do you think we can start looking for a house, Al? The spring, maybe? After the snow melts? Will we have enough money saved by April?"

"April," he said, and wondered if he'd still be alive then.

Chapter 6

The doctor swabbed the tattoo with Merthiolate, disinfecting the area, until the snake and dagger glistened; Al watched the cotton ball move back and forth across the pigment. He was reclined in the examination chair, feet crossed at the ankles. The doctor hummed *Silent Night* until he was satisfied Al's upper arm had been cleansed. He dropped the cotton ball in a waste basket and prepared the syringe.

"Lignocaine?" Al asked.

The doctor stopped humming and faced him, still holding the hypodermic, his brows arched in surprise. "Lignocaine and epinephrine."

Al nodded once in approval.

"You know about local anesthetics?"

"I read up on the procedure before making the appointment."

"What did you read?"

"Medical journals mostly. Plastic and reconstructive surgery articles. Some dermatology papers, things like that."

"Those are difficult to find at your local library," the doctor said, and resumed preparing the syringe.

"I didn't have much luck there. I found most of them at the medical school."

"At the University of Buffalo? Are you a student there?"

"I snuck in. Pretended I was a med student. The librarian was very helpful."

"You're resourceful."

"I like to be prepared."

The doctor injected him. "This works fast. You'll be numb soon. You won't feel anything."

"I know."

"Then you know what to expect," the doctor said, picking up the high-speed skin grinder.

"You're going to grind away at me like you're doing body work on an old car. The skin's going to come off layer-by-layer and the tattoo with it."

"You'll be in discomfort when the anesthetic wears off."

"I'll be in bigger discomfort if that snake doesn't come off. Let's get going."

The doctor pulled the stool closer to the examining chair and sat. The grinder whirred to life in his hand and he bent to his work. Al watched his arm turn raw; the smell of burning flesh filled the room.

****

His apartment was dark when he came home—the floodlight wasn't shining on the front door, no electric candles burned in the windows, the Christmas tree stood dark in the corner.

The anesthetic had begun to wear off and his arm throbbed under the tight bandage; he knew the pain would grow worse. He called for Lolly but there was no response. The hall closet door was ajar, and he opened it with his good hand. When he shrugged off and hung his winter coat, it felt as if the coiled snake were now striking. Its sharpened fangs sunk into his skin and the blood that had once dripped down the dagger was now his own. He could almost hear the snake's rattle.

He called Lolly a second time as he switched on a lamp, but again there was no answer; he wondered if she were down at her mother's telling her about the house they had toured as Sylvie puffed away on a Pall Mall, the baby bouncing on her lap and breathing in what she exhaled. From down the hallway, he saw a strip of light seeping under their closed bedroom door.

"Are you in bed already?" he called. "It's still early."

An image of Lolly, dressed in garters and black sheer stockings, lying on their bed waiting for him flashed in his mind, and he hurried to her. Thinking of her propped up on pillows, her legs parted, made him forget the pain in his upper arm.

He opened the door and froze.

She sat cross-legged on the bed, the empty duffle bag by her side. In front of her were green piles of money stacked the way he had them at Bobby's apartment. The .45 rested next to her leg. She looked up at him. Black trails of mascara ran down her cheeks.

"I was snooping for my Christmas presents," she said, her voice strangled in her throat. "I thought maybe you brought something back from New York for me. A bracelet. Maybe pearls. I found this in the back of the hall closet instead." She raised a handful of bills. "There's almost eleven thousand dollars here, Al. I've been sitting here counting it over and over. Eleven thousand. Every time."

The throbbing in his arm spread to a pounding in his ears. Al knew the moment he dreaded had arrived. He tried to remember the confession he had written out, the words he had memorized, but as his stood in front of his wife, he couldn't think of a single syllable.

"Where did it come from, Al? Where did you get this money? Why do you have a gun? And don't you lie to me. Don't you dare lie."

Words still eluded him. For the first time since he stole that '51 Mercury as a teenager, he felt ashamed, but, like then, he wasn't sure if the shame stemmed from his crime or from being caught.

"Answer me, Al. Where did it come from? What have you been doing? Selling guns again? Is that why you went to New York?"

He said nothing.

Lolly grabbed the .45 and aimed it at him. "It's loaded. I checked. Answer me." She flicked off the safety.

He raised his hands.

"Answer me, Al."

"Banks," he said.

She stared at him, the gun wavering. "Banks? What about banks?"

He opened and closed his mouth.

"You rob banks? Is that what you're saying? You're a *bank robber*?"

Al nodded.

Her lips moved but no words escaped. A tremor rippled through her body; the gun shook harder. The barrel strayed across his chest.

"Put the gun down, Lolly, before that thing goes off."

She gripped the .45 with both hands to steady it. "How many?"

"Lolly, put the gun down."

"How many banks did you rob, Al?"

"Five," he said, not bothering to include the one in California. That one was a long time ago and far away. They'd never pin that one on him.

"You robbed a bank yesterday, didn't you? In Brooklyn or wherever you went. That's why you needed the police radio in the car. Jesus Christ, Al," Lolly said, and got up from the bed still holding the gun. The stacks of bills collapsed into each other. She began pacing from the footboard to the window and back again. "Five banks. Jesus Christ. Are you out of your mind? Mother was right all along. She warned me. Every day she warned me."

She stopped pacing and whirled around to face him, her eyes a wild blue. Once more she leveled the gun at him. "Where's the rest of the money, Al? If you robbed that many banks you must have more than eleven thousand," she said, nodding toward the bed. "Do you have a girlfriend? Did you spend all the money on *her*? Was Mother right about that too?"

"What? Of course not, Lolly. I'd never do that. The money went into the business or I put it aside for the house." He didn't mention using the money to buy and sell guns.

"The *house*. We're never going to get a house, are we, Al? That was a lie like everything else, wasn't it? God, how stupid I am."

For a third time, he couldn't find a single word to say.

"What's going to happen, Al? What happens now?"

"I'll have to leave. Run. They'll be coming."

Lolly, still holding the gun, hugged herself as if the cold outside air had seeped through the storm windows and the layers of insulation and into their bedroom. "When?"

"Soon."

She began breathing deeply, her chest rising and falling. She staggered to the window and stared into the night. Snow had begun to fall again. Her breathing was loud. He could hear her taking air in through her nose and blowing it out her mouth, the way she had when he had rushed her to the hospital to have the baby. Deep, rhythmic breathing, the kind the doctors said could help manage pain.

"I'm going with you then," she said, still staring into the night. "The three of us. We'll go together."

He went to her and hugged her from behind, wrapping his arms around her. He nuzzled her neck and ran his hands from her elbows to her shoulders, caressing her, whispering her name over and over. He kissed her arms and back through her sweater, his lips lingering against the wool. She leaned back into him, reaching up to cradle his head, still gripping the .45.

"I can pack tonight," she said. "We'll leave in the morning."

"Lolly," he whispered. "No."

****

His father-in-law had the habit of moving a chess piece, then holding it, fearing he was making a wrong move. He'd keep his fingers wrapped around it and study the board, searching for traps and reserving the right to slide the piece back to its original spot if needed.

Al fingered the bandage beneath his shirtsleeve as he waited; he'd need to take another painkiller soon. The first was wearing off. He had plenty of them, though, and Seconal. He agreed with Bobby: they'd never take him alive. He'd lay his king down before that happened, swallowing a handful of pills and letting the barbiturates first pull him into sleep, then pull him away. It would be a gentle death, gentler than alternating electrical currents passing through his body. Even if the jury didn't sentence him to die for the bank guard's murder, he couldn't live the rest of his life locked away from Lolly.

"Chess is a lot like life, Albert," Stan said, still studying the board. "Except there are no do-overs in life." He pulled the rook back and frowned, his forehead wrinkling into ridges.

"I don't know about that, Stan. Sometimes you might get a do-over, but it's painful and usually leaves scars." He rubbed his arm again.

He was patient with his father-in-law; he enjoyed spending time with him. He liked the quiet of the apartment when they played; Stan insisted on no radio or television during chess. Sylvie would lock herself in her room to read or go upstairs to visit the baby, and the only sounds came from the settling house or a passing snowplow. Stan puffed his pipe, and cherry tobacco enveloped them. Al would use these games to test openings or strategies that he'd read about or try to prolong the game as long as possible; he could have beaten him in four moves if he wanted. Al liked using this quiet time to think, to plot. He would miss Stan.

His father-in-law moved his bishop, exposing his queen, but Al ignored it. His strategy tonight was to sacrifice as many pieces as he could, giving Stan the illusion of winning, and then checkmating him with as few remaining chessmen as possible. He squinted at the board, choosing which of his pawns would die. His arm hurt to the marrow.

Two moves earlier, he had decided on Philadelphia and then Brazil.

Philadelphia was large enough for him to disappear and assume a new life. He liked the idea of living in the Germantown neighborhood, so similar to the Polish and German neighborhoods where he was raised—Cheektowaga, Kaisertown, Buffalo's East Side. He'd feel comfortable surrounded by the accents, delis, and bakeries. It would be as similar to home as he could think of. And Philly was a mere sixty miles from Atlantic City and ninety away from New York, close enough to Bobby and Curry to plan their next job.

He would need money for Brazil.

Al pushed a pawn to the center of the board, knowing it would be taken by Stan's bishop. Stan puffed faster on his pipe, the way he always did when he saw an opportunity, and took the pawn. He hesitated and kept his mottled hand on the piece as he surveyed the board again. A minute passed as he searched for signs of Al's strategy. Once he was confident it was safe and that he wasn't overlooking anything, he pulled his fingers away. Al was certain Stan had never made a bold move in his life.

"You're not concentrating tonight, Albert," he said, placing the pawn next to Al's other captured men.

"Don't count me out yet."

He thought he'd try the Smothered Mate strategy, hemming Stan's king in the corner surrounded by his own pieces, giving him no escape when checked by his knight. He knew how Stan's mind worked. The wall of chessmen encircling his king would give him a sense of safety, of invincibility. He'd be oblivious to Al's black knight weaving its way across the board and its deadly intentions. The end would be startling.

As Al pretended to ponder his next move, he decided he'd use the alias *Carl Fischer*; he'd never used that one before. He had derived the name from two great chess champions: Carl Schlechter, the Austrian who fought Emanuel Lasker to a draw in the 1910 World Championship, and Bobby Fischer, who had become the youngest Grand Master in 1959, a few months shy of his sixteenth birthday. A man named Carl Fischer would fit in and go unnoticed in Germantown, Pennsylvania.

He advanced his black knight.

Stan checked if the knight was challenging any of his pieces, and when he saw that it wasn't, he shoved his pawn forward. Al knew Stan was trying to race his pawn to his side of the board to promote it to another queen. Fighting off two queens while he maneuvered into the Smothered Mate struck him as a worthy challenge and more fun than he'd expected to have this awful evening. The game allowed him to stop thinking of Lolly, of running, of becoming a fugitive and leaving her.

But he couldn't stop thinking.

He decided to let the pawn advance to the eighth rank and allow the queening to take place. Stan would think he had the game won, that it was the beginning of the endgame.

Al sacrificed another pawn and wondered how long before he could come back for Lolly and the baby. He'd have to pick banks carefully, making sure the hauls were big enough so he could work his plan as fast as possible. Al and Bobby would have to lay low for a while to let things cool down a bit. He was certain the FBI was making their identification and capture a top priority since a guard had been murdered. His goal was for him and his family to spend next Christmas together in São Paulo if he could outsmart the Feds for that long. There were no extradition laws in Brazil. He had checked.

The idea of robbing two banks in the same day, one right after the other, formed in his mind. While the police were busy investigating the robbery and concentrating on one side of town—Chicago? Providence? Newark?—they'd hit another bank on the opposite side of city. Maybe they'd rent a storefront and soap the windows near the second bank, giving the appearance they were renovating and getting ready to open a new business, maybe a television and electronics store. He'd hang an *Opening Soon* sign on the door. They'd start weeks in advance so they could get to know the other surrounding merchants, letting them become accustomed to seeing them in the neighborhood. Then, after the second robbery, they'd head to the storefront and lock themselves safely inside and listen to the sirens screaming by their soaped windows. The police could set up all the roadblocks and shut down all the bridges they wanted. They'd eat sandwiches and drink coffee out of thermoses and monitor the police radio, laughing at the cops as they chased the wrong suspects and searched for them far from their storefront. They could stockpile supplies and stay hidden for days, weeks. He'd have two chessboards and play Bobby and Curry simultaneously and beat them both, the lone danger being locked up with Bobby for that long. Then, when the police and Feds decided the mysterious bank robbers must be miles away, when the roadblocks came down and the bridges reopened, they would sneak to the next town, the next job, the next bank, another step closer to reuniting with his family.

He wondered if Brazil looked as nice as the photographs.

*****

She was awake when Al came upstairs after checkmating Stan. The apartment was dark except for the Christmas tree and the burn of her cigarette; the ashtray on the coffee table was filled with grounded butts and bent fags. Her eyes were red and swollen from tears and menthols. Looking at them made the fire return to Al's stomach. She hadn't smoked in over a year since the doctor had told her she was pregnant. He stepped toward her, his arms open.

"Don't," she said.

He stopped and lowered his arms. "Are you okay?"

"Christ, Al. How could I be okay?"

"I'm sorry."

"Sorry? My God, Al. Sorry? You apologize when you forget the milk, not after confessing that you rob banks."

She picked up the pack of cigarettes from the coffee table and shook one loose. She lit it with the cigarette stub she held between her thumb and forefinger before grinding it in the ashtray, adding it to the growing pile.

"Sorry?" she asked again. "What are you sorry for, Al? For ruining our marriage? For showing me how stupid I am? Or for getting caught?"

"They haven't caught me yet."

"*I* caught you. Me, the naïve little wife who doesn't know anything. If I can catch you, don't you think the FBI can, too?"

"I have a plan."

"You told me your plan. Your plan is to leave without me."

"I can't take you and Alison with me, Lol. It's too dangerous. Or at least it will be soon."

"How can I stay here? Do you have any idea what it will be like for me once word gets out that you're a wanted criminal? I'm not going to be Lolly Nussbaum or Lolly Majchorowicz or whoever the hell I am anymore. Everyone's going to call me the Bank Robber's Wife once this hits the papers. They'll be gossiping and whispering behind my back when I walk by. And do you think any parents are going to let their children play with Alison when she's older? Do you think anyone is going to have anything to do with us at all?"

He started to apologize again but stopped.

"And what about my mother? Can you imagine what it's going to be like living with her? How many times will I hear that she was right about you? How many times will she tell me that I was stupid and ruined my life by marrying you?"

"Lolly, I…"

"How can I stay here without you, Al?"

"I can't take you, Lolly. I wish to God I could. But I swear I'll come back for you and Alison. I need to work things out and get enough money together."

She snorted and twin smoke streams jetted through her nostrils. "Yesterday I would have believed you. This morning I would have believed you." She looked at her watch. "Six *hours* ago, I would have believed you. But not now, Al, and not ever again will I believe a single word you say."

The phone rang before he could respond.

"It's been ringing for the last hour," she said, picking a dry tobacco flake from her tongue. "Every time I answer, they hang up."

"Probably kids," he said, walking to the kitchen. He lifted the receiver with his good arm and barked "Hello" in the mouthpiece to scare them.

He heard a cacophony on the other end of the line: jumbled voices, laughter, ringing slot machines. "Hello," he said again louder.

"They picked up Curry," Bobby said, shouting above the noise.

Al froze, words again eluding him. He looked at Lolly, her lids heavy and half-closed from smoke.

"Did you hear me? They got Curry."

"I heard you. When? Where?"

"Queens. He went home to say goodbye to his mother. They were waiting. I told him not to go, but he wouldn't listen."

"Jesus."

"He's gonna rat, Al. You know him. He'll cut a deal sure as shit and give us up. You especially since you masterminded everything. I hate rats."

So, I'm the mastermind now, Al thought. *Not the coward hiding in his car.* He didn't think Curry was the only one who would give him up if given the chance.

"It's time to run, Al. For good. And there's no going home again either, or you'll end up like Curry."

The line went dead in his ear, and he pictured agents in dark suits grabbing Bobby by the arms and wrestling him to the casino floor, pulling guns and money from his pockets. Al hung up the receiver. Lolly was standing in the kitchen doorway, her arms folded across her chest.

"Who was it?" she asked.

"Bobby," he answered. "I have to go."

Chapter 7

Lolly lay on her side of the bed, the other half of the mattress cold, empty. The clock on the nightstand ticked toward dawn. The house felt abandoned, the same way her grandparents' house had felt after her grandfather had died, as if something large and permanent had vanished, leaving behind a quiet vacuum.

The tears had stopped. Her side hurt from retching after the vomiting had ended. A shiver rippled through her and she covered herself with the blanket folded at the end of the bed. It weighed her down, pushing her deeper into the mattress. She imagined it woven from steel, not wool, the bulk of it powdering her bones and compressing cartilage until there was nothing substantial left. If the blanket were then lifted, a breeze could easily scatter her remains, mixing them with the fallen snow. Whatever lingered would be washed clean in the spring, carried away by the thaw and April rains, leaving no trace of her behind.

She rolled on the side that didn't ache, curling knees to chest, and drifted into that gauzy realm between sleep and consciousness where fantasy blended with uneasy dreams. She saw herself hurt—struck by a skidding sedan or slipping on the ice and striking her head on the glazed sidewalk. Her perspective was from above, looking down on her fallen body and the gathering crowd. Blood, red and rich, spread across gray ice. Sylvie stood close, holding Alison to her breast with Stan by her side. Others were there, an incongruent group that could only be formed by the subconscious—Maeve, the shoplifter, her second-grade teacher, the butcher from The Broadway Market. More people arrived: strangers, neighbors, friends from East High School that she hadn't seen since graduation. They all encircled her, but no one offered to help. She tried to call out but there wasn't enough air in her lungs.

Neither Al nor an ambulance arrived.

When she awoke, the dream was forgotten, and she thought of the plans that needed to be made. But Al was—had been—the planner in the family, not her. She'd have to tell her parents of course, a conversation she dreaded. Or maybe she would wait until Al's picture was splashed on the *Courier Express*' front page or hung on the post office bulletin board, and then she would have to nod and say: "You were right all along, Mother. I am a stupid little fool."

She would have to get a job. Al had left her half the stolen cash, hidden behind her dresser until she could open a safety deposit box in the morning, but the money wouldn't last. He had told her that he wouldn't be able to send any more when he was underground, that the FBI would be monitoring her mail and phone calls, trying to trace him. It would be up to her to provide for herself and Alison until he came for them.

The stillness exploded.

The downstairs front and back doors were battered open at the same moment, shattering glass and splintering wood.

Lolly sat straight up; the baby wailed. An army of boots thudded up the back and front stairs, and then the apartment door and the kitchen door were both kicked off their hinges; Sylvie's doors downstairs exploded inward as well, adding to the noise and confusion. Lolly jumped from the bed as light blinded her and she was ordered to freeze, to raise her hands, to not move a single goddamn muscle. She did as she was told, feeling naked and afraid in her thin nightgown. Gruff voices yelled "Clear!" from each of the rooms, and then every lamp and ceiling fixture was turned on so the apartment was bright and glowing, the way it would if a party were taking place. Sirens wailed from outside and red and blue lights flashed across houses and snow-covered lawns.

A tall, oval-faced man strode into Lolly's bedroom dressed in a dark overcoat and black fedora, the accumulated snow melting on the crown and brim. He held a gun, an extension of his hand, and scanned the bedroom. "Where is he?"

"Gone," she said, her arms still raised, her nightgown still clinging.

"Where?"

"Just gone."

His eyes, the same dark color as his coat and hat, looked flat and dull, the light burned from them ages ago. "Get dressed."

She lowered her arms and grabbed her robe from the foot of the bed and pulled it on, thankful to be covered. "My baby," she said, and tilted her head toward the wailing.

"Get her and meet me in the kitchen. Now."

She hurried past him to Alison's room, ignoring all the unsmiling men who filled her apartment. Her bare feet stepped on the snow they had tracked in that puddled on the floor. She scooped the baby in her arms and held her as she searched the crib for her pink pacifier, feeling under the elephant blanket until she found it. She tucked it between Alison's lips and gently rocked her as she hurried to the kitchen. Tears streamed down both their cheeks.

The oval-faced man was already seated at the kitchen table in Al's chair; the fedora rested next to the Atlantic City ashtray. The gun was nowhere to be seen. Lolly slid into the chair opposite him. His black hair was cropped short and receded to the top of his head, adding to his face's oval shape. Pale and waxy skin contrasted with what was left of his dark hair. She guessed him to be around forty.

"I'm Special Agent Alexander of the FBI," he said. "I'm in charge of the Nussbaum investigation."

She nodded, the words *Nussbaum investigation* reverberating in her brain. From the various rooms of the apartment, she heard drawers opened and furniture shoved aside.

"You and your husband are in a lot of trouble, Mrs. Nussbaum," he said. "Your best hope is to cooperate with us."

"*I'm* in trouble?" she asked, a new fear taking hold of her. "How am I in trouble?"

Special Agent Alexander leaned back in his chair and unbuttoned his coat, revealing a plain black suit that reminded her of a pall bearer's. He crossed his leg at the knee. "We've linked your husband to at least five bank robberies in the eastern United States over the last year, ma'am. There may be more. You expect the U.S. government to believe that you were unaware of what was taking place? He was living here with you, wasn't he?"

"I don't know anything about bank robberies."

Another agent burst in the kitchen holding the duffle bag. He opened it and showed Alexander the money. "From behind the dresser."

"Count it and bag it. Run the serial numbers."

Now I have nothing, she thought.

Alexander swung back to her. "I suggest you tell me everything, Mrs. Nussbaum, before I arrest you and put that baby into foster care."

She held Alison tighter. "I didn't know about the bank robberies until last night. That's when I found that money and Al told me what he'd been doing."

"You lived under the same roof with him, shared the same bed, and you didn't know your husband was a bank robber and a murderer? That's what you're telling me?"

The kitchen floor buckled beneath her; she grabbed the kitchen table with one hand and clung to Alison with the other. "Murderer?"

"That's right, Mrs. Nussbaum," Alexander said, uncrossing his legs and leaning across the table. "A bank guard is dead, and a New York City policeman is fighting for his life thanks to the Nussbaum Gang."

"The Nussbaum Gang," she repeated.

"Eyewitnesses have identified a one-eyed man as the shooter…"

"Bobby Wilcoxson," she blurted.

"…but all participants can be charged with murder when it occurs during the commission of a felony."

"Oh."

"And you know nothing about this?"

"I don't. I swear."

She heard hurrying footsteps up the backstairs and another younger agent, his cheeks red from the cold, entered the kitchen carrying a wooden crate. He tilted it so Alexander could see the clock parts, keys, and wire.

"From the garage," the agent said, his nose running.

"Tag each piece, then compare them to what we already have," Alexander said, pulling a small notebook from his inside coat pocket. He reached in his other pocket and brought out thick-framed glasses, the same color as his suit, and perched them on the end of his nose. The younger agent hurried down the backstairs as Alexander flipped through the notebook. "Has your husband ever been to Washington, D.C., Mrs. Nussbaum? Recently, I mean?"

From her parents' apartment, Lolly heard a crash. She wondered if a cabinet had been knocked on its side or perhaps a dresser. "Mother," she said, and rose.

"Sit," he ordered.

She gazed at the backstairs, her head cocked, waiting for the next crash of furniture.

"Sit," Alexander repeated.

She sat, still looking toward her mother's apartment.

"Has your husband ever been to Washington, D.C?" he repeated.

"Yes," she mumbled. "For business."

Alexander peered at Lolly over his glasses, his lips curling to a smirk. "Business? That's what he told you? That he was taking business trips?"

She nodded and felt stupidity blush her cheeks.

"When did he go to Washington on this business trip, Mrs. Nussbaum? Do you remember?"

"The spring," she answered. "May or June."

"On June fifteenth, two bombs were set off near the White House," he read from the notebook. "Did you know that, Mrs. Nussbaum?"

She shook her head.

"It was in the papers and on the news."

"Maybe I read about it. I don't remember."

"Calls were made to the police supposedly by white supremacists protesting the integration movement. They said there were more bombs planted near the White House and the Capitol and set to detonate. Most of the D.C. police force began searching around Pennsylvania Avenue. The White House itself was placed on lockdown. Bomb sniffing dogs were brought in, as well as experts from the military and various federal agencies. While that was taking place, a bank was robbed on the other side of town. Nearly twenty thousand dollars was stolen. There weren't any police even close enough to chase the robbers. They were all looking for bombs."

"Were there anymore?" she asked, her own voice foreign to her. "Bombs, I mean."

"One," Alexander said, removing his glasses and holding them. "It failed to detonate. Even your genius husband makes mistakes."

She heard paper being torn and realized the FBI were ripping open the giftwrapped presents under the Christmas tree and going through them.

"How much do you want to bet, Mrs. Nussbaum, that the homemade detonation device on the unexploded bomb matches the parts in that crate?"

Her head was spinning; she gripped the table firmly. "Was anybody hurt when the two bombs exploded?"

Alexander stared at her, his face unreadable. "They exploded in abandoned buildings."

"So no one was hurt?"

"Not a soul."

"And if the bombs went off in abandoned buildings," she said, her thoughts gelling, "nobody could have possibly *been* hurt. No one was *intended* to get hurt."

"There's always the possibility that innocent people will be killed or injured when bombs explode, Mrs. Nussbaum. Your husband is a dangerous man."

A shorter, stockier agent entered the kitchen from the backstairs. His dark overcoat was open; his shirt collar strained against his thick neck. He was perspiring, despite the cold.

"They're still tossing the downstairs apartment, but it looks clean so far," he said, wiping his face with a handkerchief.

Alexander nodded. "Mrs. Nussbaum, this is Special Agent Brause. He's assisting on this case."

Brause said hello as he shoved the handkerchief into his pants pocket, but he was looking past Lolly to the Simon Pure Ale calendar that was tacked to the wall behind her. He hurried across the room and removed it. "Do you mark things on this calendar, Mrs. Nussbaum?" he asked, flipping back the months. "Doctor appointments, birthdays, anniversaries?"

"Yes."

"And your husband's business trips?" Alexander asked.

"Yes."

Alexander asked Brause, "June fifteenth?"

Brause flipped to June and read, "Al Out. D.C."

Alexander reperched his glasses on his nose and looked at his notebook. "August thirty-first?"

"Al Out. Rochester."

"Bag it," Alexander said, and then told Lolly that the Lincoln-Rochester Trust was robbed of fifty-seven thousand dollars on August thirty-first.

"We found street maps too," Brause said. "Rochester, DC, all of them. Escape routes are drawn on each one."

Her stomach rolled.

"Mrs. Nussbaum?" Alexander asked.

The room shifted and roiled under her feet.

"Are you all right, Mrs. Nussbaum?"

She stood, knocking over the kitchen chair. She hurried across the room and handed Alison to the startled Brause and then retched in the sink, bringing up only bile. She gripped the counter until her stomach settled. Her hand shook as she took a glass from the drying rack, filled it, then rinsed her mouth.

"I'm sorry," she said, turning to face the agents and leaning against the sink.

"Don't be," Brause said, handing Alison back to her.

"Do you love your husband, Mrs. Nussbaum?" Alexander asked.

"What?"

"It's a simple question, maybe the easiest you're going to answer all day."

She closed her eyes and rolled her head, her neck and shoulders knotted. "Nothing is simple with Al."

"Do you love him?" he repeated.

She opened her eyes. "I love the man who dotes on this little girl. I love the man who spends quiet nights at home with his family reading or playing chess. I love the man who can't keep his hands or eyes off me. This other man, the one who sets off bombs near the White House and robs banks, I don't know him at all."

"If you love him, you'll help us," Brause said, his face once again shining with perspiration.

"How can I help you when I don't know anything?"

"We think you do, Mrs. Nussbaum. We think you know a lot," Brause said.

"But I don't. You know more than I do. Everyone knows more than I do."

"Let me explain how this is going to unfold, Mrs. Nussbaum," Alexander said. "As of two hours ago, Albert Frederick Nussbaum and Bobby Randell Wilcoxson have been placed on the FBI's most wanted list. That means their picture has been sent to every law enforcement agency in the United States and Canada, as well as to Interpol. Their wanted posters will hang in every post office in the country. Cars will be stopped at the Canadian border and searched. They will be considered armed and dangerous, which means if either of them so much as flinches during their arrest, our agents will open fire."

She felt the tears slide down her cheeks again, surprised that she had any left to shed.

"The regular cops, the police, won't even wait for them to flinch," Brause added. "They shot one of their own and we don't know if he's going to make it. If that officer dies…well," Brause shrugged his thick shoulders, "most cop killers aren't taken into custody alive."

"The FBI needs to find your husband first, Mrs. Nussbaum," Alexander said. "That's his best chance of surviving and *you* are our best chance of making that happen."

"But I don't know anything," Lolly said.

"Was there a special place that he liked to go—a cottage up in Canada, a hunting lodge in the south towns, a cabin somewhere in the Adirondacks?" Brause asked.

"No, we didn't have a second place. We were saving for a house."

"Saving for a house," Brause repeated, shaking his head. "That's a good one."

Alexander pushed his fedora aside and picked up the Atlantic City ashtray from the table. "Where did this come from?"

"Atlantic City," she answered. Alexander's eyes bore into her until she added, "Al brought it home from one of his trips."

"No banks were robbed in Atlantic City," Brause said, to Alexander.

"Alert our office in A.C. that Nussbaum might be coming their way. Put them on alert. Make sure every tollbooth collector between here and Jersey has Al's wanted poster. Emphasize to everyone that he is armed, extremely dangerous, and military trained. Tell them to take him alive…if they can."

*****

Lolly stood at the front window, gazing at the dawn sky streaked pink, red, and purple. *Red skies at morning, sailors take warning*, she thought. Or is it *mourning*? Below, all the snow-covered lawns remained untouched white blankets, pure and even, except hers. A dozen sets of footprints crisscrossed her driveway and grass, giving the snow a cratered appearance.

The house was quieter as most of the agents had left. Drawers had been yanked from dressers, their contents

STEPHEN G. EOANNOU

strewn. Cushions had been pulled from the couch and both the mattress and box spring leaned against her bedroom wall. Books had been taken from Al's handmade barrister bookcases, their pages riffled, and then tossed aside; a crack snaked across one of the bookcase's glass doors. Some of her grandmother's ornaments had been brushed from boughs by broad, passing shoulders and lay shattered next to torn-open gift boxes, the presents scattered; a single footprint, the ridges of the sole plain to see, stained a Christmas sleeper intended for Alison. Even the picture of her and Al in his groom's hat had been removed from its frame and dropped next to the magi who lay on their sides. What were they looking for inside the picture frame? A folded treasure map? A safety deposit key? A combination scrawled on the photograph to some hidden safe?

She thought of running away. Not with Al or to look for him, but packing Alison and some clothes and driving somewhere, anywhere far from her wrecked apartment, her wrecked marriage, her wrecked life. Maybe she'd drive to Florida where it's sunny and where nobody has ever heard of the Nussbaum Gang. She would use her given name, Alicia— Lolly suddenly sounded so juvenile—and start over. How wonderful it would be to leave Lolly behind with all her flaws and mistakes and become someone else, creating her own history, designing her own future that didn't contain guns or bombs or her possessions taken as evidence in plastic bags. Then she remembered that she didn't have a car to pack or cash to get them to Miami. Even if she still had the station wagon and the money Al had left, wouldn't the FBI come after her too? Wouldn't they think her fleeing was some admission of guilt, confirming her involvement in these five bank robberies? Or would Alexander think she was far too slow to be involved but would follow her anyways, tracking her every move, hoping she would lead him to Al?

She sighed, the noise a deflating sound, and realized she didn't have the option of running like Al, and that the dark fantasies of being hit by a car or hurt in some other accident would never occur and would never take her away from her awful life. She would need to somehow live through this with as much dignity as a fugitive's wife could muster, but she had no idea how to begin.

"I hope you don't mind, but I made coffee," Alexander said, startling her. He had removed his coat and jacket, revealing his shoulder holster. His tie was loosened; the night had exhausted him as much as it had her. She breathed in and realized the smell of percolating coffee had filled the apartment. It reminded of her of all those days Al had risen before her and started breakfast. She would lie in bed, warm and safe, as the smell of coffee and frying eggs drifted to her.

"I could use some," she said, fearing she'd cry if she lingered on mornings that were gone forever, and stepped toward him. Something crunched under her feet, but she didn't look to see what it was. She didn't want to know.

She followed Alexander into the kitchen, and he told her to have a seat. As she sat at the kitchen table, watching him slide an oven mitt on his hand and lift the pot from the stove, she wondered if he made coffee for his wife every morning and pancakes for their children on Sundays. Did he wear a shoulder holster along with an apron when he mixed the batter? She shook her head, realizing he probably wasn't home many mornings or many Sundays because he was out hunting criminals, dangerous and desperate men like Al.

"I hope it's not too strong," he said after handing her a mug and sitting across from her.

She blew the steam away and sipped. "It's fine."

Alexander sat angled towards her, leaning back in the chair. "Al is smart. He didn't leave much for us to find."

"Al thinks things through."

"And he played it smart too. He never called attention to himself. We didn't know who was robbing those eastern banks. He had all that money, but he never flashed it around. He didn't spend it on women or cars or a big fancy house."

She winced, the house on Lafayette coming in then out of focus.

"Don't get me wrong, Mrs. Nussbaum. You have a very nice home here."

"I did yesterday," she answered, and nodded towards the counters stacked with the dishes, glasses and pans pulled from cabinets. She waited for Alexander to apologize for tearing her apartment apart.

"He took care of you. I can see that," he continued, the apology never coming. "That's why I'm convinced he must've had a plan for taking care of you if he had to run or was arrested."

"If he had a plan, he never shared it with me".

"He must have left you money."

"You found it."

"Where's the rest?"

"I have no idea."

"That's hard to believe."

"This is all hard to believe."

"We found his car outside Rochester. No sign of your husband, though. He disappeared into the storm."

"Can I have the station wagon back?" she asked, the idea of running to Florida returning.

Alexander shook his head and sipped his coffee. "Can't," he said. "Evidence. We impounded it."

She needed a job and wondered if anyone would ever hire someone like her. Without a car, she would be forced to walk through snow or shiver on Bailey Avenue corners waiting for the number nineteen bus to get to work. That is, if anyone would hire a bank robber's wife.

Alexander looked past her to the wreck and chaos. "No, he took care of you, protected you from knowing about his other life with Bobby. He loved you, I'm sure of it. He'll be back for you, Mrs. Nussbaum, and I'll be waiting."

*****

Despite an ache felt deep inside muscle and bone, Lolly didn't try to sleep. Instead, she began putting the kitchen back together. She wiped out cabinets and replaced the contact paper. She washed the FBI off each glass and plate, wiped the dishes dry to remove any lingering trace of them, and then placed them back on the shelf. The rim of one poinsettia mug was chipped and she cradled it in her hands, trying to remember if the chip had been there before or if some uncaring federal agent had knocked it against another cup, damaging it beyond repair.

"Mrs. Nussbaum?"

The strange, male voice startled her. She sucked in her breath and dropped the mug and it shattered on the floor, the broken pieces spreading across the linoleum.

A hatless man stood in the backstairs doorway. He wore a gray overcoat that fit loose in the shoulders and fell baggy across his middle. Whiskers darkened cheeks and chin; he looked too disheveled to be a federal agent.

"Who are you?" she asked. "How did you get in?"

"I didn't mean to frighten you. I'm Morton Lucoff. I write for the *Buffalo Evening News*. The door was open. Well, actually, there was no door. I stepped over it."

"Get out."

"You are Mrs. Nussbaum, right? Al's wife? The bank robber?"

"I said get out!"

"I have a few questions."

She rushed towards him, the pieces of the poinsettia cup crunching under her slipper, and she shoved the reporter hard in the chest with both hands.

"Out!"

Lucoff was pushed back a step or two towards the stairs. "Do you know where you husband is, Mrs. Nussbaum?"

She pushed him again. "Goddamnit!"

"Has your husband killed others?

"Get out!" she yelled, reawakening the baby.

"Do you think Al is still in Buffalo, Mrs. Nussbaum?"

She didn't have to push him a third time. Stan had heard her yelling and raced up the stairs. He grabbed the reporter by his collar and belt and partly carried, partly dragged him down the stairs to the shattered door.

"Do you think he'll get the electric chair, Mrs. Nussbaum? Will you go to watch if he does?"

She heard a dull thud, a body being slammed into plaster, and then there were no more questions.

*****

Sylvie's familiar footsteps shuffled up the backstairs and Lolly cringed. She had been up all night being questioned by the FBI but dealing with her mother seemed far worse. Sylvie entered the kitchen wearing two sweaters, mittens, and earmuffs. Lolly waited for her to erupt, to eviscerate Al, to gloat that she'd been right all along, but she said nothing. Instead, she went to Lolly and took her in her arms. Lolly hugged her back and pressed her face into the tall woman's sweater that smelled of fried sausage and cigarette smoke. Sylvie held her daughter as she wept and kept holding her until her tears and trembling slowed, then stopped.

"Why are you dressed like that?" Lolly asked, breaking their embrace and pulling a tissue from her robe's pocket. She dabbed her eyes and blew her nose.

"It's freezing in my apartment. They kicked in both doors. The cold and snow are blowing in. Your father's trying to fix them," Sylvie said as hammering started from downstairs. Sylvie surveyed the wrecked living room. "Your place is worse than mine. I'll help you clean up."

"No," Lolly said. "I want to do it. I want to do all of it. The kitchen is almost done. I want to wash and sweep and put things back the way they were. I don't want to think about Al or the FBI or bank robberies. I want to fix this place. And when I'm done here, I'll come downstairs and clean your apartment. Then I'll curl in bed and sleep until summer and wake when it's warm and everything is back to normal."

Sylvie didn't say anything. Lolly bent and slipped a Christmas album inside a jacket with a red bow and ribbon on its cover, certain that the vinyl had been scratched.

Part 2:

Middle Game

...my profession at the time was a bank robber.

—Al Nussbaum

Chapter 8

Al carried boxes from his car to his third floor walk-up in Germantown. This apartment was smaller and cheaper than the last one; money was tight. Three mismatched wooden chairs dating back to the war encircled a kitchen table. The surface was scarred with burns and gouges; folded gray cardboard had been placed under one leg to keep it from wobbling. Half the apartment windows were propped open, their sash cords either severed or missing, but the rooms still smelled stale and dry. He wondered how long it had been since someone had lived there. The other windows were painted shut.

He was sweating in the late summer heatwave. Sweat trickled between his shoulder blades and down his thighs. He set the box next to the bare metal-framed bed, no wider than his cot had been in Chillicothe. His reflection in the dresser mirror surprised him. His hair was dyed black to match the pencil mustache he'd grown, and he wore thick-framed glasses, the lenses clear. The lifts in his shoes made him almost two inches taller. Months ago, a hard crust had formed where the snake and dagger had been tattooed. The crust had fallen off revealing pink scar tissue. He looked far different than the clean-shaven, crew-cut picture on his FBI wanted poster.

Bobby had told him the Feds had printed and distributed one million copies to post offices, hotels, and bus stations. Bobby would know; he was keeping a scrapbook. Each day, he'd go to the library on Logan Square and thumb through the New York and Buffalo papers searching for any mention of their names; he carried a pair of scissors in his shirt pocket in case he found an article about them.

The stairs creaked as he went down for another box from the light blue Chevy's trunk, the car he had bought with cash under the name Carl Fischer after he had ditched the station wagon; he had kept the police radio. He grabbed the last carton of books and climbed the stairs. Another man was coming down from the second floor. He had a shy smile and apologetic eyes that shifted and roamed, never settling on one place for more than an instant.

Al nodded as he passed him on the stairs, but the man stopped. "You must be the new tenant in 3-A."

Al stopped too. He didn't want to, but that's what neighbors—not fugitives—did. "Yes, Carl Fischer. Nice to meet you. I'd shake your hand, but..." Al raised the box and smiled down at him.

"Oh, I understand," the man said, not looking at Al directly. He pulled a handkerchief from his pants pocket and mopped his forehead. "You sure picked a hot day to move."

Al kept smiling. "I sure did."

"I'm Leonard Weiss. 2-B."

"Nice to meet you, Leonard."

Leonard rose on his toes and looked into the box Al held. "That's a lot of books, Carl. You a teacher?"

"Writer," he answered, the word out of his mouth before he could stop it, but he knew he had given the correct answer. Summer would eventually end, and a teacher would return to school, but a writer could stay home. He could spend long stretches hiding in his apartment and if asked where he'd been and what he'd been doing, he could answer "Writing," and they would pretend to understand. If they asked what he was working on, he would smile coyly and say that it was too early to talk about the project, that he didn't want to jinx it, that surely they understood. They would nod, wise to a writer's strange ways and clap him on the back, telling him to keep up the hard work, that they were looking forward to reading his book someday, whatever it was about. They would chuckle as they left him and call over their shoulders not to forget them when he's famous. It was the perfect cover. Neighbors would start calling him Shakespeare when they greeted him.

"A writer? Really? That's interesting," Leonard said. "What kind of writing do you do?"

Al shifted the box to his other arm, the lies coming easily. "Crime fiction. Stories about bank robbers, guys on the run, things like that."

"No kidding? The pulps, huh? I read that stuff. Maybe I've read some of yours."

He tried to mirror Leonard's shy smile and apologetic eyes. "Well, I'm not published yet."

Leonard wiped the back of his neck with the handkerchief; his cheeks still shone with perspiration. "I'd be happy to take a look at what you've got. Give my opinion, that sort of thing. I'm a pretty avid reader."

"Sure, I may take you up on that...when the manuscript is ready."

"Of course," Leonard said looking pleased, his eyes darting from Al to the box he held and back again. "I better let you get back to unpacking. This day isn't going to get any cooler. It was nice meeting you, Carl."

"Likewise," Al said, making a note to buy a secondhand typewriter as he climbed the stairs to his sweltering apartment.

He dropped the box in the living room, placed his hands on the small of his back, and pushed his hips out, the soreness from moving already setting in. He surveyed his new home, deciding it was no better than a cell. There were no gangs or guards or fear of being jumped in the yard, but it was a prison nonetheless, a prison holding a single inmate. For the thousandth time he thought, *If Bobby hadn't killed that guard...*

Maybe it was his fault.

Maybe he should have drilled into Bobby's and Curry's thick skulls not to kill anyone, to only wound them if they had to fire their weapons, but he knew that Bobby didn't listen to him the way he had when they had first met in Chillicothe. Al had watched him in the yard and in the laundry where they had worked, recognizing immediately the danger Bobby emitted, the kind that could intimidate bank tellers and potential witnesses. For weeks, he worked close to him and ate at the same table, eavesdropping on his conversations, deciding that Bobby wasn't stupid, but that he wasn't smart enough to think things through. He talked loudly to give the impression that he was in charge, but at best he was a bully. Al knew that he could mold him, turn him into a well-armed pawn that would do his bidding.

Gradually they became friends and on a gray autumn day where the wind and air promised colder weather to follow, he and Bobby huddled together on the yard's bleachers out of earshot of both guards and prisoners. Al outlined his plans for robbing banks to seed legitimate businesses like importing electronics from Japan, and illegitimate businesses like gun trafficking. Bobby had hung on his every word, the strategies and capers so complex he'd shake his head, his good eye glinting, and ask him how he came up with this stuff.

If Al didn't need him, he would disappear from Bobby's life that very afternoon and never look in that dead eye again.

But he did need Bobby.

He needed him to go inside banks and rob the money required to go back for Lolly and the baby. He needed Bobby to grab stacks of unmarked bills by the handful, the armful, the bagful, and bring it to him for Brazil. He needed Bobby to clear out bank drawers and safety deposit boxes and vaults. But most of all, he needed Bobby to do what he was told.

Al was too tired to shower the moving-day sweat off him. Instead, he plugged in the ancient Emerson oscillating fan that sat rusting on his dresser. The fan whined as it swirled hot air around his bedroom. He sat on the edge of the metal bed, ran his fingers through his dyed hair and wondered if it was this hot in Buffalo, if Lolly was wearing a sundress the same shade as her eyes, if her shoulders had been honeyed by the sun. If he was home on a stifling day like today, he would have filled a plastic wading pool with the garden hose for Alison and let her splash and squeal and slap the water with tiny hands. He'd stand close by, smiling but keeping an eye on her, making sure she didn't duck beneath the surface. Or maybe he'd film her with his Bell Howell eight-millimeter camera that he kept in the hall closet, capturing all the giggling and splashing on home movies so he and Lolly could watch and remember when they were old and Alison had her own babies.

He wondered if Alison was walking yet.

Something opened inside him. It started as a small hole, then expanded until it was black and gaping, filled with loneliness and loss, and its own gravitational pull drew him in.

If Bobby hadn't killed that guard...

He rose from the bed, the box spring squeaked, relieved to be unburdened, and started pacing the small room. He needed to do something to occupy his hands and mind to escape that widening hole before it consumed him. He dropped to his knees in front of the bed, not to pray for forgiveness or guidance but, rather, to pull Bobby's Thompson submachine gun from underneath the bed. He carried it to the wobbly kitchen table and dug through a carton until he found his gun cleaning kit. The kitchen chair also teetered when he sat on it, but Al didn't bother to shim it steady. Instead he leaned forward, balancing on the two even front legs, and began field stripping the machine gun for the third time that week.

He'd once told Bobby that he'd fallen in love while in the army—with guns. He loved how each piece fit and had its special, deadly function. He loved the power the rifle held when it was assembled and loaded, and he loved the way it made him feel when he pulled the trigger, felt the recoil, saw the results; it didn't take him long to earn his army marksmanship badge. The drill sergeants always wanted to see how fast he could breakdown his rifle and reassemble it, and he was always the fastest in his unit no matter if he was blindfolded or had someone screaming in his ear to distract him. That day, in the oppressive apartment heat, with sweat coating his grip, he took his time stripping the weapon, enjoying the way each part felt and the rich smell of gun oil.

Al dropped the magazine and pulled off the butt stock. He slammed the bolt forward, set the safety to *Fire* and the selector switch to *Full Auto*. The gun, lighter in his hands without the stock, felt like a toy. He flipped it upside down and set it on the gouged table. He slid the rear assembly handle back and squeezed the trigger and lifted up to pull the assembly free. In the army, his fellow recruits would struggle to release the buffer pilot and spring and would curse him for how easily he could do this. Nothing had changed since his discharge.

He eased the bolt all the way back and lifted it out, moving it from hand-to-hand, measuring its worth and guessing its weight before setting it on the table. He hooked his thumbs through his front belt loops and leaned far back in the chair until he was balancing on the unstable back legs and admired the unassembled parts spread before him. Separately, none of the pieces—trigger, barrel, bolts—were dangerous, but together they were deadly. He thought of all the times he had fired weapons—Tommies, shotguns, automatics—and the countless hours he had spent at firing ranges or in the woods aiming at targets. In all those years, through all those fired rounds, both in the army and as a civilian, he had never once fired at a human being.

The chair, threatening to splinter, made a groaning sound as Al settled it on the floor. Before reaching for his cleaning kit, he arranged the parts in the gun's outline like a schematic drawing and imagined each piece labeled: rear grip, fore grip, bolt handle. Al wet the patch in solvent, attached it to the rod and ran it down the barrel; the wet patch affixed to the end would have broken up old powder and lead residue if there had been any. As he worked the rod up and down inside the barrel, he wondered if Officer Accardi was back on the job or if he was still recovering from the chest wound that this gun had given him. Would he wear the badge dented by Bobby's round as a lucky talisman to protect him for the rest of his law enforcement career? Or had he framed it and hung it on the same wall as Saint Michael's icon, patron saint of police officers? Or maybe Accardi had quit the force, having lost his nerve after being shot by a one-eyed bank robber. A Thompson blast can change your mind about so many things.

Al extracted the rod and inspected the patch. It was so clean it was as if Bobby's submachine gun had never been fired, and he wished that was true.

****

He was drowsed on the stained mattress when he heard the knock: three quick ones, a pause, then a single rap, another pause, then three more quick ones. The knocking was louder than usual, more insistent and impatient, almost a pounding. Al wondered if it was really Bobby. He pulled a .45 from under his pillow and went to the door in his boxers and sleeveless undershirt.

"Yes?" Al said, through the closed door. "Who is it?"

"J. Edgar Hoover, smart guy," Bobby answered. "Who the hell do you think it is?"

Al unlocked the door but left it chained. He cracked it open and stared into Bobby's dead eye.

"Jesus, open up already."

He unchained the door and opened it. Bobby burst in, his body alive with energy, and paced around the small apartment. "We made it, man. We're big time. Top of the charts. Number one with a bullet."

Jackie Rose followed, carrying an armful of magazines. She wore lime pedal pushers and a green and blue striped top. Her hair, dyed a sandy brown, was pulled into a ponytail and her face, makeup free, was tanned and freckled. She looked like a high school girl who had spent every day of summer vacation lying in the sun, her skin shiny with baby oil. She kissed Al's cheek; her fingers rested on the scar where the snake had once coiled.

Al locked and chained the door then pulled his sticky t-shirt away from his body. Another old fan rattled in the living room window, trying to draw some of the heat from the apartment. He didn't feel big time at all.

"What are you talking about, Bobby?"

He set the gun on the couch and watched Bobby orbit the living room, bouncing from one side to the other. His quick movements contrasted with his appearance. Al had aged him as part of his disguise, shaving back his hair to increase his receding hairline. His temples were dyed silver and he wore black horn-rimmed glasses; there was nothing that could be done to hide that eye. He looked like a middle-age man; he and Jackie Rose were traveling as father and daughter.

Bobby reached in his back pocket and tossed Al the current issue of *Reader's Digest*. "Read all about it, smart guy. I'm Mickey Mantle! I'm Babe Ruth! I'm John Goddamn Dillinger!"

Al stared at the beach scene on the cover: a pale blue sky above sand littered with seashells, driftwood, and coral. A lone seagull hovered in the corner. "What is this?"

"Open it. You'll see. Page forty."

The article's title was written in red: "Most Wanted Criminal Since Dillinger." Bobby's mugshot was outlined in a matching red box with the caption "If You See This Man, Phone the FBI." Printed in the upper margin of each page were the words "$10,000 Reward."

"Dear God," Al said, and sat on the couch to read the article.

Jackie Rose dumped all but one of the extra copies she carried next to him and then hurried to an open window; she fanned herself with the one she had saved. Bobby stood behind Al and pointed over his shoulder.

"See there? At the bottom? 'Most-sought desperado since Dillinger.' They're talking about me, smart guy."

Bobby began pacing the apartment again, his arms swinging in wide arcs as if he were loosening his shoulders before stepping into the batter's box. He grinned the whole time. "Public Enemy Number One. Top of the list. Famous. I'm in the goddamn *Reader's Digest*! Everybody knows my name, isn't that right, baby girl?"

"That's right, Bobby," she answered, still fanning herself and looking out the window.

Al flipped the page. The Feds had Bobby linked to all the robberies: November 5, 1960, First Federal Savings & Loan, Buffalo, witnesses said there was something unusual about the robber's eye, that it didn't focus; January 12, 1961, M&T Bank, Buffalo, one of the robbers had a bad eye; June 30, 1961, Bank of Commerce, Washington, D.C., the machine gunner had a glass eye.

He stopped reading. "Bobby, when you were inside the banks, did you leave the sunglasses on like I told you?"

Bobby waved away Al's words. "Too hard to see with them inside. Took the damn things off every time."

Al's stomach burned.

Bobby began shadow boxing, bouncing on his toes and shuffling his feet. "Look at me. Cassius Clay. Olympic champion. Gold medal, baby. Readers fucking Digest." He danced around the couch until he was in front of Al and threw lefts and rights in his direction.

Al was first mentioned on the article's third page. They had everything: his description, his arrest record going back to that stolen Merc, his mug shot on the fourth page.

"Curry must have talked," he said.

"Curry's a rat. A fucking rat. He'll get what's coming to him. All rats do."

Al read that, as a public service, *Reader's Digest* was offering ten thousand dollars to the person or persons who supplied information leading to his or Bobby's arrest.

"Help catch the men who killed a Brooklyn bank guard and wounded a New York City police officer!" the article screamed.

A year earlier, the *Digest* had offered a similar reward for the capture of Joseph "Killer" Corbett, the man who had kidnapped and murdered Adolph Coors III, heir to the family beer fortune; Corbett was arrested a week after the article and his mug shot had run in magazine.

Al lowered the *Digest*. "You realize this isn't a good thing, right? What's the circulation of this?" he asked, holding up the magazine. "A million? Two million? More? Bobby, the people who'll read this and see our pictures live all around us. Anyone can spot us. Hell, with a bounty on our heads, *regular* people will be looking for us not just the cops. The FBI's tip line will be ringing off the wall."

Bobby stopped throwing punches. "You know what we should do? Rob a bank. Today. Show them we can't be stopped. Show them it don't matter if we're in *Reader's Digest.* Show them why I'm Public Enemy Number One."

"What are you talking about?"

"I'm talking about robbing banks, Al. It's what we do. It's what I'm good at. Let's knock one over today."

Al shook his head. "Nothing's planned. Don't be stupid."

"We need the goddamn money. We haven't done shit since Brooklyn. I'm tired of you saying we got to let things cool down. It ain't ever gonna cool down for us. Not ever, and I'm running out of cash."

Al looked at Jackie Rose for help.

"He's right, Al," she said from the window. "We're almost broke."

"You must be running low too," Bobby said, looking around the apartment. "Or you wouldn't have rented this dump."

Al stared at Jackie Rose sitting on the sill, her smooth legs folded under her. She was still fanning herself; sweat glistened in the hollow of her neck. It had been months since he'd been with Lolly. He wondered if he'd ever see her again.

"This makes us hotter than ever. Even you, Jackie," he said. "Your picture is in here too. Aiding and abetting."

"We still need money, Al," she said.

"Everybody will be looking for a one-eyed man and his girlfriend," he said to her. "Who wouldn't want a free ten grand?"

"It's not just me and Bobby, Al. You need money too. For Lolly and the baby and Brazil like you're always talking about."

"Yeah, you don't have a hope in hell of getting to Brazil if we don't get back to work," Bobby said.

Fatigue pumped through Al's veins, weighing down his muscles and eyelids. He wanted to crawl back to his stained mattress and close his eyes, shutting out Bobby and Jackie.

"Well?" Jackie prodded.

Al rubbed his temples.

"You know we're right," Bobby said. "You're not the only one who can be right, you know."

He pressed his palms into his eyes; his hands smelled of gun oil.

"What do you say, Al?"

He pulled his hands away and blinked first at Jackie and then at Bobby, their faces full of want and need as they waited for him to answer. His goal, the fugitive prayer he chanted each night before falling asleep, was *Christmas in Brazil, Christmas in Brazil.* He would never be able to answer his own prayer if he stayed holed up in dingy apartments.

"Well," he said, the word struggling out of his dry throat as he tried to sound fearless. "These banks won't rob themselves. I'll start planning something tonight. Maybe that bank in Pittsburgh we saw a few weeks back. That looked like a tin can."

"Atta boy." Bobby leaned in and grabbed the magazine from him. He held it in his palms and grinned at the cover, his good eye glinting.

"Show him the other article, Bobby," Jackie Rose said, fanning herself faster with the *Reader's Digest.*

"There's a second article?" Al asked.

"Oh," Bobby said. "Yeah." He shifted the magazine to one hand and reached in his back pocket, pulling out an unevenly folded newspaper clipping. He shoved it at Al. "That Morton Lucoff guy from the *Buffalo Evening News* is queer for you."

"That guy, again?" he asked, unfolding the article, its edges jagged where it was torn from the newspaper. Al wondered what happened to Bobby's scissors. Maybe he only carefully cut out the articles about himself.

"That's the fourth story he's written about you. I've been counting. Why you?" Bobby asked. "Can't he write about someone else?"

"I'm the Buffalo boy gone bad," Al said, scanning the article. "A local interest."

Lucoff had travelled to Ohio and interviewed the Chillicothe guards and warden who all described how Al had been a model prisoner, never caused trouble, and was paroled early for good behavior. The warden mentioned how Al played chess every day and how he had won correspondence tournaments while behind bars. A photograph of his empty cell accompanied the article. He didn't read to the end.

Al folded it, matching corner to corner, and handed the clipping back to Bobby. "Do what you want with it. Put it with the others or burn it. I don't care."

"Don't go getting a swell head because that hack writes about you all the time," Bobby said, stuffing it back in his pocket, wrinkling it. "Remember one thing, smart guy."

"What's that?"

Bobby bent down and leaned in close, his glass eye inches from Al's face. "If I'm Mickey Mantle, that makes you Roger fucking Maris."

****

After Al had bought the second-hand Smith-Corona, he started writing long letters to Lolly. He propped a tape recorder next to the typewriter to capture the sounds of hammers striking paper, the single bell at the end of the margin, the carriage being returned. While he read or slept, he played the recording so his neighbors would think the reclusive writer was hard at work and would pass his door without knocking. He was leaving his apartment less frequently, venturing out only when he needed food and supplies, magazines and books. He tried telling himself that he was playing it smart, that the fewer people who saw him the better, but he knew fear was keeping him locked in his apartment. Anyone could recognize him. Rolling through a stop sign could lead to a car chase and shootout. *How many people did subscribe to the Reader's Digest?* he wondered.

The first letters he wrote to Lolly were apologies, asking for forgiveness for leaving her and Alison. He was sorry that he wasn't the man she thought him to be and tried to explain the surrealism that surrounded planning crimes, pulling them off, outsmarting the police. He filled pages describing what it felt like to sit in the car while Bobby and Curry were inside a bank doing and saying what he had instructed. If anyone noticed him waiting behind the wheel, his face would reveal nothing—not excitement, or nervousness and certainly not fear. They would walk by, never suspecting that at that moment he was feeling more intoxicated than he ever had from alcohol and higher than he had gotten from any drug. When Curry and Bobby returned to the car, their bags stuffed with stolen money, he wanted to explode with laughter. He'd pull away from the bank as cool as a movie star but with pride puffing him until he felt bigger behind the wheel. They had worked *his* plan, *his* design, *his* baby. He had taken pieces from the small and innocuous—fake mustaches and sideburns—to the large and imperative—exit plans and contingency strategies—and put them together like he was reassembling a machine gun. He wrote to her that robbing banks was the best job he ever had.

Except for Brooklyn.

The muffled gun blasts had blown away any feeling of pride or desire to laugh. Up until then, there was a dream-like quality surrounding each of the robberies, and they never felt quite real to him. There had been no repercussions. He had been so careful, had planned so thoroughly. The crimes were puzzles to be solved, chess strategies to master.

It felt real now.

He wrote about loneliness, the pain of being away from her, how he missed watching the baby sleep, how he jumped when he heard car doors slam. Hundreds of words were spent listing all the things he loved and missed about her—her gentleness, falling asleep in her arms, the way she tucked her hair behind her ear when she bent over a drinking fountain. His typing grew faster, the hammers striking the paper harder when he described how he wanted to make love to her—in which rooms, in which positions, the places he wanted to kiss and taste and probe—until the typing would stop and he'd curl on his dirty mattress and masturbate quietly, quickly, sometimes with tears falling, as he had in prison.

The second batch of letters was about Brazil.

He explained how he had used money from bank jobs to buy guns that he then sold to another ex-con from Chillicothe named Luiz, who would smuggle them to Cuban rebels fighting Batista. In prison, Luiz had boasted how he could get all the real passports and visas he wanted, not the phony ones that would get him stopped at customs but the ones that could get a person safely out of a country and into another. This, he wrote, was how they would get to Brazil and be a family again. It would be expensive, but he would get Luiz the money; maybe his cut of the Pittsburgh job would bring in enough. In Brazil, they could start over. He'd get a legitimate job. There was so much he could do: mechanic, locksmith, electronics. Even Sylvie knew he was good with his hands, calling him Mr. Fix-It as he repaired everything and anything in both apartments, the sole compliment she had ever given him. Maybe he would become a writer. Who could write about crime and criminals better than he? Instead of planning heists, he'd plot stories. He could write novels or screenplays under a pseudonym. Brazil would be their paradise where they could raise Alison together in tropical sunlight.

After he finished typing a letter, he would read and re-read it, his sweat leaving smudges where he held the pages. He'd correct typos and replace words with ones that were stronger, more exact, that expressed precisely what he wanted. Sometimes he balled entire letters and started over if he wasn't pleased with the tone or the way he had described something. He had rewritten a paragraph three times that explained how counting stolen money right after a heist felt like Christmas morning. When a letter was perfect, written as well and as honestly as he could, he would stand in front of the toilet and burn it. Maybe the letters would have made Lolly feel better, at least she would know he was alive, but he couldn't take the chance. The FBI might be monitoring her mail, so he'd watch his words curl and char. He held them as long as he could, turning the paper to spread the flame, seeing how close the fire would get to his fingertips before dropping the letters in the bowl. The burnt pages hissed when they hit water.

In the background, his recorded typing filled the apartment, the sound seeping under the door, into the hallway and out the open windows for all to hear.

He thought about Pittsburgh.

Chapter 9

Lolly stood behind the bookstore's counter, the *Reader's Digest* shaking in her hands. Words swam and blurred as she struggled to read the article. Six thousand federal agents were looking for her husband, but she didn't trust her eyes and re-read the sentence. *Six thousand? My God. What chance did Al have of surviving this manhunt?*

The word echoed in her skull.

Manhunt—to hunt a man. She knew every successful hunt ends in a kill.

Her focus faded until the sentences became unreadable. She flipped to page forty-four, to Al's mugshot, her fingertip trailing over his lean face, a face she missed so much it hurt to look at the photograph. Why was Jacqueline Rose's photo next to Al's? The article had identified her as Bobby's girlfriend. Shouldn't she be next to his picture and not her husband's? She was pretty, Lolly admitted, in a peroxide way. Did Al like that? Was she with him on all those nights he travelled away from home? She was Bobby's girlfriend, wasn't she?

The bell above the door jingled and Lolly tossed the magazine under the counter as if she had been caught reading something obscene. Agents Alexander and Brause entered.

"I'm at work."

"We need to talk," Alexander said, his skin waxier than she remembered with dark circles under his eyes. She wondered when he had last slept. Days ago? Weeks ago? Maybe the last good sleep he had was the night before the Brooklyn robbery.

"I'm at work," she repeated, unable to keep the annoyance out of her voice.

"We could always bring you down to headquarters, Mrs. Nussbaum," Brause said, daubing his red face with a white handkerchief. He had sweated the starch from his shirt, and it clung to him in wrinkles.

Maeve peeked out of the office. "It's okay, Lolly. It's slow today. No one is out in this heat. Take as long as you need."

"Let's walk then," Lolly said, her blue eyes taking in Brause's discomfort.

Alexander held the door for her, the bell tinkling overhead, the sun almost blinding her as it reflected off parked cars and sidewalks. She strode quickly, her sandals slapping the pace; she heard Brause next to her, already breathing hard.

"So, what's so important that you have to bother me at work?" Lolly asked. "What *haven't* you asked me?"

"Was your husband political, Mrs. Nussbaum?" Alexander asked, slipping on sunglasses.

"Al? My God, no. He hated politicians. He thought they were all idiots. He didn't think much of the police, either."

"What were his views on Cuba?" Brause asked, a slight hop in his step. Lolly wondered if he could feel the heat rising from the cement through his leather soles. She walked faster.

"He had none, as far as I know. He doesn't drink rum or smoke cigars. He likes Hemingway, though. Didn't he live in Cuba?"

"I suggest you take this seriously, Mrs. Nussbaum," Brause said. "Or you can answer our questions downtown."

She sped up and heard Brause wheeze. They crossed the street in front of a carload of teenagers waiting for the light to change. Their windows were rolled down; Elvis had finished singing "Good Luck Charm" and DJ Tommy Shannon was giving WKBW's call letters at the top of the hour.

"I flew in from Washington this morning, Mrs. Nussbaum," Alexander said. "I met with Director Hoover about your husband."

She stopped in the middle of the intersection, Alexander's sentence braking her. The two agents stopped on either side. "J. Edgar Hoover knows about Al?"

"Of course. Your husband is at the top of our most wanted list. He's been eluding us for months. Mr. Hoover called him the most cunning fugitive alive in our meeting."

The light changed and the teenagers leaned on the horn, startling her. The kids yelled for them to move. She resumed walking, slower, as the car took off behind them with their tires squealing; "Take Good Care of My Baby" blasted from their open windows. She should have realized that the Director of the FBI would know about Al, but it still shocked her that her husband was so infamous that Hoover would know of him and rewards would be offered.

"We have reason to believe your husband was arming Castro's men," Brause said, his face a deeper red, his neck blotchy.

She stopped a second time at the corner. She let the statement sink in, turning it over in her mind, trying to make sense of what it meant. "*Castro*? Al?"

"We've found guns hidden all over New York State, Mrs. Nussbaum. Not a gun here or there, but caches of guns and hand grenades stored on farms and in warehouses that we've traced to your husband," Alexander said.

Brause pulled his notebook from his suit coat; it looked damp. "Did your husband ever mention Cowlesville, New York, Mrs. Nussbaum?"

"I've never heard of it."

"There's a farm there," Brause read. "In the barn we found eight German machine guns, fourteen automatic pistols, sixty hand grenades, two anti-tank guns, and thousands of rounds of ammunition."

"Anti-tank guns?"

"Castro," Brause answered.

"We believe he was using his share of the bank robbing money to buy and sell arms for an even greater profit," Alexander said.

"Cowlesville is just one of the locations we found. There are others." Brause raised his notebook, pointing it at her. "Some contained even more weapons than this."

She felt a wisp of hair fall loose against her neck and left it there. For a moment, the house on Lafayette came into view, then vanished. Had Al set aside any money for a new home? Or had it all gone towards guns? She started walking again, directionless, and the agents fell in step with her. People passed her, some pointing and whispering to their companions. Others said nothing, but she could tell they recognized her. Their eyes would dart away. From behind, she heard "That was the bank robber's wife!" whispered above flowing traffic.

"Has your husband been to Florida?" Brause asked, placing his notebook back in his pocket. His hair was matted across his forehead.

"I think it should be clear by now, Agent Brause, that I have no idea where my husband has been or who he has been with, except for maybe Bobby. I'm ashamed that I don't— ashamed of what my marriage was—but that's the truth."

"We believe that your husband has extensive contacts in Florida from gun running. He might be down there as we speak. Did he ever mention Florida, Mrs. Nussbaum?" Alexander asked, his face so waxy in the sunlight she thought it might melt.

"I was the one who would bring up Florida," she answered, turning the corner to avoid more Bailey Avenue stares. "As soon as Christmas was over and the decorations were packed away, I'd want winter to be over too. I'd complain to Al that I was sick of the cold and wanted to feel sand between my toes, to look across the water at night and see boat lights and the opposite shore."

"He never took you to Florida, Mrs. Nussbaum?" Brause asked. "There was no special place he liked to visit? Miami? Lauderdale? Tampa? We think he was down there quite a bit and he never took you?"

"No," she answered, and imagined Jackie Rose tanning in the Florida sun, her skin turning golden, her hair blonder. Lolly wondered if Jackie had been there with Al while she'd been home pregnant and alone. "Never."

"You expect us to believe that, Mrs. Nussbaum?" Brause asked.

"Do you expect me to believe all this about my husband, Agent Brause?" she asked, gesturing with her hand beyond her neighborhood, beyond Florida, beyond territorial waters to distant Cuban shores.

"Director Hoover believes, and I agree, that if your husband was stockpiling weapons across the state, he must have been hiding money across New York as well. We believe that's how he's been managing to avoid capture so far. He's very smart and he has access to money," Alexander said.

"My father always says that Al is the smartest guy in the room."

"We need to know where that money is, Mrs. Nussbaum."

Lolly laughed. "You think *I* know where the money is?"

"The Director does," Alexander answered.

"How much money has my husband stolen or made from selling guns? Thousands? Hundreds of thousands? Do you think if I knew where that money was hidden that I'd be working two jobs and living in my parents' apartment? Do you think I *enjoy* sleeping on their couch?"

"The money has to be somewhere," Brause said.

"What I think," Lolly said, the idea forming as she spoke, "is that you and the Director and all six thousand agents looking for Al are desperate. Why else would you keep coming back to me and asking me questions when it's obvious that I know nothing about Al's secret life? Guns? Castro? Hidden money? My God, you have no idea where he is, do you? The *Reader's Digest* said that Al has been 'lost from view' since December. Lost from view? What does that mean? He's invisible? If anyone could pull off *that* trick, it would be Al. I'm beginning to think he *is* some sort of magician. He certainly fooled me, and it seems like he's fooling the FBI too. That's why Hoover knows about him. Because Al is making everyone look bad. He's making you two look the worst of all."

"It's only making things worse for your husband, Mrs. Nussbaum," Alexander said. "The longer this goes on, the angrier Mr. Hoover will become. More and more agents will be added to the case. When he's captured, there won't be leniency."

"*If* he's captured," she said and hurried back to the bookstore, leaving Brause and Alexander sweating in the sun.

*****

Lolly crossed Bailey Avenue looking no better than Brause. Her hair fell limp, and her clothes were sticky with sweat. Her pace quickened as she neared the bookstore and the promise of air conditioning. The door opened as she approached.

"Come in where it's cool," Maeve said, holding the door for her. Her eyebrows pinched, ridging her forehead. "I've been waiting for you. I've been worried."

Lolly stepped into the store, and the perspiration dried on her face. "It feels glorious in here."

"Sit down before you fall down," Maeve said, locking the door and turning the Closed sign toward the street.

"You're closing early?" she asked, as she sat in one of the old wingback chairs that were scattered throughout the store for customers to relax in and thumb through books.

"There's no business today anyway. Too damn hot to be out in this heat. Stay there while I get you some water," she said, hurrying to the office.

Fergus jumped on Lolly's lap, but he felt heavy and warm, so she pushed him to the ground. He sulked away.

"Are you all right?" Maeve called from the office.

"I'm fine. Just hot. I should have let them question me here, but I wanted to make them sweat for a change, especially Brause, the shorter one. I don't like him."

Maeve reentered the store carrying a tall glass of water, the ice cubes clinking together, and a damp cloth. "Drink this," she said, handing her the water and cloth.

Lolly shut her eyes and drained half the glass.

"They were frightening. Who were they? Detectives?"

"FBI," Lolly answered, wiping her forearms and neck with the cloth. "They don't scare me anymore. I guess I'm used to them. Or maybe I'm getting tougher. Once a week, they'll come by and ask me questions I don't know the answers to. It's comical, really. I'm sorry they came here, though. That's not good for business."

Maeve leaned against the front counter and dismissed the apology with a wave of her hand. "What did they want this time?"

"This week they wanted to know where the money is hidden. Last week they wanted to know where the guns were hidden. Every week they want to know where Al is hidden."

"What did you tell them?"

"What can I tell them? I don't know anything."

"Would you tell them if you did?"

She sipped the cold water, studying Maeve over the glass. Her circle of friends had grown smaller over the last eight months. People she had known all her life called or stopped by the apartment under the pretense of checking on her, to see how she was holding up, to make sure she was doing okay. At first, she welcomed the company and was surprised that so many were concerned about her. Then she realized that most were there hoping to learn gossip about Al. As she shut out one person after another, she felt something harden in her core, toughening her from the inside, and making her skeptical of everyone's intentions. And now with *Reader's Digest* offering the ten thousand dollar reward, she didn't know if she could trust anyone.

The phone rang, and Maeve hurried into the office to answer it leaving Lolly to ponder her question. She had asked herself the same question on countless sleepless nights on her parents' couch—would she help the FBI catch Al if she could? She could hear Sylvie answer for her: "Of course you would. Why wouldn't you? What has he done for you except break your heart and lie to you? You don't owe him anything, but you owe it to yourself and to your baby to get free."

Still.

There was the other Al, the one who would put his hand on the small of her back to guide her through restaurants; the Al who tried so hard to console Alison when she was colicky; the Al who would bring her a single burnt orange rose, her favorite, for no reason at all. She didn't want to see him hunted, handcuffed, and locked away like an animal. Part of her, a very small part, still imagined a life with him.

"Sorry," Maeve said, walking out of the office. "That was my mother. I told her I'd call back." She rolled her eyes. "How's your mom doing?"

"She's okay. Tired, though. She's not used to watching the baby all day and night while I work."

"Where would you be without her?"

"Lost. Alone. I don't know how I would manage."

Maeve studied her. "You look better. Your color is back. I don't think you're going to die from heat stroke anymore."

"The water helped. I wish we had air conditioning in my mother's apartment."

Maeve frowned. "I have a confession to make. While you were out with the FBI, I read the *Reader's Digest* article."

"You don't need to confess. I'm sure everyone in the city has read it. At least everyone in this neighborhood."

"I couldn't believe I was reading about Al. I mean, I saw his picture and read his name, but it didn't match up with the Al I know, the quiet guy who would come in and buy books about chess."

"Wouldn't it be nice if they had the wrong guy and this was all a big mistake?" Lolly asked, looking towards the non-fiction corner where books on chess and true crime were shelved near each other. She set the water glass on the floor next to her chair.

"That would be nice, wouldn't it? But they don't have the wrong guy, Lolly."

"I know."

"This is hard to say," Maeve said, "but you should start thinking about the reward."

"The reward? Why? What about it?"

"You could use the ten thousand."

Everything inside Lolly accelerated: her heart, lungs, rushing blood. A noise whirled inside her head, like a propeller had started to turn and would soon gain speed and lift her toward the ceiling. She gripped the arms of the old chair.

Maeve didn't give her time to answer. "You need to help the FBI and tell them what you know. You have to think about yourself and the baby. I don't know how much you make at the restaurant, but it can't be a lot if you're working here too. You could start over with ten thousand dollars. You could move away or at least get out of this neighborhood where everyone knows you. I have a cousin who's a banker. He could tell you how to invest it if you want. He helped me get this store."

Lolly stared at her friend, taking in her red hair, green eyes, the smooth skin sprinkled with freckles and not recognizing a single feature.

Maeve squatted and placed her hand over Lolly's. "I know it would be difficult…"

"Difficult?" Lolly said, her voice sounding deeper, harder. "You think it would be *difficult* to betray my husband?"

"Lolly, I…"

She pulled her hand away from Maeve's. "What kind of person betrays her own husband? It's not like Al is a killer or kidnapper or threatening to hurt anyone. Then, sure, I'd help, but he just robs banks."

"It would be for the best, Lolly. This would all end and you could move on with your life. That money would help you."

"It would destroy me. And what if I did know where he was hiding and told the FBI? What if they killed him instead of arrested him? How do I live with *that*? What do I tell Alison in ten years when she asks what happened to Daddy? That I had him killed so I could move to the suburbs? That I did it for ten thousand dollars, money that wouldn't last a year? What kind of person does that make *me*?"

"A smart person, Lolly. Al would do it if he was in your position. He'd know it was the right move to make. The *only* move. You have to think what's best for *you*, not Al. You can't tell me you don't need ten thousand dollars."

Lolly pushed herself up from the chair, knocking over the glass, spilling the remaining water. "I should have run away with him like I wanted."

"Lolly, wait."

She brushed by Maeve and unlocked the door to the waiting heat.

*****

Alison's highchair was pulled close to the kitchen table when Lolly came home from the bookstore. The baby cooed and raised her arms when she saw her mother, and Lolly pulled her from the chair and kissed her cheeks and neck as the baby giggled. She held Alison close, her eyes shut tight, breathing in lotion and powder, relaxing for the first time since her walk with Alexander and Brause.

"I just got her settled in that chair," Sylvie said, stirring the baby food at the counter. "She's been fussy all day."

"It's the heat," Lolly said, pretending to nibble Alison's little hand to make her laugh. "It must be a hundred degrees in here."

"It's not that hot," Sylvie said, setting the Minnie Mouse bowl on the table next to an opened copy of *Reader's Digest*. "Feed her before you have to go to work again."

Lolly slid Alison back in the highchair, tied a bib around her neck, and then sat next to her, ignoring the magazine. She made airplane noises, flying a spoonful of baby food in the air until it landed in Alison's mouth.

"I took her to Mass today," Sylvie said, striking a match several times until it sputtered to life. She lit her cigarette. "She was a good girl."

"Of course, she was," Lolly said, flying another spoonful in for a landing. Some baby food dribbled on Alison's chin.

"We stayed afterwards and talked with Father Jozef," Sylvie said, blowing smoke towards the ceiling.

"Oh?" she asked, dabbing at Alison's chin with a cloth. "About what?"

"I wanted to show him the magazine," she answered, gesturing to the *Reader's Digest* with her cigarette.

The spoon stopped in midair. "Why would you do that?"

Sylvie raised a thin shoulder and let it fall; she had lost more weight since Al left, smoking more and eating less, telling Stan the stress was gnawing at her. "It doesn't matter. He had already read the article."

Lolly scooped more strained peaches onto the spoon. "Well, I'm sure that piece of journalism gave Father Jozef and the nuns something to gossip about."

"Don't be disrespectful. We had a nice talk."

"About what? The article?"

Sylvie nodded. "But mostly we talked about you, and Al, and an annulment."

Lolly put the spoon down. "What?"

"You need to start thinking about it, Lolly."

"Annulment? What does that even mean?"

Sylvie took a long drag on her cigarette then shot smoke through her nostrils. "Don't play dumb. You know what it means."

"No, I don't, Mother," she said. "Does that mean my marriage never happened? That I *imagined* the last two years? And what about Alison? Does an annulment mean that she doesn't exist, either? Is she annulled as part of the package?"

Alison slapped the tray with her hand as she stared at the spoon. Lolly pressed the peaches between her lips.

"Father Jozef says you have an open and shut case, just like the FBI."

Lolly ignored her and waited until Alison was ready for the next spoonful.

"According to the church, you can declare your marriage invalid because of fraud, concealment, failure to consummate, close blood relation of the parties, coercion, or misunderstanding. You can claim three of the six reasons," Sylvie said, ticking them off. "Fraud, concealment, and misunderstanding, which makes your marriage voidable."

Lolly wiped the baby's mouth with the cloth and then lifted her from the chair. "Voidable? Like a check?"

"Like a check that never should have been written," Sylvie said.

Lolly put Alison on her shoulder to burp her, patting from her lower back to her shoulder blades and down again. "This conversation is absurd, Mother. I'm not getting an annulment."

"What are you going to do then?" Sylvie asked, crossing her arms. "Hope they shoot him and you become a widow? Or waste your whole life waiting for him to get out of prison? Imagine what an animal he'll be after twenty-five years in jail. He'll come out worse than he went in…if he comes out at all."

The baby burped and Lolly wanted to run from the apartment, from her life. Even waitressing nights at The Greek's place was better than staying here. She handed her mother the baby. "I got to get ready for work."

"Father Jozef said you don't even have to wait for a civil divorce because your case is so unusual. Al robbed banks! A man is dead because of him! The archdiocese won't hesitate to grant you an annulment and free you from that monster."

"Don't forgot Castro," Lolly said, hurrying to the living room.

"Castro? What?" Sylvie followed her.

Lolly undressed, letting her blouse and skirt fall to the living room floor, not bothering to shut the front drapes.

"What's this about Castro?" Sylvie asked, the cigarette bouncing between her lips.

"Nothing," she said, grabbing her waitress uniform from the corner, the spot where she kept all her folded clothes. She and Stan had emptied her apartment and stored her dresser in the basement because there was no room for it in her parents' living room. "Forget I said anything."

"I want to know," Sylvie demanded, stubbing out the Pall Mall like she was jabbing it in Al's eye. "What's Cuba got to do with anything?"

She stepped into the white polyester uniform, pulled it up, and then reached around to struggle with the zipper. "You'll read about it in the paper soon enough. Or in *Reader's Digest*. Then you and Father Jozef will have more to talk about."

Lolly picked up the white waitress shoes from the corner where all her shoes were piled, some in boxes, some not. She stepped into them and hurried to the front door without tying the laces—grabbing her purse on the way without stopping.

"I want to know about Castro," Sylvie repeated, louder. "Don't you walk away from me."

But Lolly was already gone.

*****

She stood at the corner, waiting for the number nineteen bus to take her to the New Genesee Restaurant, The Greek's place. Large sunglasses, the kind the first lady sometimes wore, covered much of her face even though the skies were darkening with a coming storm. Her waitress uniform clung to her body, fitting snug at her hips and across her breasts. Angelo, The Greek, had told her it was good for tips when he had hired her. Men stared as they passed, and she noticed cars slowing as they approached the corner, even when the traffic light was green. She was convinced they weren't looking because they recognized her as the bank robber's wife. She shifted her weight to one leg, jutting a hip. A car horn tooted as it drove by and she allowed the corners of her lips to curl into a small smile. If the tips were good this week, she was thinking of making an appointment at the beauty parlor and having Irene style her hair differently, maybe in a flicked-up bouffant like Mrs. Kennedy wore. She needed to make changes.

Since Al had left, she imagined her life like a library card catalog with rows of drawers running vertically and horizontally. She was learning to fill those drawers with what haunted her—the FBI, the reward, and now the annulment. She was cramming the drawers until they were hard to close; some opened in the middle of the night, terrifying her to tears. As she stood sweating on the corner, she imagined pushing hard, trying to shut a drawer on her mother.

The silver NFT bus rattled to a halt in front of her, belching black exhaust as it braked. The doors unfolded and she felt her uniform slide up her leg as she stepped high to climb onboard. The driver, a man too old to be looking, winked as she dropped her coins in the box. She took a seat near the front of the bus and caught the driver staring at her in his wide mirror before he shut the door and put the bus into gear.

It was a fifteen minute ride to Genesee Street, but she dozed in the swaying bus, exhausted by her conversations with the FBI, Maeve, and her mother. She hadn't slept well since she had moved to her parents' apartment. The combination of worrying about her future, worrying about Al, and the narrow living room couch made sleeping difficult; she was up more during the night than Alison. She would pace the apartment or sit in the darkened kitchen sipping wine at three in the morning, the only sounds reaching her would be a police cruiser creeping past her house or a lonely train whistle drifting over from the Central Terminal on Paderewski Drive. Bailey Avenue had become the safest street in Buffalo as black and white patrol cars crawled up and down the street throughout the night, hoping to catch Al returning for a visit although she had almost given up hope that he would ever come back. Sometimes the police tracked their spotlight across the front yard and bushes, and Sylvie's living room would flash with light, which jarred Lolly awake if she happened to be dozing. The police spotlight was powerful enough to find Lolly's card catalog and open drawers, releasing all that chipped at her until she would shatter.

The driver called out Genesee Street, and Lolly—not quite awake—reached up and pulled the bell cord, her arm awkward and slow moving. The air smelled of approaching rain when she stepped off the bus. As she crossed the street to the restaurant, she hoped the thunderstorm would cool things off but would end before she had to make her way home; she was tired of standing at bus stops in the rain.

The New Genesee Restaurant hadn't changed much since The Greek's father opened the place forty years earlier. Booths still lined three walls, and tables—some with matching chairs and some without—were scattered in the center. A lunch counter fronted by a dozen swivel stools faced the kitchen. The pattern on the linoleum floor had worn away years ago and was only visible in the corners where foot traffic was light.

The restaurant was open twenty-four hours and didn't draw much of a dinner crowd; the place was busiest for breakfast and lunch and when the bars closed at four in the morning. The Greek called it "The Floor Show" when drunks stumbled in. When Lolly arrived that night, one man sat at the counter and an older couple with dark hair and matching olive complexions, maybe Greeks, sat bent over their plates in a booth. Lolly called hello to The Greek, who was cleaning the grill.

"You look like a movie star with those sunglasses, *koukla,*" he said, calling her 'doll' in Greek.

She smiled as she took off the glasses and dropped them in her purse. She liked The Greek from the moment she had walked in and asked if he was hiring. He had her sit at the counter and fill out an application. When he read it in front of her, she saw his heavy eyebrow arch when he read her last name, but he never asked about Al or if she was his wife. Instead, he hired her for the slowest shift, from after dinner until midnight, and she learned to wait and bus tables.

"You think every woman who comes in here looks like a movie star, Angelo," she said, walking to the kitchen and punching in to start her shift.

"Only you, *koukla,*" he answered. He grabbed a coffee can half-filled with water and poured some on the hot grill. The water sputtered and bubbled across the top. Steam rose, reddening The Greek's face. He returned the coffee can to its spot and grabbed a wide-edged paint scraper and began scraping the baked-on food that had blackened and browned the grill's surface.

She waved at the new dishwasher, a thin teenager with pocked skin who did not return her smile.

"That's Stavros," The Greek called, as he covered the grill in oil. "My wife's cousin from the old country. Dumb as a stump. Doesn't speak a word of English."

"It's nice to meet you, Stavros," Lolly said, and the boy nodded and slumped back to the stack of dirty dishes.

"Dumb as a stump," The Greek repeated as he sprinkled cleanser on top of the oil and then shook salt on top of the cleanser for friction. "Washes dishes like a shoemaker."

She tied an apron around her waist and watched as The Greek placed a new pad in its plastic holder and began scrubbing the surface, cleaning the grill from right to left in sections as wide as the scouring pad.

Storm clouds rolled in from the lake. Lightning flashed and she counted until she heard thunder. The air grew still, and then the sky emptied. Rain fell hard and fast, exploding against the pavement in diamonds.

"It'll be a slow night if that keeps up," The Greek said, wiping the grill with paper towels.

She stared at the pelting rain through the front window; she couldn't afford a slow night. The tables and booths needed to be filled with heavy tippers. She had applied for every advertised job that she qualified for—receptionist, counter girl, warehouse worker. Each time the manager would scan the application and ask, "Are you the bank robber's wife?" After she answered, they would pretend to read the rest of her application and then promise to call or keep her paperwork on file in case there were openings; soon she started answering that she was Al's sister hoping that would make a difference. Only Maeve and The Greek had hired her. Both, she was certain, out of sympathy.

The door opened and a man hurried in, his hair and suit plastered to him. He blinked rapidly, looking astonished that there was still a dry place in Buffalo the downpour hadn't touched. His face, shadowy with whiskers, was wet. He wiped it dry and then wiped his hand on his trousers.

"Take your jacket off and hang it over there to dry if you want," Lolly said, nodding to the coat tree. "Coffee?"

"Yes, thanks," the man said, shrugging off his suit coat and hanging it where he was told. "Black."

She poured him a cup, thinking the man looked familiar but she couldn't place him. Maybe he had eaten at the restaurant previously or had come into the bookstore. She set the cup and saucer at the counter and a menu next to it as the man came closer, smoothing his hair with his hand.

"It's coming down hard out there," he said, sliding onto the stool. "The sky is black over the lake. They say it's going to rain all night."

Lolly frowned, realizing she would work another long night without making any money. She would check the want ads on her break to see if there were any new listings.

The man sipped his coffee, his gaze alternating between the menu and Lolly. He ordered an open-faced beef sandwich with gravy and French fries instead of mashed potatoes. Lolly scribbled the order on her pad and turned toward the kitchen, certain he was staring at her back. She tore off the order ticket and placed it on the carousel at the pass-thru window and spun it toward The Greek.

"Order in," she called.

"You don't remember me, do you?" the man asked.

She faced him and studied his dark eyes, the sharp nose. He looked around Al's age, but his hair was already turning gray. "You look familiar."

He extended his hand. "Mortin Lucoff."

It took a few seconds for the name to register, and then she took a step back, ignoring his outstretched hand. "From the *News*," she said.

Lucoff nodded and pulled a fresh pack of cigarettes from his shirt pocket and tapped it twice against his palm. "That's right. We met in your apartment."

"We didn't meet. You were trespassing."

He tore the cellophane from the pack. "I would have knocked, but the door was on the ground."

"Well, that one works fine," Lolly said, nodding towards the restaurant door. "I suggest you use it."

"Hold on. I have a proposition for you."

"I bet you do."

"Is everything all right here, *koukla*?" The Greek asked, emerging from the kitchen with a carving knife in his hand.

"Hear me out," Lucoff said, shaking free a cigarette. "Then I'll leave if you still want me to."

"It's okay, Angelo," Lolly said. "Thank you."

"You yell if you need me. And you," he said to Lucoff, pointing the knife at him. "Watch yourself."

Lucoff lit his cigarette with a silver Zippo and snapped the lid shut.

"What do you want?" she asked, after The Greek went back in the kitchen.

"Have you been following my articles about your husband, Mrs. Nussbaum?"

"I don't read the paper anymore. Only the want ads."

He tilted his head and blew smoke at the tin ceiling. "You haven't read my series on Al?"

"Occasionally someone will clip one out and mail them to me anonymously, but I throw them away. I always thought it was some spiteful person sending them, but now I wonder if it was you."

"It wasn't me. It's a shame you didn't read them, though. They were good."

"What do you want, Mr. Lucoff? Why are you here? I'm sure you didn't come all the way to Genesee Street in the rain for roast beef."

"Here's the thing," he said shifting on the stool. "I did a nice job on those articles, Mrs. Nussbaum. I'll probably get nominated for an award because of them."

"Good for you. What do you want?"

The man at the end of the counter signaled for his check, and she took it to him, worrying that he had overheard the conversation and was leaving because of it. She was certain The Greek was listening.

"Between my articles and this," he called to her, pulling the *Reader's Digest* from his back pocket, "everyone knows Al's story, Mrs. Nussbaum, but no one knows *your* story."

"I don't have a story," she answered, after handing the man his check and walking back toward Lucoff. "Get out."

"Sure you do. You have a great story. The unsuspecting wife learns that her husband is the most wanted man in America? That he's stolen more money than Dillinger and she never knew? That he abandoned her and their child, and she's left to pick up the pieces alone? People want to hear *that* story, Mrs. Nussbaum."

"Well, I don't want to tell it. It's hard enough living it without having to read about it in the *News*. Leave. I'll pay for your dinner."

"You know other things too. Mrs. Nussbaum. Things about Al."

She snorted, her hands on her hips, and looked up as if she could see through the tin ceiling, past the roof, to the storm clouds hovering above. "God, you and the FBI. I don't know anything about the money or the guns or where he is. I don't know how many times I have to say that."

"I'm not talking about guns or money. You know things about Al only a wife knows. The human-interest angle, Mrs. Nussbaum. You know what makes Al tick."

"Jesus, I don't. I wish I did. He's as much a mystery to me as he is to everyone else."

"How does a smart, middle class kid raised by both parents from a good home and with every opportunity this county has to offer end up running from the FBI? Al should have ended up in college, not prison. How did this happen? Readers want to know."

"I don't know," Lolly said, her voice softer. She had asked herself the same sad question almost every day, and she couldn't come up with an answer.

Lucoff pulled hard on the cigarette, studying her. "I'm not talking about the *Buffalo Evening News*, Mrs. Nussbaum," he said, exhaling smoke. "This," he said, tapping a finger on the *Reader's Digest*, "changes everything. Al is a *national* story. Everyone knows him. Walter Cronkite ran a segment on the CBS News about him last night."

"So?" she asked, moving to the cash register where the man from the end of the counter waited with money in hand.

"So, you need to think bigger than the local paper, Lolly. Can I call you Lolly?"

"No." She rang the man out and handed him his change.

"Editors will pay for your story, Mrs. Nussbaum. Maybe *Reader's Digest* will do a follow-up. Maybe the *Saturday Evening Post* will be interested, or *Playboy*, or *Life*. I'm sure somebody will pay a lot for this story. I already have *Inside Detective* calling me."

"*Inside Detective?*" she asked and shook her head. She had seen the magazine in the racks at Van Slykes's Pharmacy and sometimes Al would bring a copy home. Usually there was a busty blonde on the cover—someone who reminded her of Jackie Rose—wearing a tight sweater ripped at the shoulder and tied to a chair. She couldn't imagine ever doing an interview for them.

"I can't help you. I don't know what makes Al tick. I wish I did," she said, as the man at the register handed her a tip before turning up his collar and heading into the storm.

Enough for bus fare, she thought. *Jesus.*

Lucoff leaned forward and whispered, "You can make stuff up, Mrs. Nussbaum. No one will know."

"*I* would know," she said, clearing the man's plate and glasses. "And Al would know. It would be betraying him, which is what it seems everyone wants me to do today."

Lucoff leaned back on the stool. "Betraying him? No disrespect, Mrs. Nussbaum, but Al *betrayed* you. A single mom, no money, no skills. How are you going to survive? You need this money. Besides, you may never see Al again."

"What's in this for you?" she asked, wiping the counter with a wet rag. "You can't possibly care how, or if, I survive."

"I'll get paid too. More than I'll get at the *News*, that's for sure. And I'll get credit for an article in a national magazine. Who knows where this might lead for me? It could open doors."

"I wish you would open that door," she said, pointing towards Genesee Street. "If I didn't want people in Buffalo reading about me, why would I want people all over the country to?"

"For the money, Mrs. Nussbaum. For the *money*. These editors will pay top dollar, and not just for this one article but for those that follow."

"There will be others?"

"Sure. One now, another when he's arrested, another during the trial. Maybe a final article after the verdict comes in. They'll definitely pay big money if Al gets the death penalty."

"Get out."

"Think about the money, Mrs. Nussbaum."

"Get out."

"Order up," The Greek said, bringing Lucoff's plate out instead of sliding it through the pass window; he still gripped the carving knife.

"Mr. Lucoff won't be staying," she said. "Wrap his order to go."

Lucoff raised his hands in surrender. "Fine. I'll go. But think about it, Mrs. Nussbaum. The offer stands." He left his business card on the counter.

She watched him slide from the stool and walk to the hall tree.

"Think about it, Mrs. Nussbaum," he said again, shrugging on his wet sport coat. He opened the door, hesitated, then dashed across Genesee Street.

And she did think about his offer. Would three articles pay as much as the *Reader's Digest's* reward? Would it be enough to get to Florida? Or enough for her to work one job instead of two? Would it pay for the secretarial program at Bryant and Stratton Business School so she could support herself and the baby? She thought of Alison and all the things she would need; she was outgrowing her clothes so fast. It would be so nice if she could afford her own car, even if it was old and barely running, so she wouldn't have to rely on Stan and public transportation for rides. Or she could get her own apartment, away from her mother and her talk of annulment and how Al had ruined all their lives.

Still, the proposition felt wrong. Not as vile as turning Al in for the reward but, rather, that she'd be exploiting him somehow and cashing in on the wreckage of his life. Images of Al flashed in front of her: Al handcuffed, Al in the back of a police car, Al looking at her from across the court room. In each image, she saw the hurt, the disappointment, the recognition that she had let him down and how that was far worse than any judge's sentence. She tried to shove those images away, but none of the drawers in her card catalog would open.

"Who was that guy?" The Greek asked. "Some reporter? Why didn't he wait for his food?"

"He's nobody, Angelo," she mumbled. "Nobody important, anyways. Give his dinner to Stavros."

Thunder clapped right above the restaurant, rattling the front windows. The lights flickered but stayed on, and she knew she'd be waiting for the number nineteen bus in the rain again. More lightning strobed and the peals of thunder that followed sounded like combat. After The Greek went back to the kitchen, she crumpled Lucoff's business card in her fist.

*****

The rain had stopped before her shift ended, leaving everything dripping and steaming. Sitting in the bus on the ride home, she watched the world pass through a wet window, the view of parked cars and people emerging from dark doorways distorted by running droplets. A bum shuffled down the street wearing red and blue bowling shoes. His nose was flattened and his ears cauliflowered. He threw punches at imaginary opponents—jabbing, jabbing, jabbing before throwing a right; a rope held up his pants.

Her tip money jingled in her pocket, and her thoughts returned to Lucoff. The glass felt cool when she leaned her forehead against the window and wondered how much *Life* magazine would pay for her story. Five hundred? A thousand? More? What's the going rate for a series of articles? *I should have asked him*, she thought.

When she got home, she took off her white shoes in the front hall and tried not to make a sound as she entered her parents' apartment. Sylvie had not left a lamp on for her, so she felt her way to Alison's room in the dark. The baby was sprawled on her tummy, legs and arms stretched wide like she hadn't stirred in hours. The apartment was so stifling that Sylvie had put her down only in a diaper. Lolly touched her daughter's back, and her skin felt warm; she would need to buy a small fan if the heatwave that gripped the East Coast continued much longer. Fans couldn't cost much.

Her stockings made a whispering sound on the hardwood floor as she padded her way to the kitchen and switched on the single light above the sink. A bottle of Chablis stood on the counter. She poured the wine into a water glass, telling herself it would help her sleep even though her legs were exhausted from standing all day. She sipped, then opened the freezer for ice cubes and dropped them in the glass, raising the wine to the rim. Turning, she saw papers stacked on the kitchen table labeled "Initial Gathering of Proofs." She flipped through the documents—a formal petition of annulment, suggested witnesses' certificate, the appointment of a procurator form.

Mother.

She set aside the procurator form and picked up a questionnaire. There were fifty questions, and she flicked on the ceiling light to read them; the paper trembled between her fingers.

"How did you meet your spouse?"

The question made her feel naïve and stupid. What would she put down if she were to answer? That she was a silly fourteen-year old girl swept off her feet by the smartest, most handsome boy in school? That she should have listened to her mother when she told her that it was dangerous to date a boy three years older? *Even Mother didn't realize how dangerous you were and how even more dangerous you'd become*, she thought.

"Was your courtship ever broken?"

She pulled a chair back to sit, not caring that it scraped against the linoleum and might wake her mother; she picked up the pen Sylvie had left by the papers. Yes, she wrote in a swirling hand. Our courtship was broken while Al served gun running and parole violation sentences at the Chillicothe Correctional Facility in Ohio. He wrote poetic letters promising that he had learned his lesson, and that all he wanted was to spend the rest of his life with me. No, your holiness, I didn't think taking him back would be a mistake.

"Did anything unusual or significant happen during your courtship or engagement?"

Please see above regarding the Chillicothe Correctional Facility.

"Did anyone advise you against your marriage?"

It might be easier if she listed those who had advised her to go *through* with the marriage; that list would be much shorter. Instead, she wrote that both her Mother and Father Jozef had thought that Al was an unreformed, unrepentant criminal and that the marriage was doomed from the beginning; a copy of his arrest record could be attached as supporting evidence. Or maybe she could include his wanted poster that some vindictive neighbor had shoved under her door. Shouldn't that be part of the gathering of proofs?

The "Our Life Together" section was the most difficult part to answer; she felt the tears well as she read the questions but brushed them away, determined never to cry again.

"Briefly describe the beginning of your marriage."

Should I start on our wedding day and how handsome you looked in your white jacket? Lolly thought. *Or should I go farther back to how exciting it was to go dress shopping with Mother and that I loved how my dress billowed and rustled when I moved like it was telling secrets with each step? Should I skip the wedding day Polish breakfast of ham and kielbasa and how I couldn't eat a crumb because I was so excited? I could tell the church Fathers how my face hurt from smiling. Maybe I should describe moving into the apartment above my parents. You were such a good sport picking out furniture and paint colors with me. And you—Mr. Fix-It—replaced all the door and window locks and repaired the kitchen cabinets. Even Mother, who was so miserly with her compliments, said there was nothing you couldn't do, nothing you couldn't fix. But she was wrong. You can't fix our marriage—our lives—can you, Al? Those are broken forever.*

"Were there problems in your sexual relationship?"

This question made her laugh. She wanted to write "God, no!" She thought more about this question and the laughter stopped and her smile disappeared as she realized that what Bobby had offered—guns, banks, money—was far more exciting than anything she had offered Al in the bedroom. She wondered if she had said or done something differently, if she were prettier or sexier, if she were more like this Jackie Rose, that he would have stayed home and not gone off with Bobby to Washington or Rochester or, God, Brooklyn.

She left the question blank and gulped her wine. Most of the questions didn't interest her and she skipped those or wrote "Dumb" as an answer.

Number twenty-seven left her in tears, first from laughing and then from weeping, and she was angry with herself that she had cried again.

"Were there any serious problems or disturbing discoveries during your marriage?"

This was perhaps the easiest question to answer; she could make a list, starting with discovering eleven thousand dollars in the back of the hall closet. Most housewives would've been excited to find so much cash. Their thoughts would have leapt to vacations, a new car, college funds, but she knew Al had gone back to crime as soon as she found the duffle bag and that gun sitting on top of all that money.

"But I was wrong, wasn't I, Al?" she said aloud, as if he were again sitting across the table from her. "You didn't go *back* to crime, did you? You never left it. That was another 'disturbing discovery' I made, wasn't it? And all the other discoveries that followed—the bank robberies, the murdered guard, the FBI Most Wanted List—all go back to that one."

"Did you and your spouse communicate honestly and effectively?"

Lolly snorted and pushed the page away. She took another swallow of wine. Her head, already fuzzy from working too many hours and eating too little, grew fuzzier. Radio static played between her ears.

"Describe the personality of your spouse."

Which personality? she thought. *How could the same man who was so gentle around the house, so protective of me and our baby, turn out to be so dangerous?*

"Describe your roles in the care of your home and family."

This question hurt her the most, because Al was a good husband and father when he was home. She knew she could never write an answer to this one. It would be easier to submit photographs—Al holding Alison for the first time at the hospital, both he and the baby crying, or Al lying in bed, cradling Alison in his arms like he'd never let anyone harm her. Maybe pictures from their first Christmas together as a married couple would make convincing evidence, one of them in front of the tree, or opening presents, or kissing under the mistletoe.

Goddamn you, Al. God damn you.

"Was anyone involved in the break-up of your marriage?"

Lolly wrote "Bobby Wilcoxson" and underlined his name with two violent strokes. She pictured Bobby's face, how one side of his mouth slanted into more of a snarl than a smile and how that eye, dead and glassy, always chilled her to gooseflesh.

She scribbled over Bobby's name.

Bobby may have been involved in the breakup of the marriage, but Al was the one who was responsible. "We could have led a nice quiet life on Bailey Avenue," Lolly said aloud again. "I didn't need that house on Lafayette. We wouldn't have been rich, but we could have been happy, we could have been normal, we could have been together."

Goddamn you, Al.

Goddamn you again and again and again.

Chapter 10

Al and Bobby sat parked across from the Western Pennsylvania National Bank off Route 30 going over Al's plan. Potted hydrangeas guarded either side of the main entrance, the white flowers full and round. The terra cotta building had originally been built in 1930 as a Ford dealership with a forty-foot tower and a flagpole attached to the top; the Ford banner had flown under the American flag until the dealership failed during the Depression. The building had remained empty. Some of the bronze and frieze windows were broken by thrown snowballs and rocks, until the war started and Western Pennsylvania National acquired the building for one of its branches. Al knew they'd never put a bank so close to a highway today; it's too easy to merge the getaway car with the fast-moving traffic and blend in with all the innocent commuters. He was convinced this should be an easy job, a real tin can; there wasn't even a bank guard to worry about this time. He hoped his share was enough so he could drive to Florida for new passports and visas for the three of them. Then maybe another big bank job or two, and he'd have enough start-over money and could go back to Buffalo for his family.

Christmas in Brazil.

In the bank's front window, a fully restored 1934 Ford V8 cordoned by velvet ropes faced the street as a tribute to the original purpose of the building; Al liked the nod to history, but it also worried him. What did this say about the bank president? That he thought differently and was a wild card, which meant he could be more dangerous than an armed bank guard? That the bank was special to him and worth defending? Al hoped he just liked old cars, but he didn't trust bank presidents in their three-piece suits and their names painted on their office doors. The idea of one doing his bidding, being moved like a chess piece, appealed to him very much. The Ford was beautiful, though. The roadster's black body was buffed to a glossy shine and reflected the summer sun. An Aurora Red pinstripe ran from the chrome grill to the rear fender, the color matching the spoke wheels.

"You won't be carrying a Tommy on this one, just a .45," he said. "You'll need a hand free to collect the money. I'll steal two cars. One for the getaway and another waiting a few exits away at that burger place we spotted. We'll dump the getaway at the burger joint and then we'll drive to my car and drop the second stolen car there. We'll split the money at your apartment in Germantown."

"That's a good omen," Bobby said.

"What is?"

"That Ford in the window. That's a good sign."

"Why?" Al asked, turning to face the roadster.

"Dillinger drove a '34 at the end, smart guy. He liked that big pushrod V8 and dual carb. I've been reading about him. He could outrun the cops in that baby. Hell, he could've driven that one for all we know. He might've even pulled a few jobs with it before they killed him. It's a good sign. A damn good sign."

Al nodded, troubled by Bobby's inability to focus. He wondered how many more times he'd have to go over the plan with him.

"When did you start reading about him?" Al asked. "I've only seen you read comic books."

"After the Reader's Digest article. Jesus, we should steal that car, Al."

"Steal it?"

"Fuck the money. We should steal Dillinger's car."

"That's not Dillinger's car, Bobby."

"We could drive it right through the front window."

"It probably doesn't even run. Besides, what would we do with it?"

Bobby's good eye narrowed in disbelief. "What are you? Stupid? We'd rob banks with it, of course. We'd be on the front page of every newspaper in the country if we pulled a job and got away in that," he said, pointing to the Ford. "Walter Cronkite would talk about us again."

"I don't want Walter Cronkite talking about us again. I don't want anybody talking about us again."

"We'd be goddamn legends."

Al thought of all the counterarguments—that its gas tank was probably empty, that it's thirty-year-old engine couldn't outrun a modern police car, that a 1934 Ford V8 with a red stripe was conspicuous as hell—but he knew there was no point in reasoning with Bobby. Instead, he said, "Let's go over the plan one more time."

"What's to go over?" Bobby asked. "I go in the side door, do all the work, and come out the front while you hide in the car."

"Bobby…"

"I'm going to look at the Ford."

Bobby got out the passenger side and crossed against traffic. Horns blared but he ignored them, drawn to the roadster that he was certain Dillinger had driven. He placed his palms on the window and peered inside. Al wondered if anyone—the bank manager, a teller, maybe a customer— noticed the one-eyed man with his face tight against the glass.

A police callbox stood in front of the bank near where Bobby was pressed to the window. Al hadn't seen it used in all the times he had cased the bank and was certain it was no longer in operation, but he still worried a patrolman would blunder by in the middle of the robbery.

They didn't need another Brooklyn.

*****

The night before the robbery, Al lay on his bed reading, his recorded typing setting a background rhythm that he no longer noticed. Everything was ready for tomorrow: guns loaded, gas tank filled, the police scanners ready to install in the cars he would steal in the morning. He had checked and rechecked the batteries in the walkie-talkies and had driven

Route 30 so many times he could close his eyes and see every curve and exit. His refrigerator and shelves were stocked with food and canned goods; he'd hole up here for two weeks letting things cool down before heading to Florida for the passports. He had told Bobby to stay locked in his apartment with Jackie Rose after the robbery but knew he wouldn't listen. After a day or two, Bobby would grow anxious and start pacing, talking faster and faster about Dillinger and Mickey Mantle and how Al didn't deserve an even cut. The apartment would shrink into a cell, the walls and ceiling closing around him until he'd have to bust out, first stopping at the library to check the Pittsburgh newspapers—the Gazette, the Sun-Telegraph, the Pittsburgh Commercial—for articles on the robbery and a mention of his name before driving to Atlantic City. He'd spend his money at the roulette wheel or on clothes and jewelry for Jackie Rose. He'd start pestering Al for another bank to knock over as soon as he got back from Miami, and that would be fine with him. He was already thinking about that Boston bank.

Christmas in Brazil.

Al read the final page of Dan J. Marlowe's *The Name of the Game Is Death*. He shut the paperback and stared at the cover, the title in white lettering except the word Death, which was colored blood red. The artwork depicted a shadowy figure shooting a man in the back while he stood inside a phone booth. He was crumpling toward the ground, the receiver released from his hand and dangling. The price, thirty-five cents, was stamped in gold in the upper right corner and worth every penny; it was the best book Al had ever read about a bank robber. The amorality and callousness of the main character, Chet Anderson, reminded him of Bobby. The novel was written in the first person and reading Anderson's thoughts and feelings was like reliving past conversations he'd had with Bobby. All Anderson needed was a glass eye, he thought.

He wanted to ask Marlowe if he had ever robbed a bank or served time. He was convinced that he had. How else could he have captured such realism? And if Marlowe was just a writer and not an outlaw, had he known someone like Anderson in real life? Had he met Bobby somewhere, maybe in California before Bobby had fled east? Was he the inspiration for his main character? Al swung out of bed and hurried to the kitchen table, still clutching the paperback. He shut off the tape recorder and fed a piece of paper into the Smith Corona and began typing his questions: where did you get your idea for the story? Did you know that the novel would end in fire and death when you started writing? How long did it take you to write the book?

He picked up the paperback and flipped through the pages. The book had been published by Gold Medal Books, part of Fawcett Publications. He was certain he could call their New York office and con some receptionist into giving him Marlowe's phone number. Even while he was thinking this, other questions for Marlowe were forming, questions about structure and plot points, point-of-view, and dialogue. He put down the book and struck the keys hard, the hammers hitting the paper like a firing machine gun. His brain flooded with thoughts. The faces of people he had known—inmates, prison guards, gun dealers—hovered in front of him in an array of floating mug shots. He could see their scars from lost battles, the distant stares of the morally bankrupt, the tensed muscles of those about to explode into violence. He knew how to physically describe them to the finest detail. But Al was one of them and could also describe first-hand the fear when running from the police, the adrenalin rush of pulling off a job, the bite of handcuffs locked into place. He was certain he could make readers see what he had seen and feel what he had felt.

He yanked the questions for Marlowe from the typewriter and rolled another sheet into place. His fingers danced across the keyboard, nimble and quick, listing out story ideas: a teenager joyriding in his first stolen car, a confrontation in a prison laundry room, a fugitive leaving his family behind. Al knew loneliness and loss, what it felt like to be hunted and the sense that there was something innately wrong with him, perhaps a genetic condition, which drove him to banks and guns and Bobby. But he also knew the hope that all criminals possessed—the hope for a bigger score, for an early release, for getting away with it all—and he clung to it during his empty days and emptier nights.

Christmas in Brazil, Christmas in Brazil, Christmas in Brazil.

Putting it all on paper should be as easy as robbing the Western Pennsylvania National Bank, he thought, typing faster. As the carriage approached the right margin, the warning bell sounded.

*****

Neither spoke as they drove to the bank in the stolen Dodge. Al held the wheel with gloved hands, driving with the flow of Route 30 traffic and listening to the police radio for any reports of two stolen cars. He scanned the highway for anything out of the ordinary—road construction that might slow them down, accidents that could bog traffic, more state troopers patrolling than usual—but saw nothing unexpected. Bobby sat next to him in the passenger seat, breathing hard, his left leg bouncing, a .45 in his hand. Every few minutes he would check to see if it was loaded.

"Put the gun away," Al snapped. "You're not a kid going out on his first job, for Christ's sake. That's all we need is for a trucker to pull next to us and see you holding a piece."

Bobby holstered the gun in his shoulder strap under his sport coat, his leg jittering faster. He looked out the windshield, the side window, down at his gunless hand, everywhere but at Al. "I've never gone in by myself before," he said. "I always had Curry with me."

"You'll be fine," he said, but studied Bobby for signs of cracking. He needed him functioning for a few more jobs, then he could explode into a thousand violent pieces for all he cared. "Small bank, no guard, a highway on their doorstep. We'll be in and out before they know what happened."

"Jackie Rose should be driving," Bobby said, chewing his thumbnail. "We've always worked in pairs inside."

"Maybe next time we'll try something different," Al said, having no intention of going into a bank on these last robberies before fleeing to Brazil.

Bobby reached under his suit coat, pulled out the .45, then holstered it again. He started gnawing on his other thumbnail.

"You got the pillowcase?" Al asked.

Bobby patted his suit coat pocket as an answer. "Aren't you hot in them gloves?"

"Yeah," he answered, flexing his hand. "Better than leaving fingerprints in here. I don't want to make it too easy for the Feds. Where are the gloves I gave you?"

"Who wears gloves in the fucking summer?"

Al exited Route 30, watching Bobby out of the corner of his eye. As they approached the bank, Bobby's leg calmed, and he stopped chewing his nail. He fitted the walkie-talkie's earpiece into place, then put on his sunglasses. Al pulled to the curb and left the engine idling. Bobby got out of the car without saying a word and stared at the 1934 Ford in the window.

Al thumbed on his walkie-talkie. "Test," he said.

Bobby nodded without turning and strode toward the bank's side entrance. Other than two boys, maybe ten or eleven years old, who rode past the bank on bicycles, the sidewalks were deserted. Bobby looked straight ahead, fixated on the side entrance, never checking the street around him or turning back to Al. He disappeared through the door, the bank swallowing him.

In and out, Al thought. A tin can. Nothing to it.

He checked his watch, marking time, already counting off how long it should take Bobby to move the customers against one wall and work his way down the teller cages, leaving empty cash drawers in his wake.

A single shot.

Loud.

Al had fired so many .45s in his life he could recognize the report even if he was in a coma.

Christ, he thought. Not again.

He shifted the stolen car from park to drive but kept his foot on the brake. He expected Bobby to burst from the bank, firing shots behind him as he ran, but the front door remained closed and the street quiet. He waited for more gunshots but didn't hear the .45 again or any returned gunfire. He put the car back into park and tried to slow his breathing. He checked the time. The first two tellers should have been cleaned out by now.

"Only big bills, Bobby," he said aloud, and wondered if Luiz in Florida had read the Reader's Digest article and would charge him more for the passports and visas, the price rising because of the notoriety and increased risk.

"Just the big bills," he said again.

The police scanner crackled to life with an all-units call. A silent alarm had been tripped at the Western Pennsylvania National Bank off Route 30. The dispatcher's words jarred him more awake than he had ever felt before. He registered every sound, smell, and object around him. His skin tingled.

He picked up the walkie-talkie, his gloved hand shaking. "Abort, Bobby, abort. An alarm was tripped. The cops are on their way. Get out of there."

He rolled down the window and heard approaching sirens; he shifted the Dodge back into drive.

"Come on, come on, come on," he barked into the walkie-talkie, fighting the urge to press the accelerator and leave Bobby behind.

The bank door swung open and Bobby ran out, the pillowcase clutched in his hand but not bulging as much as Al had hoped or needed. Bobby jerked open the passenger side door and tossed the pillowcase in the backseat. He wasn't wearing his Ray-Bans.

"Go!" he said, slamming the door. "Drive!"

Al accelerated faster than he wanted toward Route 30; the sirens were growing louder behind him, but no flashing lights appeared in his mirrors. He could feel the sweat bead on his face and wiped it away with the back of his glove.

"Too many people in there," Bobby said, his words blasting in bursts. "Customers. Free transistor radios if you open an account. They wouldn't listen. They stood there. Frozen. Scared shitless. Bunch of hicks. Fucking coal miners. Farmers' wives. Fired a round in the ceiling to get them to move."

Thank God, Al thought.

"We need two people in the bank. Two. Not one. Stop being a pussy. I can't cover everyone. Jackie…"

"Shut up," Al said, and raised the volume on the police scanner. The Dodge had been reported stolen. Bobby's description was given. Roadblocks were going up on Route 30 in both directions. He and Bobby were considered armed and extremely dangerous, possibly with machine guns, hand grenades, and home-made pipe bombs. The cops already had them identified. They must be guessing, Al thought. They had to be.

"Fuck," Bobby said. "Fuck. Fuck. Fuck. We should have brought the Tommies."

"Relax. We're fine," Al said, fighting to keep his voice level as he exited Route 30. He worried that if he didn't act calm, Bobby would become uncontrollable. But Al wasn't calm. Every cell in his body was singing. He could hear his blood thrumming in his ears and pulsing in his neck and wrists. Each breath carried a different emotion: fear, excitement, joy. He laughed as he drove toward the burger place where he had parked the stolen Ford Fairlane. "They don't know about the other car yet."

"Yet. Yet," Bobby said, his leg jumping again, his good eye darting. "We shoulda brought Tommies."

Al pulled around to the back of the restaurant where the cream-colored Fairlane was parked by the garbage cans. "Grab the money," he said, opening his door, glancing around the deserted parking lot. The restaurant didn't open until noon. After Bobby pulled the pillowcase from the backseat, Al locked the keys inside the Dodge.

The Ford, with its bigger engine, roared to life. It would take fifteen minutes to drive to the back road, far from Route

30 and the roadblocks, where his Chevy was parked in a stand of trees. Bobby opened the pillowcase that rested on his lap and peered inside.

"Good haul?" Al asked, looking over as he lit a cigarette with the Fairlane's lighter.

"Not really. Maybe five grand."

"That's it?' he asked, ramming the lighter back into place. He was hoping his cut would be four times that amount. Brazil slid further away, becoming another faraway country outlined on a map. "Curry dropped twice as much last time."

Bobby's leg started dancing, his good eye darting. "That little shit bank teller. The second one I got to. He couldn't have been more than eighteen. He was playing games, the pimply fuck. I bet he's the one who tripped the goddamn alarm."

"What kind of games could he play with a .45 pressed against his forehead?"

"Fuck you, Al. I was covering the customers."

"Why? Did someone point a transistor radio at you?"

"I should press this against your fucking head," Bobby said, raising the .45.

"What game did he play?" he asked, a second time, almost certain Bobby wouldn't shoot him while he was driving fifty miles an hour.

Bobby lowered the gun and reached in the pillowcase. He brought out a fistful of singles and fives. "He dropped the big bills in the trash can when I wasn't looking."

Al hammered the steering wheel with the bottom of his fist. Brazil was as far away as Mars. "I said nothing small!"

"I know that, you motherless fuck! When I caught on to what he did, it was too late. You were already screaming like a girl into the walkie-talkie about the cops coming. I had to get the hell out of there."

"You couldn't have grabbed the trash can?"

"It takes two people to rob a fucking bank, Al. You know that. You taught me that. One to cover and one to clear. If you send me in alone, I should just pass a note to a single teller and rob only her. Is that what you want? To leave all that money in the other cash drawers? Any pussy can pass a note. Hell, even you can do that."

"No, that's not what I want," he said, through clenched teeth, anger tearing through him like he was the one who had been robbed, that Brazil had been stolen from him. He took a moment to form his thoughts. The dispatcher's voice called out the positions of the roadblocks on Route 30. An ambulance was on its way to the bank; an older customer was having chest pains.

Al took a deep breath. "The next time you go into that bank, you'll be carrying a Tommy gun. What I want is for you to walk right up to that pimply-faced motherfucker and shove the barrel into his mouth and say real loud for everyone to hear that if anyone tries something funny, if anyone trips another goddamn alarm or hides the big bills, the back of that kid's skull is going against the wall. Get another teller to go up and down the line clearing out the drawers for you. No, get the bank president to do it. Order that rich bastard around. Make him steal the money for you. You don't move. You keep that gun right in that punk's mouth. You do that, no one will give you any trouble and you won't have to fire a shot. You won't need a second person inside with you. That bank president will bring all the money to you like a goddamn errand boy."

Bobby's good eye gleamed. "We're going to rob the same bank twice? I don't even think Dillinger did that. Did Dillinger do that?"

"I don't know, but we're not going to find an easier bank to rob than that one. I'll be goddamned if we only get five grand out of there."

"Not even Dillinger did that," Bobby said, looking out the window. "In fact, the only thing better than robbing that bank twice is to rob it three times."

Al shook his head. "If we rob it twice, they'll hire guards for sure. The cops will patrol more often. They'll reactivate that call box out front."

"We'll bring gas cans with us," Bobby said, staring far off with a clairvoyant's gaze. "Big ones. Like in the army movies. I'll carry two and you'll carry one and cover everyone with your free hand. I'll pour my cans into the gas tank. If Dillinger's old Ford still won't start, you splash gas all over the fucking place and light a match so we can escape. We'll set that sonofabitch bank on fire, money and all. We'll make the news for sure."

"You think of that plan all by yourself, Bobby?"

"Every part."

"I thought so," Al said, pulling off the road where his car was hidden.

*****

Al pulled in front of his apartment, shut off the ignition, and leaned his forehead against the steering wheel. Twenty-two hundred dollars, half the take, was tucked in his jacket pocket, the smallest amount they had ever robbed. Not even enough to get him to Florida and back. The last month weighed down on his shoulders—the running, the hiding, the paranoia every time he left his apartment to buy books or hair dye. Every sedan that drove by contained federal agents, every police car was after him, every good citizen saw through his disguises and recognized him from his wanted poster. It took him an hour this morning to raise the courage to leave his apartment and rob the bank, and he was coming home with nothing but bologna money to show for it. He would spend the next two weeks locked in his hot apartment for a little more than two grand.

He got out of the car and Leonard Weiss and another older tenant were sitting on the apartment steps with bottles of beer and a transistor radio between them.

"Carl!" Leonard called. "Join us!" He turned to his friend. "This is the writer I was telling you about. The one in 3-A."

Al shut the door to his Chevy and willed a smile. He was in no mood to make small talk with Leonard and his old sidekick. The smart thing was to get off the street.

"You've got to hear this!" Leonard said, the beer making him shout and giving him confidence to look Al in the eye. "It's incredible!"

The radio was tuned to WABC AM out of New York, whose signal could be heard up and down the eastern seaboard on clear nights. Al would lie sweating in bed reading or having imaginary conversations with Lolly and listen to Cousin Brucie play all the hits or to the Mets bumbling their way to another loss.

He nodded to the older man. "I'm Carl Fisher."

The older man struggled to his feet. He was tall, over six feet, but thin and stooped. His hair was stringy and gray and needed cutting; stains from past meals dotted his yellow Banlon shirt. He shook Al's hand and smiled, revealing a missing bottom tooth. "Marty Stroger. Nice to meet you."

"Marty, hush!" Leonard said. "He's pitching."

Al heard the Mets' announcer, Lindsey Nelson, describe Sandy Koufax's wind up and delivery, and Ray Daviault—the Mets' relief pitcher—swinging and missing.

"Another one! He struck out another one!" Leonard yelled, his smile broad and pure, reversing time so he looked twelve years old. "That makes eleven already."

Marty grimaced and sat back on the steps. He rubbed his knee. "So, he struck out the other pitcher. Big deal. I could strike out Daviault, and I'm half dead. Besides, the Mets are the worst team in history. No one can hit the ball."

"Good game?" Al asked, resting his foot on the bottom step.

"Koufax has a no-hitter going. In the first inning, he struck out all three batters on nine pitches. Nine!"

"He'll blow it," Marty said. "The kid always gets wild late in the game."

"He's no kid anymore. He's twenty-six or seven."

"Everyone's a kid to me. And he still gets wild."

"You're just sore because the Dodgers left Brooklyn."

"I left Brooklyn too," Marty said, to Al. "To live here with my sister after my Ethel died."

"Losing your wife and leaving your home is tough," Al said.

"Ever been to Brooklyn, Carl?" Leonard asked.

"Nope," Al said. "Never."

"Me neither. Been to Manhattan a couple times but never Brooklyn. Say, have a seat. Grab a beer."

"Thanks, but I should get back to my novel."

"Nonsense," said Leonard, and held up a sweating bottle of Schmidt's. "You gotta hear if Koufax gets the no-hitter."

"Sit. Sit," the old man said and patted the space next to him.

He took the beer, deciding it would seem suspicious if he didn't accept their invitation. "I guess I can stay for an inning or two."

"Or until Koufax throws this game away," said Marty. "Whatever comes first."

"Attaboy," said Leonard, ignoring the old man. "Relax. Loosen your tie. Aren't you hot in that suit coat?"

"No, I'm fine," Al lied, but he still wore the shoulder holster under his jacket. He took a small sip of beer. He didn't want to sit but thought he'd be less noticeable if he did. If a police car cruised by, they'd look like three friends sitting on the front stoop listening to a ballgame and having a drink. Except one was wearing a sport coat in a heatwave. He sat next to Marty and tried to look small by leaning forward and resting his arms on his thighs; he bent his head, pretending he was hanging on Lindsey Nelson's every word.

"We started listening to the game in Marty's apartment—he's on the first floor in the back—but his sister kicked us out. Said we were too loud."

"It was like an oven in there anyway," Marty said. "No breeze in the back of the building. Damn heat."

"Is there a score?" Al asked.

"Dodgers up four nothing. They scored all their runs in the first."

"That bum Miller didn't even last an inning. He's no big league pitcher," Marty said and reached for another beer, the back of his hand liver-spotted. "Hell, there's not one big leaguer in the Mets' whole damn rotation."

"How's the book coming?" Leonard asked. "I hear you in there working all the time."

Al sipped his Schmidt's and thought about his answer. He might have to keep up the pretense of being a writer and playing the recorded typing for a long time. "Slow," he said. "I thought I'd be further along."

"I can't imagine writing a novel," Marty said and shivered. "Just the thought of it brings back unpleasant memories from high school English class with Mrs. Kratzenberg. How do you come up with all them words anyway?"

"I just write one at a time," Al said, staring at his car. "That's the trick."

"One at a time. That's pretty good. You hear that, Leonard? He writes one word at a time."

Leonard smiled, his eyes glassy from beer.

It was a mistake parking the Chevy in front of the building, he decided. He must be getting tired or sloppy. Any patrol car looking for it would spot it right away. After he breaks away from Marty and Leonard, he'll pull it around back, maybe park it behind the next building, but would that make a difference? When they come for him, they will be coming from every direction.

The Dodgers didn't score in the bottom of the sixth. Nelson had to raise his voice to be heard over the Dodger Stadium crowd as Koufax took the mound in the seventh.

"He should be pitching in Brooklyn," Marty said. "The Dodgers played there since 1884. All of a sudden Brooklyn's not good enough for them? They move out west and we get stuck with the Mets."

Al tried to relax, to slow his mind. He envied Marty and Leonard. They could sit outside on a summer night and argue about baseball and complain about the heat; their lone care at that moment was the next pitch. This is what normal men must do. He thought of Bobby and how they had argued

197

because Bobby wanted to drive back to Pittsburgh the next day and shove the Tommy gun in that punk teller's mouth. Al knew they would have to wait. Investigators would still be on the scene, canvassing the area, even tracking down those two kids on their bikes to ask if they saw anything unusual. Then he'd have to re-case the bank, making sure they hadn't hired guards or changed their routine. He wondered if Bobby was psychotic enough to try to steal the old Ford in the window on his own.

Kanehl grounded out to short to start the inning, but Koufax walked the next batter, Mantilla.

"He's done," Marty said. "You watch. He'll start walking them. One after the other. Maybe a wild pitch here, he'll hit a batter there. Next thing you know he's blown the no-hitter."

"You're crazy. Koufax is the best in the business," Leonard said. "The left arm of God."

"Mistakes add up. Sooner or later it all catches up with you," Marty said, and Al knew that was true. He stared at his Chevy again.

"Drink your beer," Leonard said.

Frank Thomas, the Mets' most dangerous batter, hit into a double play ending the inning.

Leonard, beaming, slapped Marty on the back. The old man spilled his beer, adding new stains to his yellow shirt. "Six more batters, gentlemen, and we'll have a no-hitter. We're listening to history being made."

Al counted days. If they waited until August to rob the Pittsburgh bank again, maybe they could hit the Boston bank in September. That would give him two months to get to Florida, find Luiz, and make all the arrangements to get out of the country. The beer soured in his stomach as he thought of all the tollbooths he'd drive through, all the state troopers he'd pass, all the gas station attendants and hotel clerks between Boston and Florida who might recognize him.

Ron Fairly struck out looking at a chest-high fastball to start the inning for the Dodgers, but big Frank Howard, all six foot seven of him, swung on the first pitch and crushed the ball over the left field wall. Leonard stood, arms in the air, fists balled, and howled in joy.

"Five nothing," he bellowed.

"There's still time for Koufax to throw it all away," Marty said. "Sit down for God's sake."

If all went well—if he found Luiz, if he had enough money for the documents, if he wasn't shot or captured along the way—he could go back for Lolly in November.

Christmas in Brazil.

He couldn't stop thinking, and his thoughts shook him so hard he wondered if he had made a noise like he'd been gut punched. If he had, it was drowned out by Leonard still celebrating Howard's towering homerun and Marty telling him to stop yelling before someone calls the cops.

What if he went back for Lolly and she refused to go with him? What if she wanted nothing to do with him or Brazil? What if she called the police or the FBI as soon as she saw him?

Both Roseborro and Burright popped out to end the inning.

Al propped his elbows on his thighs and covered his face with his hands. What if Lolly hated him?

"Don't worry, Carl. Koufax has this locked up," Leonard said, still standing but wavering from the beer. "You can throw away the key on this one."

Al straightened, pulling his hands away from his face, and frowned, pretending his only concern was Koufax facing the middle of the batting order.

"Don't get too sure of yourself," Marty said. "Don't get all cocky. There's still a lot of baseball left. The game isn't over until it's over."

Koufax struck out Cook to start the eighth inning.

Al realized he had no backup plan if Lolly wouldn't leave with him. Would he go on to Brazil alone? What would he do there without her? What would be the point? He tried imaging a life in South America on his own, but he saw nothing without Lolly and the baby. Certainly, he couldn't go on robbing banks until his luck ran out or Bobby got them both killed.

Hickman, the number six batter, flew out to center and Lindsey Nelson's voice went up an octave.

He'd have to think of a way to talk Lolly into going. There must be a dozen reasons why they should run to Brazil together—that they love each other and always have since high school, that they could be a family again, that South America offered a fresh start. He'd write it out ahead of time—he'd start tonight after moving his Chevy—to make sure he thought of everything and left nothing out.

Koufax walked Elio Chacon, the Mets weak-hitting shortstop, and it was Marty's turn to stand.

"Chacon? He walked Chacon?" he said, struggling to his feet. He held Al's shoulder to steady himself. "Does Chacon even have a batting average? How could he walk him? This is the beginning of the end, my friends."

Al had always been able to talk Lolly into things, and he had to sugar talk her one last time. There was no promise he wouldn't make to convince her. There would be no more bank jobs, no more gun deals, no more stolen cars, and he knew he would miss it, but he'd give it all up to be with Lolly again.

Chris Cannizzaro, an even a weaker hitter than Chacon, struck out on three pitches to end the side. WABC didn't break for a commercial between innings and the Dodger crowd kept cheering throughout the pause in play; Lindsey Nelson talked louder to be heard over the noise. The cheering grew louder when Koufax came out to lead-off the bottom of the eighth. They began chanting San-dee! San-dee! even when a curveball froze him, and he struck out looking.

"He bats like a Met," Marty said, sitting and opening the last bottle of Schmidt's.

Al imagined Lolly tanned year-round, her hair highlighted by the South American sun. He pictured her in thin clothes and bathing suits, dancing to Brazilian rhythms, her arms raised, her hips swaying. An ache covered him; his arms felt heavy. He closed his eyes and tried to conjure the smell of her perfume but couldn't. The next time he summoned the courage to leave the apartment, he'd buy a small bottle of Interlude so he could sprinkle some on his pillow.

Lindsey Nelson didn't speak when Koufax came out of the dugout to pitch in the ninth; he let the radio audience up and down the East Coast listen to the roaring Dodger fans. The crowd quieted while Koufax pitched, letting him concentrate, and all thirty thousand of them groaned in one voice when he walked Gene Woodling.

"He's going to choke in the end," Marty said. "He won't be able to pull this one off. He's always been a choker."

"I've got faith," Leonard said. "I'm rooting for him."

The crack of the bat came out of the transistor radio like a gunshot. Leonard straightened, Marty grinned his missing-tooth smile, even Al leaned toward the small speaker. Maury Wills, a golden glover, scooped up the grounder and flipped the ball to second, but they couldn't turn the double play. Fielder's choice.

"Jesus. Don't hit it to Wills," Marty said. "Hit it to anybody but him."

Al decided he'd carry the bottle of perfume with him in his pocket as a charm or maybe dab some on a handkerchief. Then, when sadness and loneliness overcame him, he could simply reach in his pocket for his hanky and touch it to his nose and no one would give it a second thought. He could close his eyes and pretend Lolly was by his side like she was supposed to be.

Kanehl grounded out to third, but again the Dodgers couldn't turn the double play. Another fielder's choice.

"What the hell's wrong with Burright?" Leonard demanded, looking at Marty and then to Al and then back to Marty for an answer. "Since when can't he turn a double play? Is his arm shot? He can't make a throw to first base? What kind of second basemen is he? Christ, he's not helping Koufax at all."

"Koufax is a Jew," Marty said. "Christ isn't going to help him."

"Sure he will. Christ was a Jew. But Koufax doesn't need Christ's help. He needs Burright's help, that weak-armed bastard."

But it was Maury Wills, the future Hall of Famer, who helped Koufax. Mantilla swung on the first pitch and Wills fielded it cleanly and made a straight throw to second to end the game, giving Sandy Koufax his first major league no-hitter.

Leonard cheered with the Dodger crowd. Marty tilted the bottle of Schmidt's and drained the last of it. Al stood, thanked them for the beer he'd hardly touched, and told them he was going to move his car and then go up to his apartment.

He had some writing to do.

Chapter 11

The Greek's daughter, Elena, was to be married the Sunday before Labor Day and Lolly was invited. She was reluctant to accept the invitation. Apart from going to her jobs and running errands, she hadn't been out of the house socially since Al had become a fugitive. There had been no lunch dates with girlfriends or matinees at the North Park Theater. She had even stopped going to church because of the whispering in the pews when she sat down, and because of Father's Jozef's mournful eyes when he saw her and implored her to come in for a talk.

Angelo had insisted that she attend the wedding.

"It's my only child, *koukla*," he had said. "You can't say no. Everyone is invited. I'm even closing the restaurant."

She compromised, promising The Greek that she would go to the church for the ceremony.

"The church?" he had bellowed, as he cleaned the grill. "What fun is that? At the reception there will be food and dancing and ouzo! We've been saving money for Elena's wedding since she was born. You're coming to both!"

As the wedding approached, Lolly grew excited. She would hardly know anyone there, and she hoped none of the Greeks would know her; she could be Lolly again, at least for a few hours. The idea of styling her hair and wearing makeup and lipstick made it feel like a holiday. She had bought a lavender cocktail dress a year ago, hoping to wear it to a special occasion with Al; the tags still hung from the label on a length of thick thread held in place by tiny brass pins. The bodice was fitted with a scooped neckline that accentuated her clavicle, a part of her that Al had always admired. He would run his fingertips and tongue the length of it and back again before moving up to kiss her neck, her ear, her lips. The full skirt flared and was gathered on the left side in an elaborate rose; the hem brushed the slope of her calves. Taffeta rustled as she shifted and spun in front of the mirror in Sylvie's room, her head twisting over her left shoulder and then the right, inspecting herself from all angles. She worried the pellon lining would be too heavy for the relentless heatwave that would not break, but she had nothing else appropriate to wear. Before she left, she worked her wedding band off her finger and left it on the kitchen counter.

The ceremony was held at the Greek Orthodox Church on the corner of Delaware and West Utica. She had never been to this church or to a Greek wedding and gaped as she stared up at the limestone bell tower. The sun was hot on her bare arms as she walked through the open oak doors into the narthex. The heavy smell of incense hung in the air. Candles burned on a sand-topped table to the left of the doorway. She lit a candle, not knowing if she should say a prayer for the living or the dead but whispered one for Al—hoping he was still alive.

She was seated in an aisle by an usher with dark curly hair, the same black shade as his tuxedo. Lolly felt his breath on her neck when he leaned down and whispered his name, Yianni, and that he hoped she would save him a dance at the reception. As she sat on the maroon-cushioned pew, her cheeks warming, she wondered if Yianni whispered that to all the dateless women he escorted to their seats. She decided that he most likely did and that it didn't matter. She tried to remember the last time she had danced and a vague memory of Al waltzing her around their living room took shape. She felt his hand on her back holding her close and remembered the smell of his aftershave as she rested her head on his shoulder. The memory faded, melted by the heat, and she realized she wanted to be held again. A pale line from her wedding band circled her tanned finger, and she folded her right hand over it.

The organ played as the guests were seated. Yianni smiled at her every time he escorted another woman down the aisle, the woman's date or husband following a step behind. Sometimes she wouldn't look up but could sense him close and could feel his eyes on her. When she did glance up, she returned his smile. She would save him a dance, maybe more than one.

The church was not air conditioned and no breeze blew in from the open Delaware Avenue doors. She fanned herself with a hymnal and looked around the church. There were no statues or stations of the cross like at the Visitation of the Blessed Virgin Mary Catholic Church where she and Al had been married. Instead, an oak screen of Byzantine icons depicting sad saints and tired angels separated the nave from the altar; in the middle of the screen was a wide opening, and she could see a priest dressed in white robes moving about the altar. Stained glass windows lined the church's southern wall and depicted scenes from the Old Testament—Moses raising the tablets, Noah leading the animals, martyrs resigned to their fates. The windows on the north side depicted scenes from the New Testament—the Nativity, the Crucifixion, the Resurrection. Sunlight streamed through the stained glass, illuminating Judas' red hair, John the Baptist's drawn countenance, and the curls in Christ's beard.

She closed her eyes, the heat and organ lulling her. If nearby guests had recognized her and were gossiping, they were doing so in a beautiful foreign language, their words unrecognizable and harmless, bouncing off her like grains of thrown rice. For the first time since she had found the stolen money in the hall closet, she felt at peace as she sat surrounded by strangers who either didn't know or didn't care who she was or what her husband had done. There were no federal agents or reporters watching her from the choir loft or from behind the pulpit; the photographer hired by Angelo was taking pictures for the wedding album, not the front page. She felt weightless and about to float toward the ceiling on coiled smoke from burning incense and wanted the feeling to last. She only opened her eyes when Yianni walked by with the other usher toward the front of the church and squeezed her shoulder.

A door on the icon screen opened inward giving the impression that Archangel Gabriel was flying backwards; the groom, Basil, and his best man emerged. Basil was tall and lanky with a pronounced Adam's apple that bobbed in his throat when he gulped air. She remembered how calm Al had acted on their wedding day and realized she had never seen him nervous, not when they were in high school and were learning together in the backseat of his father's car, and not even when he was throwing clothes in a suitcase getting ready to run from the FBI.

The organist played the traditional wedding march, and the congregation rose and faced the back of the church. A flower girl, maybe three or four years old, threw fistfuls of pink petals straight down at her shiny patent leather shoes before turning the basket over and dumping the flowers in a pile. Two bridesmaids followed, their features so similar— high cheek bones, thick eyebrows—that Lolly was certain they were sisters, maybe cousins. Then the bride appeared, her arm linked with her father's, her smile wide and electric, her dark eyes lighting as the camera bulbs flashed. She wore a long-sleeved, A-line wedding dress with a beaded high collar that hugged her neck. Delicate lace work spanned the bodice and shoulders. The filigree swirled and curled in an intricate pattern of open roses. The dress was old and must have been a family heirloom. Lolly hoped that Elena's grandmother and mother had both worn the dress on their wedding day.

The Greek looked straight ahead. Tears glistened on his cheeks and his chin quivered. She remembered walking down the aisle with Stan and how his voice had trembled when he tilted his head toward her and had whispered, *There's still time.*

When The Greek and Elena reached the small table in front of the altar, he kissed her, shook Basil's hand, and gave him his daughter. The priest, standing on the other side of the table facing the congregation, began singing a Greek prayer, his voice deep and echoing throughout the old church. Lolly didn't understand a single syllable but was certain the words were beautiful, holy, and ancient.

*****

The reception was held at the Statler, the finest hotel in Buffalo. The brick building was built in English Renaissance Revival style and towered eighteen stories above Niagara Square, overlooking City Hall, the federal courthouse, and the county jail. Millard Fillmore's mansion, known as the Castle for its corner towers, turrets, and covered parapet walks, was demolished in 1920 to make room for what the *Buffalo Evening News* had described at the time as Ellsworth Statler's monument. Lolly crossed Delaware Avenue, her gaze fixed on the words "Hotel Statler" etched in gold on the black marble above the revolving front doors. She had never been inside the grand hotel and thought this might be her last chance.

She pushed through the spinning doors and stepped into cool air conditioning. She took a few steps into the Botticino marble vestibule, which stretched the length of the building from Delaware Avenue to parallel Franklin Street, then stopped—frozen in place like a stunned tourist as she took in the crystal chandeliers, twenty-eight-foot-high ceilings, and hand-painted tapestries. Her first thought was, *My God.* Her second thought was, *I wish Al could see this,* and she knew he never would.

The receiving line was setup outside the Golden Ballroom. As she waited to congratulate the families and the newly married couple, she couldn't stop staring at Elena. The bride's smile was constant. She greeted each guest with a kiss or hug. Her laughter rang across the marble floors and echoed off the high walls. Lolly wondered if the girl—she couldn't have been more than twenty—would ever feel this happy again. Basil stood next to his bride and whispered something in her ear. Her eyes misted and she rose on her toes to kiss his cheek and Lolly felt sorry for her, knowing that whatever Basil had whispered, Elena had believed completely.

"*Koukla!*" Angelo bellowed as Lolly made her way down the line. "You came!" The Greek hugged her tight. He released her but kept a hand on her shoulder. "This is Lolly, from the restaurant," he said to his wife.

"I'm Chrisoula. Thank you for coming," the woman said, her dark hair streaked with gray and piled high.

"Thank you for having me. And congratulations to both of you. Your daughter is a beautiful bride."

"Lolly," The Greek said, in a voice loud enough for everyone to hear. "I closed the restaurant today. I invited everyone to the wedding—waitresses, dishwashers, cooks, even Stavros, that dumb stump. I've never closed before and I don't remember my father ever closing either. We've always been open twenty-four hours, seven days a week. But today is special! My only child's wedding! And guess what?"

He didn't give Lolly time to answer.

"I couldn't find the key to the front door! I don't remember ever locking it! I thought it was hanging in the office!"

Everyone laughed, even the white-gloved waiters passing plates of appetizers and sparkling glasses of champagne.

"What did you do?" Lolly asked. "You didn't leave the door unlocked, did you?"

"No. I would've been robbed for sure. There are crooks everywhere. I hired that bum who walks up and down Genesee Street wearing bowling shoes to sit in the restaurant and scare away all the other bums! He used to be a boxer."

There was more laughter and Lolly kissed Angelo's cheek before moving down the line. She found herself standing in front of Elena, staring into her bright eyes. Happiness and optimism radiated from her. Lolly remembered feeling the same way at her own wedding, certain that every future day with Al would be just as joyous and perfect. Her mind clouded, the appropriate congratulatory words failing to form.

She could only think of condolences.

*****

Her heels clicked against the parquet floor as she entered the Golden Ballroom. Three large crystal chandeliers, identical to the ones hanging in the vestibule, were suspended from the ceiling. Gold leaf accentuated the crown molding, the balcony railings, and the Corinthian pillars, giving the impression that the ballroom was indeed golden. Round tables covered in linen were set for ten, the silverware gleamed from the chandeliers' light. Candied almonds wrapped in white netting and tied with a silver ribbon were set on each plate. On the stage at the far end of the ballroom, Taki and The Aegean Singers were playing Greek music—the band's name written in Hellenic blue on the drum kit.

Yianni approached her, a tulip glass in each hand. "You look thirsty," he said, handing her champagne.

His sudden appearance startled her, and she felt her cheeks warm as they had when he whispered her name at the church. "I do?"

Her fingertips brushed his as she took the glass.

"Parched," he said, smiling.

She searched for something to say, realizing it had been years since she had flirted with anyone but Al and was out of practice. "To the bride and groom," she finally said, and raised her glass.

"*Es ta thee ka su*," Yianni replied, tapping his glass against hers, the crystal ringing.

"What does that mean?"

"It translates to 'and to yours', meaning to your future wedding. It's an old Greek wish spoken to all the single people at the reception."

"To the bride and groom," she repeated, and sipped the champagne, the wine sweet and cold on her tongue. She glanced around the ballroom, afraid to look at Yianni. "Everything is perfect."

"All my Uncle Angelo does is work, work, work. For years I ask, 'Uncle, why do you work so hard? Why don't you take a day off? Go on a vacation once in a while. Go back to Greece for a visit.' And he always answers, 'Day off? Go back to Greece? I got Elena's wedding to pay for.' And I always say, 'You work this hard to pay for a wedding?' And he would say, 'Ah, Yianni. It's going to be some wedding.'"

"He was right," Lolly said as a waiter offered her a tray of stuffed grape leaves. "This is some wedding."

"And yet," Yianni said, spearing a grape leaf with a toothpick, "you come to this fancy wedding alone. Why doesn't a beautiful woman like you have a date?"

"What are these?" she asked, picking up the candied almonds from the closest place setting and studying them, avoiding Yianni's penetrating eyes. "Almonds?"

"*Bomboniere*, wedding favors. The almonds are called *koufeta*. They are sweet on the outside but bitter inside. The hope is the newlyweds' life will be more sweet than bitter."

She frowned as she held the almonds and thought of them as rare and expensive jewels, something Al might steal.

"There are an odd number of nuts," Yianni continued. "Either five or seven, I forget which. Do you know why?"

"No," she said, imagining her own marriage as an almond and the sweet coating dissolving, leaving only bitterness. She counted the almonds. Five. "Why?"

"Odd numbers are indivisible. It symbolizes that the married couple will share everything and never be divided."

She set the *bomboniere* down and then drained her champagne. "That's a lovely thought."

"My uncle is waving at me. I think it's time for photos. We will dance later, yes?" he asked, his eyes wide and hopeful.

Lolly started to nod then stopped. "We'll see."

She took a few steps before smiling at him over her shoulder.

*****

Lolly took another glass of champagne off a waiter's tray and strolled amongst the tables, searching for the place card bearing her name. She found it at Table 12 near the bandstand, and guilt rippled through her when she read *Lolly Majchorowicz* written in swirling calligraphy. She had started using her maiden name on job applications, certain that 'Nussbaum', spoken so much on the radio and television and kept alive by Morton Lucoff's constant articles, was preventing her from getting better paying jobs. Over the summer, she began using Majchorowicz more and more as she signed checks, paid bills, and addressed envelopes. She felt less guilt each time she wrote out her maiden name. But here, in this beautiful hotel, wearing a pretty dress and her wedding band left at home, using her old name seemed like a betrayal.

She grew angry with herself.

How many aliases had Al used since he drove away on that snowy night? She tried to remember the ones that Agent Alexander had read to her: Karl Kessler, Al Nest, Bump Newman, none of which she recognized. She set her purse down on the table, pushing Al out of her thoughts, and read the other place cards, relieved that she didn't recognize a single name. When a waiter offered her another glass of champagne, she accepted it even though she still held one in her hand.

*****

During dinner, the Aegean Singers left Taki alone on stage to strum his *bouzouki*, his notes drowned out by knives being tapped against crystal goblets, urging the newlyweds to kiss. The guests at Lolly's table were old friends and tried to include her in the conversation, but she was soon forgotten, and punch lines to jokes setup in English but delivered in Greek were lost to her. She didn't care. Her head buzzed from champagne. Whenever her glass was empty, a waiter or someone at the table or Yianni passing by would stop to fill it. She ate food she had never tasted before—roasted lamb, *spanakopita*, cheese doused in brandy and set aflame. Besides the wedding cake, there were trays of *baklava* and walnut sugar cookies called *kourabiedes*. Each bite offered new tastes and unexpected surprises that she savored. She tried everything and wasn't shy about reaching for more. Through all the courses and all the glasses of champagne—too much champagne—she didn't think of Al a single time, or worry about money, or what the next day might bring. She didn't envision picking up the *Courier Express* or *Buffalo Evening News* and seeing the headline that Al had been captured or killed like she always feared when she opened a newspaper; there were no thoughts of an accompanying bullet-ridden photo that would haunt her to her grave. Tonight, she was enjoying and spoiling herself. A full, satiated feeling overcame her as she listened to the best man toast the newly married couple in Greek. She smiled when everyone else smiled, laughed when they did, and joined in with the applause when he had finished, pretending she had understood every word. The champagne tasted so sweet.

The Aegean Singers rejoined Taki on stage, and they played a slow song for the newlyweds' first dance and then another as the bridal party and families joined them on the dance floor. She swayed in her seat. Her head, heavy and fogged from too much wine, tried to move to the rhythm. The chandeliers dimmed, at least she thought they had, and she closed her eyes, lost in melody. Numbness spread through her, and she wondered if there was a couch in the Ladies Room where she could rest. Someone called her name, and when she opened her eyes, Yianni was standing in front of her, offering his hand. He spoke but she couldn't make out the words. *Did he speak in Greek?* she wondered. She took his hand, and he led her out to the dance floor. Then she was in his arms; it had been so long since she had been held, she almost cried. He pulled her closer; she didn't try to keep her chest off his. Their bodies melded like they had danced before. They did not speak. Her heart punched through her dress and she wondered if he could feel it through his shirt and against his skin. The ballroom grew darker, her vision tunneling. Her mind swirled, surfacing memories and images: dancing with Al at their wedding reception, pulling into the Imperial Hotel in Niagara Falls on their wedding night in a borrowed—stolen?—Cadillac, the train station across the road from their honeymoon suite and the boxcars that rumbled past their window throughout the night. From the corner of her eye, standing at the dance floor's periphery, she imagined she saw Morton Lucoff sipping champagne and holding a camera, shimmering like a ghost. Then the ballroom dimmed to darkness.

She thought she was floating and realized she was leaning into Yianni. He gripped her around her waist as he partially carried, partially dragged her out a side door into the night.

"You need air," he said, his words muffled, sounding as if he was far away.

"Too much champagne," she mumbled, as headlights from passing cars blurred by.

"Breathe," he said, and she did, and felt the world tilt.

He steered her down an alley. She took another deep breath and lost her balance. He caught her, his hands encircling her arms, and leaned her against the hotel's brick wall. Then his lips, soft like Al's, touched hers and she returned the kiss. She closed her eyes, lost in the memory of a thousand other kisses and the way things once were. Tears fell then and, for a moment, he was back with her, stroking her arm, brushing the hair from her face, his breath warm against her neck. Her head spun and she was certain she'd float away if his arms weren't holding her. But the aftershave was stronger and the beard too rough. The lips became insistent. The thousand memories were forced away and the dark alley and the bricks, uncomfortable against her back, returned. His weight bore against her and she struggled to breathe.

"Enough!" The Greek yelled, shattering the sweltering night.

The world tilted at a greater angle and she slid with it.

*****

The sensation of movement. Humid air smelling of rain rushes against her face. Her head lolls from side-to-side, up and down. Darkness. Two male voices, one The Greek's, the other a stranger's, drift in and out, like a radio station out of range.

"That goddamn Yianni," The Greek says. "He was always bad, even as a kid. I should have drowned him twenty years ago."

"Do you even know where we're going?"

"Bailey Avenue."

"Christ, this is going to take forever. We should have poured her in a cab and sent her on her way."

"When you have a daughter, you'll understand."

"I understand your wife is going to drown *you* if you don't make it back before the kids leave for the airport."

"This, I also understand," The Greek says.

The radio station's signal weakens and the voices fade. Time passes, but Lolly doesn't know how much. The car bounces over potholes or railroad tracks and she moans, as if something deep inside her is broken and has been jarred. She begins to drool.

Laughter.

"This is funny?" The Greek asks.

"I was thinking of Yianni's face when you told him who her husband is."

"I think he shit his tuxedo."

"Did he really kill five people?"

"I don't know. Something I heard. Or maybe I made up. One for sure in New York. A cop or bank guard. Maybe both. I was trying to scare that bastard Yianni."

"But with a machine gun, right? He mowed them down?"

"I don't know."

"That's what you told Yianni."

"That's when he shit his tuxedo."

Laughter.

"Jesus, and you hired her?"

"She didn't rob any banks."

Darkness.

The absence of sight and sound, all thoughts taken flight. Only sensations: her face against the car seat, her stomach churning, a growing ache behind her eyes. Voices again. Far away and then in front of her. Everything slowing.

"Which one is it?"

"I think that one."

"There are no lights on. Are you sure?"

"What's the number say?"

"1202."

"That's it."

Stillness. Then a light shining red through her closed lids. Weightlessness. Levitation. Movement. She is flying, soaring above houses, above trees, ascending higher to the clouds, to the stars, to the moon, towards Al.

She opens her arms.

*****

She woke on Sylvie's couch still wearing the lavender dress, the hem ripped and dangling. Sunlight streamed through the windows. She covered her eyes and smelled the cigarette before she heard the voice.

"Is there anything else you can do to embarrass this family?" Sylvie asked, throwing the newspaper on her. "Marrying a bank robber and killer wasn't enough for you?"

Lolly forced herself up, her head cleaving. She squinted at the morning edition of the *News*. A picture of her and Yianni dancing—her arms around his neck, her body pressed against his—appeared above the fold in the City section. The caption read, "Bank Robber's Wife Moves On." The byline belonged to Lucoff. She let the paper fall.

"How did I get home?" she asked, her mouth dry and tasting of bitter almonds.

"Your boss carried you in. Your dress was torn. Babbling about flying."

She covered her face with her hands, her stomach pitching.

"The man left his own daughter's wedding reception because of you. He was wearing a tuxedo, for God's sake."

"I know."

From the bedroom, Alison cried. The sound pierced Lolly's ears, skull, her brain. She didn't move.

"Some mother you are," Sylvie said, taking a drag off her cigarette before going to the baby.

Chapter 12

Al rolled a cold pop bottle against his forehead as he watched Bobby struggle to count their haul; Bobby's 9mm Luger rested on the stack of hundred dollar bills next to him. Recorded typing drifted out of the propped windows and mixed with traffic noise. The second try at robbing the bank on Route 30 had been much more successful than their first attempt. Al had been right: shoving a Thompson in the pimply teller's mouth had done the trick. The bank president had cleaned out the drawers himself.

"There's thirty-one grand there," Al said, irritated by the heat and the time Bobby was taking. He tipped the bottle to his lips and finished the remaining root beer.

Bobby started counting the last stack again.

"I can take over if you're tired, Bobby," Jackie Rose said. She wore a sleeveless white blouse with three buttons open and a pair of Bermuda shorts. Al tried not looking at her. The apartment smelled of her perfume. *Coriander*, he thought.

"I'm not tired," Bobby snapped. "It's that damn typing. It's driving me crazy. I can't think. Can you turn that fucking thing off?"

"No one stops by if they think I'm writing."

"I can't stand it," Bobby said.

Jackie Rose hurried to the tape recorder. She rested a slender finger on the Power button, moving it in small circles then tapped it with a polished nail, never pressing hard enough to shut off the recorder.

"Turn it off!" Bobby yelled.

"Do you ever write anything, Al, or only think about it?" she asked, clicking off the recorded typing. She turned to him with her chin raised, another pose copied from a movie magazine, he thought. "You must get tired of thinking about it. You must want to do the real thing, don't you?" She parted her lips enough so he could see her tongue.

"I write some."

"I thought so. You're always reading. What do you write, Al? Do you ever write about me?"

"Thirty-one thousand," Bobby announced.

"Good," Al said, turning away from Jackie Rose. "We match."

Bobby counted out five hundred dollars and slid the bills across the gouged table.

"What's that?"

Bobby picked up the Luger. "Your cut."

A vibration started in Al's ears, like someone was holding a tuning fork close by. The vibration grew into a tone, the volume and pitch increasing until his skull was singing.

"My cut's half," he said. "Where's the other fifteen grand?"

Bobby's good eye raced back and forth; he pointed the Luger at Al's chest. "Men get half. Drivers get five hundred."

The apartment grew hotter; Al's .45 was on the other side of the room. He could feel the sweat on his face and wiped it with the back of his arm.

"Toss that soda bottle on the couch," Bobby ordered.

He did as he was told. The bottle bounced off the cushions and rolled to the floor. He clenched and unclenched his fists.

"Pack up the money, baby girl," Bobby said, knocking over his chair, the .9mm never wavering.

Jackie Rose mouthed *Sorry*, the word almost visible on her painted lips, then said, "Yes, Bobby." She grabbed fistfuls of bills and began stuffing them in the bag.

Al tried to keep calm; Bobby's good eye was moving as fast as it had in the Chillicothe laundry room, and he knew the Luger was one wrong sentence away from firing. The tone in his head made it hard to think.

"You don't want to do this, Bobby. We made a lot of money together."

"You mean *I* made *you* a lot of money," Bobby said, walking around the table and jabbing the gun barrel at him. "You're a wheel man. That's all you've ever been. A fucking know-it-all wheel man. That bullshit's over."

"We can make a lot more money too. There's this bank in Boston…"

"You don't get it, do you, smart guy?" Bobby raised the Luger even with Al's eye. "I don't need you. It doesn't take a genius to drive a getaway car. I don't need a chess master for that. Any kid with a goddamn learner's permit will do. I'm John Dillinger."

Al's mind raced over possible scenarios, trying to hit on the one that would lower the Luger and get him half the money. The droning in his head was constant.

"You know something, Bobby? You were right. It does take two inside to rob a bank. I don't know how I forgot that. Going in alone is too risky, too tough on you to do everything. We'll go in together from now on. I'll take Curry's place like you wanted. Jackie Rose can start driving and monitoring the radio." He glanced at her, "You can do that, can't you, Jackie?"

"Sure, Al," she said, clutching bills in both hands like she earned them. "Whatever you need."

"See? She's our third. You clean out the drawers and vaults, I'll control the guards and civilians, and Jackie Rose chauffeurs us clean away. We're back in business, Bobby. The Feds will never catch us. Let me tell you about Boston. We couldn't ask for a sweeter setup. We'll walk away with thirty-one grand *each*. Guaranteed cash money."

"Shut up," Bobby said, keeping the 9mm pointed at Al's eye. "Shut the fuck up."

Al imagined the bullet penetrating the cornea, pupil, and lens before travelling through the vitreous humor, severing the optic nerve and tearing apart his brain.

"Do you think I'd *ever* take you inside a bank with me now?" Bobby asked. "Do you think I'm crazy? I couldn't trust you to watch my back. How do I know you wouldn't turn chicken shit and run when we're in Boston? You're a sidelines guy, Al. A spectator. You're good cooling your high heels in the car and smoothing your skirt while someone else does the work. I got Jackie Rose for that."

"Bobby, look…"

"No, *you* look," Bobby said, walking towards him.

Al raised his hands for the first time. He stared at a brown stain on the wall behind Bobby, a reminder of some past leak. *What a shitty place to die*, he thought.

"Do you know the only thing worse than a rat?" Bobby stopped in front of him and pressed the Lugar against Al's left eye. "A coward. And a rat is always a coward before he turns rat. I should shoot you right here so I don't have to worry about you running to the Feds."

"Al's no rat, Bobby," Jackie Rose said, the color draining from her face, making her lipstick appear redder. "You know that. Why would he rat? He's in this as deep as you are."

"He'd rat to save his ass from the chair. He'd rat louder than Curry, that motherless fuck. I can already hear Al singing in court. 'Bobby killed the guard. Bobby shot the cop. I didn't even go inside the bank, your honor.' Fucking coward. Fucking rat."

Bobby's good eye raced back and forth faster than Al had ever seen. The vibration in his head stopped and all he heard was his heart pounding like it only had a few beats left.

"Don't shoot him, Bobby," Jackie Rose said, her voice shaking and bordering on tears. "Please."

Bobby twisted the gun sideways and pressed it so hard Al thought his eyeball would be pushed back into his head. "Give me one good reason why I shouldn't turn your skull into a convertible, smart guy."

Al had nothing left but the truth. "I need to earn, Bobby. I need to work. I need money to get Lolly and the baby. You know that." He heard the weakness in his voice and knew Bobby heard it too.

"Forget about Lolly and the kid. You'll never see them again."

Jackie Rose crammed the last of the money in the duffle bag and zipped it shut; she left the five hundred on the table for Al. "It's packed, Bobby. Let's go."

Bobby didn't move. Al could hear him breathing, he could smell his breath. His eye hurt from the Luger; he wondered if it was swelling already.

"We need to leave, Bobby."

Bobby placed the gun against Al's forehead. He pressed it in tight until the skin bruised. Al forced himself not to blink. He stared into Bobby's dead eye, and made his face hard, pretending he was fearless like he had in Chillicothe. Bobby's grin was a crooked slash across his face. They stood frozen together, connected by the Lugar, two halves joined by a gun barrel. Al, who was always aware of everything around him, became aware of nothing. Everything stopped and he wondered if he were dead already. He didn't feel the pain in his eye or forehead. Traffic noises no longer seeped through open windows. That dead eye did have power after all. It transformed Al into stone as he waited for the explosion and bullet that would send him shattering. They stood that way for an hour or a minute, waiting for Bobby's finger to contract, for the trigger to be squeezed, for the move that would finally checkmate Al.

Jackie Rose pushed the play button and the apartment filled with recorded typing. The sounds of imaginary words and sentences formed invisible stories of life and love and crime that floated through the air and crushed whatever spell gripped the two men. Bobby shoved Al hard with the Luger and his head snapped back. He retreated towards the door, keeping the gun trained on him.

"Don't come after us, Al. Don't come after the money. If I see you again, I'll kill you. I won't ask questions. I won't talk to you. I won't even let you buy me a drink. As soon as I see your face, I'm shooting. Go to Brazil or Bolivia or wherever the fuck you want. Give up robbing banks. That's for men. Write books about things you don't have the balls to do. Write about me. And Al?"

"Yeah?"

"Don't you rat."

The door slammed and he heard them hurrying down the hall and then down the stairs. His entire body shook. This time it wasn't fear that was making his hands and legs tremble. It was something harder and darker, an anger metastasizing to meanness that traveled through his veins and neurons and made his limbs shudder. No one hates being robbed more than a robber, but Bobby had stolen more than money. Whatever hope he had clung to during the last nine months had been zipped up and taken away as part of Bobby's haul.

He picked up the pop bottle and hurled it at the water-stained plaster where it exploded into a thousand pieces.

*****

The armored vest's weight always surprised him; he needed to wear it more often so it became familiar, like a second skin. Rolling on the passenger's seat next to him were two live hand grenades, and lying across the backseat was a .22 rifle loaded with soft-nosed bullets, the kind that penetrate deeply and expand painfully. The .45 rested between his legs on the driver's seat.

He knew that Bobby would be leaving Philadelphia soon, if he hadn't already. Then he would have to look for him in Atlantic City, then Vegas, then Reno; he'd have to find him before he spent all the money. But Bobby was an animal of habit that needed to mate after pulling a job. They had robbed eight banks together and after each one, as he counted the money a few feet away, Bobby, fueled by adrenalin and testosterone had groped and fondled Jackie Rose like a paroled man. When the money was counted and divided, Bobby would push him into the hallway and slam the door behind him so he could be alone with her.

He was certain Bobby would head back to his apartment one last time before leaving Philly. As he drove across town, he felt neither calm nor fear, just determination to perform a needed task.

He parked the car around the corner and cut down an alley to the back of Bobby's building, avoiding the people who had escaped their oppressive apartments to the front steps hoping to find a cool breeze. He had left the .22 in the car, deciding it was too risky to carry a rifle in daylight. The back alley was lined with dented metal garbage cans, the trash inside rotting in the heat; broken glass glistened green and amber on the ground. The rear door was locked, so he pulled his tools from his back pocket. He worked quickly, inserting the thin screwdriver into the keyhole and turning it before easing in the pick. Al heard the faint clicks as he lifted the five bottom pins into the top set, pushing them inside the housing, and the lock opened.

His rubber-soled shoes fell silent as he climbed the metal steps. The second-floor stairwell door was wedged open in the slim hope of circulating air. He peeked around the frame. The hallway was deserted. He pulled the .45 from his waistband and clicked the safety off.

Bobby's door was closed. Al heard nothing from inside the apartment and worried that they had already left town. He pressed his palm against the wood, as if testing for heat, and then tried the knob.

It turned.

The door opened without a sound, and he was grateful. There was a trail of clothes inside the door: the white sleeveless blouse, a thin bra, one of Jackie's sandals. His calmness evaporated and his breath came in bursts. He thought of Lolly the night he told her he was leaving. She had stood by the frosted window watching the snow and breathed deeply and slowly like she had when she went into labor, and he'd rushed her to the hospital. He tried to breathe the same way to regain his composure and then told himself it was working.

The bedsprings in the other room squeaked. Lined outside the bedroom door were packed suitcases and the duffle bag of money. Al knew he had to open the bedroom door and pump slugs into Bobby's thrusting body. If he didn't, he'd spend the rest of his life looking over his shoulder for federal agents and a one-eyed man.

The bedsprings squeaked faster. He needed to end it. Bobby would kill him if he caught up with him. Al reached for the knob, his fingers trembling. He'd have to steady the gun with both hands when he fired. The bedroom door had recently been painted white, and he stared at it like it was a movie screen and tried to see the future projected there: the door bursting open, Bobby rolling off Jackie Rose, his good eye wide in wonderment, his bad eye frozen, the .45 exploding, exploding, exploding, the blood splattering the sheets and headboard, Jackie Rose screaming.

Al let go of the doorknob.

He could take the money and back out of the apartment, then retrace his steps down the hall and the metal stairs to the alley. He could slice Bobby's tires or pull the distributor cap to buy some time before hopping on I-95 and heading to Miami. How long would it take to drive a thousand miles? Seventeen hours? Twenty? By this time tomorrow he could be standing in front of Luiz with thirty thousand dollars in his hand. That had to be enough for three passports, new identities, and one-way plane tickets to Brasilia. If he needed more money, Florida had banks too.

But Bobby would never stop hunting him. He'd become more obsessed with tracking him down than the most dogged

FBI agent who wanted to make headlines. Bobby knew him better than anyone, even better than Lolly. He knew the type of hotels and flophouses he liked to stay at; the neighborhoods where he felt most comfortable and how he liked to live near bookstores and drugstores so he could pick up hair dye and makeup for his disguises. Bobby would check them all between here and the Keys. He'd only be safe in Brazil.

He never should have told Bobby about Miami and Luiz.

A thought hit him so hard that it made his stomach pitch and roll. Would Bobby go after Lolly? Would he hurt her to get even with him? Was he crazy enough to go back to Buffalo? Was Al? He squeezed the doorknob and then let go. He was a good shot, but what if bullets hit Jackie Rose in the confusion?

He stared at the painted door, this time searching for answers, and saw only grainy brush marks and spots the painter had missed; he no longer envisioned killing anyone. He pushed the safety back into place and snatched the duffle bag, certain he had signed his own death warrant.

He left Bobby's cut, five hundred dollars, tucked inside Jackie Rose's sleeveless blouse on the floor in case she ever needed getaway money of her own.

Part 3:

End Game

*Do you think I'd have placed my neck in the Buffalo noose
for anyone except Lolly?*

—*Al Nussbaum*

Chapter 13

Al drove through the Buffalo streets with his fatigue jacket zipped to his chin and a black wool cap pulled to his eyes. The crackling police radio filled the car. He was sweating but stayed bundled, afraid a passing driver might recognize him. The Chevy's worn wipers smeared the wet snow across the windshield, making it hard to see. Rain had iced to sleet, then hail, then finally snow; the roads were snow-covered and glazed underneath. His hollowed stomach rumbled, but he was afraid to walk into a restaurant, imagining his wanted poster hung by every cash register. He drove past diners and hamburger parlors, their windows already decorated with blinking colored lights and garland, their front doors adorned with wreaths.

Christmas in Brazil.

The .22 again lay across the backseat, covered by a drab army blanket, the wool moth-eaten in spots. He wore two shoulder holsters under his jacket, a loaded .45 in each. Live hand grenades rolled against Seconal capsules in his coat pockets. He thought of taking a capsule to slow his mind; so much was out of his control and he had so many questions without answers: Were agents watching the house or tapping the phone? Would anyone recognize him despite his dyed hair and mustache? Was Bobby out there in the Buffalo night waiting for him with guns loaded and his good eye racing? Would Lolly agree to leave with him?

He reached in his pocket and fingered the capsules. The endgame of returning home was not a smart move, even if he was monitoring the police radio. It was risky and reckless, the same mistake Curry had made, but he was tired of running and being alone. Tonight, he would either take Lolly and the baby away or he would die by his own hand or by the men who hunted him. There was no reason to go on if there was no hope of being with Lolly again.

To turn his thoughts away from shootouts and Secanol, he practiced Portuguese, speaking the English prompt and then the translation aloud as he steered over slick but familiar roads.

Good morning. Bom dia.

Good afternoon. Boa tarde.

Good evening. Boa noite.

He avoided Buffalo's east side and his old neighborhood and instead drove on the city's Italian west side, cruising past Grant Street shops, then driving up and down streets named after New England states: Connecticut, Massachusetts, Vermont. He backtracked from Seventh to Fourteenth Street and couldn't help but notice the banks and their possible escape routes, the alleys perfect for ditching getaway cars, and all the shadowy places to hide. When he drove past Balisteri's Bakery on Niagara Street, he risked rolling down his window to breathe in the smell of baking bread.

I am hungry. Eu estou com fome.

I am sick. Eu estou doente.

He slowed when he saw the payphone in front of Johnny's Rendezvous, a mob bar since Prohibition when it was a speakeasy, but worried about stumbling into a police stakeout or undercover detectives who'd recognize him. The next payphone was further up Niagara Street, but a woman stood in the booth cradling a swaddled baby, the receiver tucked against her shoulder. He was afraid to wait on the sidewalk until she finished. Who knows who might walk past?

I'm sorry. Sinto muito.

Pardon me. Perdoe-me.

He drove another six blocks before finding another phone. He pulled to the curb, his heart fluttering in his chest. A handful of people waited for the number five bus a few feet from the phone booth. Men blew into cupped hands for warmth and women flipped their coat collars up like wings to shield the wind. He imagined they all had the Reader's Digest stuffed in their pockets or crammed deep in their purses, the page with his mugshot well-worn and dog-eared. Each of them would be so eager to race to the payphone and call the FBI. They'd yell into the mouthpiece that they had spotted Al Nussbaum, the bank robber, the Buffalo boy, the FBI's most wanted fugitive. They'd give his license plate number, a description of the Chevy, and then ask if the ten-thousand-dollar reward still rode on his head.

I must go now. Tenho que ir agora.

Please help me. Por favor, ajude-me.

He killed the motor and slid farther behind the wheel. A parked car with a running engine might draw attention. The number five bus rumbled to the curb and the good citizens boarded. After it pulled away, he summoned all the courage he had left to step from the car. He shoved fists into pockets, feeling the grenades and barbiturates, and hunched his shoulders as he shuffled to the phone booth, hoping he looked like any other man hurrying through the cold. He pulled the accordion door closed when he stepped in the booth and fished a dime from his pocket. He thought of The Name of The Game is Death's front cover and imagined Bobby walking up to the phone booth and shooting him in the spine through the plastic wall. He dialed his apartment as fast as the rotary allowed.

A recorded message.

The number had been disconnected.

Please check the number and try again.

His dime was returned. He stared at the phone as if it would tell him where Lolly was living. She must have moved in with her mother, he thought as he hooked a finger in the return and retrieved his coin. Where else could she have gone? How would he find her if she had moved somewhere else? He dropped the dime again and dialed Sylvie's number. He closed his eyes and listened to the phone ring.

Twice.

Three times.

Four.

Come on. Come on, he whispered. Entrar no. Entrar no. She had to be there.

Sylvie answered, her voice crushed stone, and he wondered if a cigarette burned nearby or drooped from her lips. In the background, he heard his daughter cry and then Lolly sooth her. He cupped his hand over the mouthpiece and asked for Lolly.

There was silence on Sylvie's end, and he wondered if his cupped hand had muffled his voice too much. Then Sylvie said, "One moment, please," her voice colder than grit. The receiver rattled as she set it down. He shifted his weight from one leg to the other and back again. A passerby might think he was moving to keep warm, not knowing that hearing Lolly's voice in the background made it impossible to keep still. He wanted to shed his army jacket and feel the snowflakes on his face, neck, and tongue. He wanted to strip off his holsters and pitch his .45s in the gutter and stand there, arms outstretched, head tilted toward heaven until he was cleansed by falling snow.

When she answered, he wondered her sweater's color, if her hair was pulled back or fell loose along her neck, if she had started decorating the apartment for Christmas.

"It's me," he said, into the phone.

"Oh." The word escaped on a breath.

"I'm in town. I need to see you. We need to talk."

"I don't know," she said, whispering. "I don't know if that's a good idea."

"We'll go for a drive. Please, Lolly."

"I'm not sure..."

"Yes, you are," he said, sweating; he pushed the wool cap higher on his forehead. "You know you want to see me. Don't tell Sylvie, though. I don't trust her. Tell her you forgot to run an errand. I can be at the house in twenty minutes. Be out front. Please."

"I have to be at work in a half hour," she said, her voice balancing on the edge of tears.

"Call in sick."

"I can't."

"Please, Lolly. We have to talk. You have to listen to what I have to say. I have a plan. Let me explain it to you. If you want no part of it, I'll take you straight home and you'll never see me again." He slid his hand in his pocket, searching for the Secanol. "Please."

The silence lasted a few seconds, but to him it was like sinking in dark waters, unable to see or hear and helpless to the currents. He gripped the capsules in his fist. If she refused to meet him, where should he park the car to swallow the pills? Sylvie's driveway? Outside a bank? In front of the FBI office?

I am tired. Estou cansado.

So tired. Tao cansado.

"Okay," she said, and he was pulled from the water, breaking through the surface and gulping mouthfuls of clean air.

"I'll be there in twenty minutes. Wait for me out front."

The phone clicked in his ear.

Eu te amo.

*****

Lolly's hand rested on the receiver after she hung it on the cradle. Sweat beaded above her lip, but a shiver rippled through her. She was certain she would vomit if she had anything in her stomach to expel. For months, she had waited for Al's call, had dreamed of it and invented conversations more romantic than anything she'd ever seen on television or at the movies. Now she didn't know what to do.

"Who was that?" Sylvie asked.

She could feel her mother's eyes burning into her back like lit cigarettes; she could almost smell her sweater's scorching wool. She tried to steady her voice, her thoughts. Lolly lifted the receiver and began dialing. "A friend."

"What friend?"

"Just a friend."

"Who is he?"

"Mother, please. I'm on the phone," she said, her pulse fluttering in her neck. When she finished dialing, she wound the phone cord around her finger and then unwound it, over and over.

"What friend?"

She kept her back to Sylvie. "Jim. Maeve hired him for the holidays."

"Maeve hired an extra person? She can't even afford to pay you."

Lolly ignored her. She should have left for work as usual and called Angelo from a phone booth blocks away from Sylvie. Al could have met her on some corner. How stupid am I? she thought.

When she heard The Greek answer, she spoke into the receiver. "Angelo? It's Lolly... Not so good... I'm not feeling well. I won't be able to make it in tonight."

Angelo responded but Lolly didn't grasp the words, their meanings blurred by images of Al. She wanted to see him so much. She didn't want to see him at all.

"Thank you," she said into the receiver when he paused, her voice robotic. "I'm sure I'll be better tomorrow." She hung up the phone.

"You don't think I know Al's voice?" Sylvie asked. "I hear his lies in my dreams every night." She lit a Pall Mall.

"I need to get ready," Lolly said, shouldering past her.

Sylvie followed her to the bathroom. Lolly stood in front of the mirror, her head tilted, and began pulling a brush through her hair in angry strokes.

"I forbid you to see him," Sylvie said, standing in the doorway.

The brush made a tearing sound, the bristles digging deep until her scalp tingled.

"What if the police chase him? What if Al starts shooting? You don't know what he's capable of. He'll be like a trapped animal. You could get killed."

She brushed her hair until it was shiny.

"Why did he come back here? This is suicide." Sylvie gestured with her hand, and gray ash fell to the bathroom floor.

Lolly put the brush down and looked at her mother in the mirror. "It wasn't Al on the phone. It was Jim. He's having some crisis and wants to talk," she said, her voice low and calm, unlike everything else in her body that seemed to be breaking free and taking flight. "And if it was Al, why do you care if he commits suicide or not? I thought you'd be happy if he were dead."

"I don't care if that bastard lives or dies or is locked in prison for a hundred years. I only care about you and that baby in there," she said, pointing down the hall to Alison's room.

Lolly squeezed a ribbon of Ipana on her toothbrush.

"What does he want? Is he giving you money? Don't take it. It will make you an accomplice. God knows you need it, though."

She brushed her teeth with the same angry strokes that she had brushed her hair.

"Don't you dare let him in this house. And don't you dare let him anywhere near that baby."

She spat and rinsed her mouth. Her hand shook as she reached for her lipstick.

"Tell him not to come back. Only the police want him here. Tell him you're getting an annulment."

She looked at her watch. "I'm meeting Jim outside. I won't be late. Give the baby a kiss for me. No, two kisses."

The second one for Al, she thought.

Sylvie straightened to her full height in the doorway, the cigarette glowing in the corner of her mouth. "You're not going."

Lolly looked dead-on at her mother for the first time. Her hands balled to fists, and her eyes dulled to gun barrel blue. Cords appeared in her neck, straining when she spoke. "Get...out...of my way."

The intensity in her voice surprised her, sounding nothing like her own. She was more surprised when her mother stepped aside. She pressed by and hurried to the door, grabbing her coat from the back of a dining room chair. The front door opened, and Stan entered carrying groceries. His cheeks were red from the cold; melted snow darkened his overcoat's shoulders.

"Hi there, Lolly girl. Off to the restaurant? I'll give you a ride if you want. It's starting to come down out there."

"No, thanks," she said, rushing by.

She slammed the door behind her.

*****

Al popped another Seconal. He needed to calm down, to see the chessboard clearly, to convince Lolly to run away with him. As he drove further east, his anxiety grew, and he thought of swallowing a third capsule. Every car was an unmarked police car, every pedestrian hailing a cab or walking in the snow a federal agent. And then another fear grabbed him: what if Lolly wasn't waiting outside the house? What if she changed her mind? What if Sylvie and Stan had stopped her?

He tried to breathe.

Por favor. Por favor.

He was tired of making plans, tired of being strong. He wanted to sleep with Lolly's arms around him again, his head cushioned by her breasts. The constant fear and paranoia ate at him. He gripped the steering wheel tighter and replayed his phone conversation with Sylvie. Did she recognize his voice? Did she know it was him? Did she say, "One moment, please," with anger? Malice? How much did she hate him? He was so tired.

I want to sleep. Quero domir.

Traffic was thinning as people made their way home from work, hurrying out of the snow. Fewer cars to blend with, he thought, gnawing at the inside of his mouth until he tasted blood. He drove like Stan: both hands on the wheel, braking gently to avoid skidding on the unplowed roads, his turn signals blinking amber as he changed lanes or rounded corners, trying not to give the cops a single reason to pull him over. He cut down familiar streets without thinking. The path home was burned into muscle memory, and he made the turns without hesitation. As he entered his old neighborhood, he expected the road in front and behind to be blocked by police cars screeching to angled halts to trap him. He waited for the darkening night to be illuminated by blinding spotlights or flashes from Bobby's machine gun. Lolly should have met him somewhere far from where neighbors might recognize him. All it took was one observant person walking their poodle to end this. But there, in front of their darkened house at the end of the driveway, stood his Lolly. He pulled to the curb and she was reaching for the handle before he could roll to a stop.

Then she was in the car and in his arms. He kissed her lips and cheeks and chin, and then held his face against hers, their tears blending. Her body trembled against his; he hugged her, never wanting her to be cold or frightened again.

"You better drive," she whispered before kissing his ear. "We shouldn't stay here."

He nodded, words lost in his throat. Before putting the car in gear, he glanced at the house. All the windows were dark except one in Sylvie's flat. A single cigarette provided the lone light, the tip brightening with each drawn breath. He stared at the red glow, frightened that it reminded him of a warning light. Then the drape fell closed, and the house was again shrouded in shadows and darkness.

*****

No cars followed them; the police radio cut in and out about weather-related accidents: cars skidding off highways, trucks jackknifing, water mains bursting and icing streets. She placed her hand on his cheek, and he tilted his head to meet her touch.

"You look so tired, Al. And thin."

"It's all part of the disguise," he joked, but Lolly didn't laugh.

"Have you been eating?"

"Not much," he said, deciding to never lie to her again. He'd tell her everything, anything she wanted to know. She would be his confessor. "Sardines and crackers mostly. I've been afraid to leave my motel."

"Where have you been? Where have you been living?"

"Florida. I drove two days to get here."

"Have you slept at all?"

"In Virginia for a little while."

She stroked his gray cheek. "You didn't get much Florida sun."

"I was afraid to open the drapes."

"Oh, Al."

"It's okay," he said, turning and smiling at her. "I'm here now. We're together."

"The newspaper said you robbed banks in Pennsylvania and that they almost caught you. I thought you were living there not Florida."

"They've never gotten close to catching me. I was there for most of the year. In Germantown near Philly. It felt like home, or at least close to it. Not that it mattered. I didn't go out much, and when I did it was at night. Except to rob that bank. We hit it twice on two different days."

"What did you do all day? You must have been so lonely."

"I read. Listened to ballgames on the radio. I started writing. Nothing serious or even very good. Just some short stories to pass the time."

"What do you write about?"

"Bank robberies, mostly."

"Oh."

He wove through slick streets with no destination in mind. The police radio chattered, the voices like other passengers in the car. He told her about Bobby and the money, how he'd been hiding from him for months, how his paranoia had grown after the two of them had split, not telling her about Miami yet. That could wait.

While he talked, her hand never left him. She stroked his cheek, massaged the tenseness from his neck, unzipped his jacket and rubbed his shoulder where the snake had once been poised to strike, never commenting on the guns strapped to him.

"What about you? When did you move in with your folks?"

"After Easter. I couldn't afford the bills."

"What's it like living with her?"

"It's fine. I'm not there much. I work two jobs. During the day I'm at Maeve's, and at night I work at the New Genesee restaurant."

"The Greek's place? Waiting tables?"

She nodded.

"Oh, sweetie." He took her hand and kissed it.

"No one else would hire me."

He didn't let go of her hand. "You're not wearing your wedding ring," he said, his thumb stroking where the small diamond should've been.

"It's hard being Mrs. Al Nussbaum."

"It's been tough being Mr. Al Nussbaum lately, too."

She rested her head on his shoulder and he pulled her closer.

"Alison must be getting big," he said.

"I should have brought pictures. She's not a baby anymore. She totters around and babbles and can say 'mama.' And she loves books like you do. I'll finish reading one to her, and she'll make me read it again. I spend half my paycheck from Maeve on children's books."

Al felt something tear off inside him; he had missed out on so much already. He wondered if Alison would remember him, but he knew the answer and tried not to cry. She reached up and took off Al's wool cap and played with his dyed hair as he drove. She glanced out the window.

"Where are we going? Niagara Falls?"

"I guess so."

He hadn't realized he was driving north on Route 61 towards the Falls; he had been weaving away from the old neighborhood as fast as possible, taking a turn or road without thinking. It seemed right that they were heading where they had honeymooned. They had started their marriage in the Cataract City, and tonight it was like he was proposing a second time.

"My God, you're not going to try to sneak into Canada, are you?"

"No, Brazil."

She lifted her head off his shoulder. "What?"

"That's what I wanted to talk to you about. I want us to go to Brazil. All of us. You, me, and the baby. There's no extradition there."

She straightened, her entire body growing rigid. "Brazil? What are you talking about? How?"

"I went to Miami. I know a guy there. It took a while, longer than I thought, but it's all set. My paperwork's already done. So are yours and Alison's. We need to get your photos taken so he can finish your passport. We're the Fischers now. The plane tickets to Brazil are already bought." He pulled open his jacket and showed her the airline tickets tucked in his inner pocket near one of the .45s.

"You bought tickets?"

"Everything is set."

"This is crazy."

"I've got it all planned, Lolly. Every move."

"How would we get out of the country? Your picture is everywhere—the post office, Reader's Digest."

"The scariest part will be at the Miami airport, but the rest will be easy."

"But Brazil?" she asked, trying to remember something about the country. "I don't even speak Spanish."

"They speak Portuguese. I've been practicing. I'll teach you."

"How will we live? What will we do down there?"

"I have some money left. That will hold us until I get a job."

She angled sideways on the front seat, tucking her legs under her to face him. "I won't go if you plan on robbing banks down there, Al. I won't."

"I'm done with all that. I'm retiring. I'll find something else to do. Something legit."

"I've never heard of a bank robber retiring."

"I'll be the first."

"This is crazy. Brazil? I'll never see my family again, will I?"

"We'll be together, Lol. The three of us. We'll be a family. And I won't screw it up this time."

"Everything I know will be gone. It will all be different. It will be like I died."

"It will be a fresh start. A new chance."

"You wouldn't let me go with you when you first started running. You said it was too dangerous for me and the baby. How is it different now? Isn't it worse? Everybody's seen your picture."

"I was too hot then, Lol. Curry had talked, and they were closing in. But it's been almost a year. The Feds don't have any leads. I'm sure of it. I read that Interpol was looking for me in Europe. The time's right, honey. Christmas in Brazil. That's all I've been dreaming about."

"I don't know. None of this makes sense. When did you want to go?"

"Tonight. We'll take turns and drive straight through."

"Tonight? This is all happening so fast, Al. I can't think."

"I can't stay in Buffalo too long, honey. It's too dangerous. Someone could recognize me at any time. We got to leave." He glanced at his watch. "You need to go home and pack. Bring one suitcase and only summer clothes. We'll buy whatever else we need once we get there. We'll meet at two in the morning. That should give you enough time to get ready and your folks should be asleep by then."

"You're not going to pick me up?"

"It's too risky for me to go back to the house. Let's meet at the Statler. Drive to the train station and get a cab. Make them drive you someplace, anyplace. Then grab another cab and do the same thing. Take three or four taxis in case you're followed. Here," Al reached in his pocket and handed her a handful of crumpled bills. "You'll blend in with your suitcase at the hotel. I'll pull right in front by the revolving doors on the Delaware side. When you see my car, come out but not too fast. Walk normally."

"The Statler? I'm scared, Al."

"It's going to be fine, Lol. Trust me. But if something does go wrong, if you think you've been followed or if there are cops around, wait outside. Not in the lobby. Outside. If I see you standing there, I'll drive away. I won't even slow down."

"And then what?"

"And then I'll think up another plan."

Lolly let him pull her close. She was trembling again; he could feel her body shake through her winter coat. As he swung the car around and steered for home, he described

Brazil to her—the ocean breezes, the lush rain forests, the exotic tastes and smells. The descriptions he'd read flooded from him.

"There's a clear lake in Brazil," he told her, "that turns into a mirror on still, bright days. It reflects the sky and clouds. The Brazilians say it's where heaven touches earth."

"It sounds beautiful."

"We're heading to paradise."

****

Every light burned in Sylvie's apartment when Lolly returned. Smoke from Stan's pipe and Sylvie's Pall Malls misted the room; the air smelled of cherry tobacco. She sensed there was something wrong as soon as she entered. A silence filled the room that was so heavy and dense, she was certain she could reach out and touch it, turn it over in her hands, feel its texture and weight. Stan sat on the couch, his pipe clamped in his mouth, puffing hard on the stem. His eyes darted everywhere but would not settle on his daughter. Sylvie stood at the front window clutching open the curtains, her face close to the glass.

"What's wrong?" Lolly asked, standing a step inside the doorway, her keys still in her hand. "Is it the baby? Is Alison all right?"

"The baby's fine," Stan said, without removing his pipe. He looked past her shoulder to a spot on the wall. "Sound asleep."

"Then what's wrong?" she asked, shutting the door. "It feels like a morgue in here."

"Jesus, now they come," Sylvie said, still at the window.

Lolly heard the engines and brakes, the slamming doors, the shouting, noises she remembered from the first night she had met Alexander. She looked for something to hold onto, then leaned against the wall to support herself.

"Oh, Mother, no."

Sylvie let the drapes fall closed. She folded her arms tight across her chest as she stepped toward Lolly.

"Why, Mother? For the reward? Or do you really hate him that much?"

"I did it for you."

Footsteps muffled by fresh snow fell on the front steps. The pounding on the door made Lolly jump even though she expected it.

"Open it," Sylvie said, her voice a whisper as she lit a fresh cigarette. "Before they break it down again."

Lolly leaned away, wanting no part of what was on the other side. Alexander and three other agents pushed their way in with their guns drawn. The backdoor was kicked in and torn from its hinges. Alison shrieked. Stan hurried to her, like he couldn't get away fast enough.

"He's gone," Sylvie said to Alexander. "You missed him. What took you so long?"

"Which way?" Alexander asked, breathless and Lolly wondered if he had sprinted from the downtown FBI office all the way to Bailey Avenue. "What kind of car?"

"I don't know. Too dark to see. He always liked Chevys. Maybe it was one of them. Who can tell? They all look alike. Ask her."

"What kind of car?" Alexander yelled at Lolly.

"I took the bus. I don't know what you're talking about."

Alexander pointed to a chair. "Sit."

She unbuttoned her coat and strolled to the hall closet, taking her time shrugging it off and opening the door. She selected a wooden hanger and fitted it through the sleeves.

"Sit," Alexander repeated, then growled at his agents. Lolly heard something about roadblocks and the agents scurried outside. She glared at her mother in a long, searing stare—wishing it would ignite her—before walking back into the living room and then sitting where Alexander had pointed.

Brause and two other agents she had never seen before, the ones who had kicked the back door off its hinges, circled the chair, leaving room for Alexander in front. One side of Brause's upper lip twitched. He remained silent, but she could read the look on his face. His expression whispered We got him, Lolly. We got him thanks to you.

Alexander towered above her. "What were you thinking?"

She said nothing.

"We can charge you with aiding and abetting," Brause said.

"Where is he?" Alexander asked.

"I don't know what you're talking about. I was out with a friend."

Sylvie made a noise like she was leaking air.

"What friend?" Brause asked, taking out his notebook. "Give me a name."

She didn't answer.

"She said his name was Jim," Sylvie said. "From the bookstore. Somebody they just hired."

"Nobody new started working at the bookstore," Alexander said.

"How do you know?" Lolly asked.

"Because we'd know about it if he did, like we'd know if anyone new started working at the restaurant. Like we know that Al called you and you were out with him tonight."

"You only know that because I called you," Sylvie said. Smoked seeped out with each word.

"Is he coming back for you?" Alexander asked. "Is Al coming back here?"

Stan entered holding the baby. He bounced her gently in his arms, a pacifier between her lips. Alison reached a pudgy hand to her mother and Brause stepped between them.

"If you don't start cooperating, Mrs. Nussbaum," Brause said, "you better get used to not holding your baby. We can slap obstruction of justice on top of that aiding and abetting. We can make it so you don't see your daughter for a long time."

Brause jerked his head toward the bedrooms, and Stan left with the baby.

The room felt sweltering; she wondered if one of the agents had turned up the thermostat to make her uncomfortable just as the hovering tobacco smoke was making her lightheaded. It was impossible to think. She fanned herself with an open palm.

"You need to help us," Alexander said. "For Al's sake."

"For Al's sake?" she asked.

"If he's coming back for you, if you're close to him, he won't fight us when we take him. I'm sure of it. He won't risk you getting hurt."

Brause leaned in close, his breath smelling of cigarettes and coffee when he spoke. "But if you're not around, if we got to chase him or if he thinks he has nothing to lose, he'll start shooting. I've read his service record. I know he's a marksman, but we'll have an army with us—FBI, state troopers, Buffalo cops—and they're all going to fire back. Bullets are cheap, Mrs. Nussbaum. We're going to use them all. There won't be much of your husband left."

She leaned forward, elbows resting on thighs, and covered her face with her hands. Brause and Alexander kept talking as she sobbed into her palms, their opposing words battering her.

"We don't want to see him hurt."

"He'll end up dead in the snow."

"He'll have his day in court."

"He'll get the chair if he kills a cop."

She sat up and pulled her hands away. Mascara tears tracked down her face. She wanted them to stop talking, to leave her alone, to go away. They should have left for Miami as soon as she got in Al's car.

"You can save him."

"He'll end up dead if you don't help us."

"He'll be eligible for parole in ten years."

"You'll never see him again."

Her mind swirled. Time swirled. The room became hazier as one by one the agents who encircled her lit cigarettes. It was hard to breathe, impossible to think. From another room, the baby cried, but they wouldn't let Lolly go to her.

"Only you can save him."

"He's a dead man."

*****

A warm front blew in from the west, changing the wet snow to an icy drizzle. Delaware Avenue was puddled and almost deserted; a few cars were ahead of him, their taillights casting a red glare across his smeared windshield when they braked. Al unzipped his jacket to make it easier to get to the automatics; the rifle had already been transferred to the front seat. The safeties on all weapons were off. The police radio chirped constantly about various car accidents around the city, the sloppy roads making for a busy night. An ambulance was needed on Kensington Avenue, a fist fight had broken out over a fender bender on Seneca Street. There was always a fight on Seneca Street—the damn Irish.

He rounded Gates Circle for the first time since he and Lolly had toured the wine-colored house. He wondered if a young couple had bought it, if Christmas lights glowed on front bushes, if they had ever found a hidden safe. He didn't turn down Lafayette to check. Instead, he accelerated through the circle. Lafayette was part of the past. His future waited for him at the Statler, then down in Miami, and finally in Brazil.

A pair of headlights cut on behind him, the passenger side brighter than the driver's side. A new lamp, Al thought. Or maybe the other one is about to die.

He drove past the mansions on Delaware Avenue's Millionaire's Row—the red-bricked Goodyear estate, The Asa Silverthorne house, the stately Harlow C. Curtiss Mansion. The houses were part of the past too, the families either dead or unable to maintain the grand homes. The mansions had been converted into schools, law offices, the American Red Cross.

The mismatched headlights remained a few car lengths behind. Al's stomach began to burn. He gripped the wheel tighter and checked his mirrors every few seconds, waiting for the car to turn left or right but it remained on Delaware, its pace even with his. As they passed under a brightly lit stretch of the avenue, he noticed the license plate was white, not New York yellow. Out of state, he thought. Or government plates. The Feds.

The nearer he came to the hotel, the less he was able to control his body. The Seconal's dulling effect was negated by the fear brought on by the mismatched headlights and the adrenalin that pumped through his system. His left leg bounced by the brake; his hands drummed the steering wheel. He thought of Bobby then and the restlessness and talking jags that had gripped him following each job and wondered if maybe Bobby had just been scared too.

He told himself there were plenty of reasons for the car to still be behind him. Delaware was a busy street, even at this hour. Maybe he was heading to the Statler too. A late night check-in, a traveler from another state who has nothing to do with me. Or perhaps the driver lived down here and was about to turn at any moment.

Al sped up.

So did the car tailing him.

He slowed and the car remained the same distance behind.

He drove with one hand on the wheel, the other resting on the rifle. His leg bounced faster.

*****

Lolly stood outside the hotel in front of the revolving doors, trying to forget the last time she'd been at the Statler with Yianni. She held a plastic doll wrapped in Alison's pink elephant blanket on her shoulder, an empty suitcase by her feet. Inside the lobby, FBI agents sat in chairs pretending to read folded newspapers and magazines. More agents hovered by the Franklin Street entrance in case Al tried to sneak through the back. Unmarked cars were parked on Delaware and the surrounding streets with their engines running, ready to be popped into gear. She overheard someone tell Alexander that the sniper was in place.

She cradled the doll like it was a real baby, cooing softly in its plastic ear and kissing its painted cheeks. The blanket smelled of Alison and she pressed her face in tight, asking forgiveness.

*****

He ignored the courthouse and jail when he drove by. He didn't want to think of all the men who had been sentenced in the one building and incarcerated in the other. Men like him. He unsnapped both holsters.

The car with the one dull headlight accelerated, closing the gap. Al was breathing faster, watching his mirrors as much as he was looking ahead. He drove around William McKinley's Monument, a white obelisk dead-center in Niagara Square memorializing his assassination in Buffalo. Bright lights shown on the marble spire and the sculpted lions that encircled it. Al could see that the car behind him was red.

As he neared the hotel, he saw Lolly standing in front of the gold revolving doors, holding the baby in one arm. Their eyes locked, and he saw fear and wondered if she saw the same in his face. He pressed the accelerator to the floor, his rear tires spinning on the wet pavement before they gripped. He sped past her. The Chevy fishtailed up Delaware Avenue as headlights snapped on all around him. Sirens shrilled from every direction; blue and red lights danced across his front and rear windshield. He fumbled with a holster and laid a .45 next to the .22. He thought of his mother-in-law and the red glow of her cigarette in the darkened window, convinced she was about to become ten thousand dollars richer.

In the confusion, Al did not notice that the red car had pulled to the curb. The driver waited for all the police cars to race after Al before driving after them.

A black and white cut off Al from the north, and he had to turn his wheel hard to the right and cut down West Huron. His Chevy scraped against a line of parked cars, the sound of grinding metal mixing with sirens. An unmarked car with a revolving blue light on its dash flew at Al from a side street on the passenger side, and he spun the wheel to the left as he smashed the brake pedal to the floorboard. He skidded the wrong way down Franklin Street, then punched the accelerator. The speedometer's needle climbed, and he doused his headlights. He kept the accelerator to the floor and swerved west around a darkened corner, racing from sirens and lights that bounced against brick buildings and across rain-slicked streets.

He made a sharp left on Masten Avenue, heading north and for a moment it was dark and quiet: no lights flashed behind him, no sirens screamed. He yanked the car to the right and parked in front of a stone church, cutting the engine. He lay down on top of the rifle and held the .45 in his left hand. Sirens wailed closer. The first car whizzed by. The second car followed close behind. He held his breath, afraid the officers and agents that sped past could hear him struggling for air.

The third car slammed into the back of the Chevy.

The impact sent him sprawling to the floor mats.

Voices.

Shouting.

He dropped the .45 and reached for the Seconal. Both the front passenger and driver side doors were thrown open. He raised the capsules to his mouth. Rough hands grabbed him by his shoulders and the back of his collar and tried jerking him from the car. He fought them off, kicking and flailing his arms, the capsules still clutched in his fist. Red and blue lights lit up the night as more police cars arrived, their brakes squealing as they parked all around him, checkmating the Chevy in place.

Bright flashlights beamed into the car, blinding him. Hands and arms appeared from everywhere—the driver side, the passenger side, the back seat—pushing and pulling him out of the car. Curses and yelling mixed with the constant squawk from the police radio dangling from the dashboard by red and green wires; he kept hearing his name repeated.

The first punch landed on his right kidney, the hard fist smashing the organ and taking his breath away. Then another punch, and another, each landing on the same spot. Billy clubs smashed elbows and kneecaps, shoulders, and collarbone. The blows paralyzed him. Then, he burst from the car in a violent rebirth. Hands, too many for him to guess the number, gripped him. He still fought, not to escape but to free his arm enough so he could swallow the Seconal. He levitated for an instant and then was slammed down on the Chevy's hood. His elbow bounced off the car and his hand opened. The capsules fell from his grasp like lost and scattered dreams. They skittered across the hood and onto the street. He lunged for the strewn pills, but each one, like Brazil, like redemption, like Lolly, was too far away.

The red Impala with the one dull headlight drove past unnoticed—the driver laughing.

Epilogue

Writing is okay. What I'd really love to be doing is robbing banks.

—*Al Nussbaum*

Charles Maibach parked the car and walked toward the bank. The Salvation Santa had already started bell ringing on the corner. "Charity Drive 1982" was painted across his donation kettle in red and green lettering. As he approached, he could see droplets of sweat forming on Santa's forehead. The air felt like spring, warm and bright, not like the third day of December at all. Santa's beard and hat drooped. He seemed to be wilting under the weight of the red woolen suit. Charles dropped a dollar in the kettle, mumbled good morning, and wondered if he'd have to donate each day for the next three weeks. Santa, despite the heat, wished him a loud and joyous "Merry Christmas!", the first person to do so this year.

The bank, too, was transforming itself into the season. Small poinsettias, their ceramic pots wrapped in silver or gold foil, rested on the counter in front of each teller's cage. A large wreath had been hung above the revolving doors, and a

Christmas tree, not yet decorated, stood in the corner scenting the air with fresh pine. Charles wasn't ready for the holidays at all. As he made his way to his office, he nodded good morning to the guard, a Vietnam veteran who sometimes sat rigid in his chair and stared straight ahead with far-away eyes. Piped-in Christmas carols mixed with Santa's faint bell ringing.

He unlocked his office door, the word *President* painted on the frosted glass, and switched on the lights. A stack of reports left untouched from the previous night awaited him on his desk; he stared at the pile and frowned as he set down his briefcase, knowing he would have to slog his way through them all before his ten o'clock meeting with the board. He hung his suit jacket on the brass coat tree in the corner and when he faced his desk again, the stack of reports seemed higher. Anything would be better than this, he thought. As he settled in his chair, already reading the top report, the phone rang. He answered it on the second ring.

"Charles Maibach," he said, into the receiver. "How may I help you?"

"Call home," the male voice said. "There's an emergency."

"What kind of emergency? Who is this?"

"Call home."

The line went dead.

He stared at the phone, confused, still holding the receiver to his ear.

"What the hell?" he said, aloud. He didn't recognize the voice at all. "What kind of joke is this?"

"What kind of joke is what?" Susan, his secretary, asked while entering his office. She carried a blue mug with "Prospect National Bank – Peoria" written across it in gold letters.

He returned the phone to the cradle. "Some guy called. He told me to call home because there's some kind of emergency, then hung up."

"Who was it?" she asked, setting the coffee in front of him.

"I don't know. I didn't recognize the voice. Some practical joker."

"You better call home to be sure."

"Yes," he said, picking up the receiver again. "I better."

The same man who had called him answered on the first ring. "I'm your emergency, Charles. I'm in your house."

"Who is this? Where's Annette?"

"What's happening?" Susan whispered, but he waved her away.

"Annette's here with me. She's very pretty, Charles. Very pretty, indeed. Well done."

"Let me talk to my wife!" Charles said, his voicing rising into the receiver. His office felt small and hot. He loosened his tie.

"Calm down, Charles," the voice said, his tone smooth like a blade's fine edge. "You'll talk to her soon enough if you do exactly what I tell you. If you don't, if you try to be a hero, the next time you see your pretty Annette she'll be cut into pretty little pieces. And we don't want that, do we Charles?"

"Dear God," Charles said. He pointed to the door, gesturing for Susan to leave. "What do you want?" He tried keeping his voice as calm and level as the man's voice on the other end. He's a professional, Charles thought.

"What we all want, Charles. Money. All of it. Everything you have in the bank. Is that asking too much?"

"Jesus Christ."

"Don't be like that, Charles. It's not your money, and it's all insured. Do as I say, and Annette will be fine."

"Let me talk to her first."

"Not until I get my money. Listen carefully, Charles. Are you listening?"

He unbuttoned his shirt's top button, the starched collar and silk tie strangling him. "I'm listening."

"Good. Clear out the vault and bring the money to the payphone on War Memorial Drive across from Leonardo's Pizzeria. Do you know where that is?"

"Yes. It's maybe a mile from here."

"That's right. They make a very good pizza. Maybe not as good as in New York, but not bad for Peoria. Get the money and then get to that payphone, Charles. Do not call the police. Do not call home again. Do you understand?"

"Yes."

"Good. You have twelve minutes," the voice said, and the line crackled with static.

Charles hung up the phone and stared at it, hoping it would ring and the man, laughing, would say he was a neighbor or a long-lost cousin, and then Annette would come on the line, she laughing too, sing-songing "Gotcha!," but the phone remained silent. He grabbed the receiver again and began dialing, then stopped.

What if it wasn't a joke?

Would the man really kill Annette—cut her?—if he defied him and called home? The fried eggs Annette had made him for breakfast soured in his stomach. The man's voice was so professional and calm that he was certain the man would do exactly as he'd threatened.

Charles pushed back from the desk and jumped from his chair. He ran from his office, almost colliding with the eavesdropping Susan in the hallway, and burst into the bank manager's office across the hall, startling him.

"What in the name of…"

He cut him off and told him of the phone call, the threat, the twelve minutes—less than that now—that he had to get to the payphone with all the money.

"We have to call the police," Thomas said. "They can go to your house and rescue Annette or follow you in an unmarked car."

"I can't risk it. I can't risk Annette getting hurt. I'm taking the money."

Thomas' face drained to gray. "I'll help."

The two men rushed to the vault. Thomas held the canvas sack stamped with the bank's logo as Charles dropped in packets of money by the armful. He grabbed wrapped bills as fast as he could, his shirt pasted to his skin with perspiration.

"Time? How much time?"

"Four minutes. You've got four minutes."

"I'm not going to make it," he said, and scooped money into the bag faster. "Jesus, I'm not going to make it."

"You'll make it," Thomas said. "Leonardo's isn't far."

When the bag was filled almost to bursting, he grabbed it from Thomas and ran for the revolving doors, startling customers and causing a murmur among the tellers. The bank guard stood as he approached but didn't move to stop him; his eyes were staring eight thousand miles away.

He swung through the revolving doors and stumbled into the Salvation Army kettle, toppling it to the sidewalk. Coins bounced and skittered across the ground; dollar bills floated to the curb. Santa swore at his back, but Charles didn't slow. He sprinted to his LeBaron and tossed the money sack on the passenger's seat. The Chrysler sputtered to life, and he threw it in gear. Tires squealed as he raced into the street without looking. Horns blared around him.

"I'm not going to make it. I'm not going to make it," he repeated, tears and sweat mixing on his face.

He wove in and out of traffic, ignoring stop signs, traffic lights, the other drivers' curses. The LeBaron skidded onto War Memorial Drive as oncoming cars screeched to avoid him. He pressed the accelerator to the floor and roared towards the payphone across from Leonardo's Pizzeria, leaving a thinning blue cloud in his wake.

The phone was already ringing when the LeBaron slid to a halt in front of it, spraying pebbles like buckshot. He left the driver's side door open and the engine running as he lunged for the payphone.

"Hello!" he yelled into the receiver.

"You're cutting it close, Charles," the voice said. "I almost hung up."

"I got here as fast I could. I got the money."

"I know you do, Charles. I'm watching you."

He looked all around, scanning the pizzeria's roof and inside parked cars. He saw no one out of the ordinary. *Was he really watching me?* he wondered. *Or is he playing?*

"Pay attention, Charles," the voice said. "Get back on War Memorial. Drive west to Knoxville Avenue. Turn south. There's a phone booth on the corner of Knoxville and Nebraska. There's a Shell station right across the street. You have seven minutes."

"Let me talk to Annette!"

"Oh, Charles. You know the rules."

The phone clicked in his ear. He screamed in frustration and beat the phone with the receiver before dropping it, leaving it dangling. He ran to his car.

The LeBaron's engine knocked like something had worked free inside the housing. He gunned the car back onto Memorial Drive, ignoring both the noise and the red engine light that flickered. He knifed the car in and out of traffic, never bothering with a turn signal. For an instant, he worried a police car might spot him and chase him with the siren blaring and lights flashing. And then what? He knew he wouldn't stop for them. They'd have to run his car off the road or tackle him when he ran for the next payphone. Nothing was going to prevent him from answering the kidnapper's call. But if they did, if they boxed in his car with cruisers and trained their guns on him while he was inside the phone booth, what would happen to Annette? He slowed the LeBaron. The traffic light glowed amber when he turned south on Knoxville Avenue.

The payphone was across the street from the Shell station, as the voice had said it would be. It was one of the new, open ones, built high enough so a driver could reach it from behind the wheel and would never have to leave his car to make a call. Charles squealed to a stop and rolled down his window, the air smelling of exhaust and smoldering rubber. He answered the phone as soon as it rang.

"Much better, Charles. Much better, indeed," the voice said. "You really picked up the pace that time."

"Let me talk to my wife!" Charles yelled, more angry than panicked. The amused tone of the kidnapper's voice infuriated him. "This isn't a game, damn it! Let me talk to her!"

"She's so pretty, Charles. So much prettier in person than in the photos I took last week. But, then again, I'm not much of a photographer, especially from that distance."

"Let me talk to her, goddammit!"

"Soon, Charles, soon. You're almost done. Look straight through the windshield. Do you see Wendy's up the block? Wendy's Old Fashioned Hamburgers? The burgers are square, did you know that? Isn't that odd? They taste the same as round patties, but they're shaped like squares. I'm not sure how I feel about that."

"I see the Wendy's, damn you. Two blocks up on the right."

"Excellent. Pull into the Wendy's parking lot and drive around back. There's an enclosed stockade area there. Open the gate. It won't be locked. Inside the fence are two dumpsters—a blue one and a green one. Place the money behind the green one, Charles. Not the blue. The green. Think of the color of dollar bills to help you remember."

"And then what? What do I do then?"

"Then you drive straight home, of course. Do not stop to call the police. Annette will be waiting for you, unharmed. Once you untie her, you can call anyone you want. Oh, and Charles?"

"Yes?"

"It been a pleasure banking with you."

The line filled with static.

He hung up the payphone and pressed the accelerator to the floor, forgetting the car was in park. The tires spun and smoked. He dropped the gear into drive and the LeBaron shot ahead, the engine giving the last bit of life it held. The steering wheel shook, and he momentarily thought of damaged wheel bearings and broken tie rods before speeding towards Wendy's.

There were few cars in the parking lot at this morning hour, and none of them looked suspicious. But would a kidnapper's car look different than others? He drove to the back of the restaurant. There, as promised, stood the stockade tucked in the corner. He parked close and scrambled out of the LeBaron. He glanced around, but the rear lot was deserted. The gate was unlocked and swung without noise or effort. He wondered if the man on the phone had greased the hinges. He placed the money behind the green dumpster, closed the gate, and jumped into his car without looking around again. He was no longer worried or even curious about kidnappers or police or eyewitnesses. His sole thought was of Annette.

The LeBaron smoked and vibrated and backfired as he drove through the streets towards his house, taking every shortcut he could think of. He chanted "Please God Please God Please God," but never specified what he wanted from God. That Annette would be alive? Unharmed? That this never happened?

All of it.

He thought of all the vacations they had planned but had never taken—France, Italy, a train trip across Canada—and the hobbies she had wanted them to take up together: bridge, tennis, ballroom dancing, the ones he never had time for. He felt weighed down by all those things he hadn't given her and all the promises he hadn't kept.

Please God Please God Please God.

He thought of their girls and couldn't imagine how he could find the words to tell them that their mother has been hurt or, unimaginably, taken from them forever. How could he tell them about the man on the phone or keep them from reading about their mother in the paper or seeing her story on TV? How would he help them through the tears, the nightmares, the sadness? How could he raise them alone?

Please God Please God Please God.

Charles banked around the corner of his street; a hubcap rolled loose as he ignored the speed limit sign. He barreled into his driveway, cutting the wheel too sharply, and parked with tires on the lawn. The LeBaron sputtered and stalled before he had a chance to cut the engine. He flung open the door and smelled leaking coolant and heard the hiss from a ruptured hose, but these details all registered somewhere in the back of his mind. He still could only think of Annette.

Please God Please God Please God.

When he burst into the house, the front door swung open and smacked the wall, the knob leaving an indentation in the plaster. The screen door slammed behind him, and he screamed Annette's name. She gave a startled cry from the living room and shut off the vacuum cleaner.

"Charles? What is it?" she said, her own voice laced with fear and worry as he rushed into the living room. She froze when she saw him. "My God, what's wrong?"

He caught his reflection in the mirror above the fireplace: pale face, hair disheveled, a wild, terrified look in his eye. He, too, stopped when he saw her. Annette's hair was brushed into place; she was wearing lipstick and eyeliner, dressed to go out in maroon slacks and a soft white sweater that accentuated her bust.

"What's happened?" she asked, her voice cracking with worry. "Were you in an accident?"

He ran to her and took her in his arms and pulled her close. He buried his face in her hair and breathed in hairspray and shampoo. She smelled clean and good and he began to sob.

"Charles, what is it? What's going on? You're scaring me."

He held her at arm's length and inspected her, checking for damage. His eyes scanned from hair to shoes and up again. "You're not hurt?"

"Of course not. Why would I be hurt?"

He looked around the house. Everything was as he had left it that morning. Each chair stood in its place. The pillows on the couch had been fluffed. There was no overturned furniture, or broken windows, or any sign of an intruder. Everything was as it was supposed to be.

"No one broke in? You weren't held hostage?"

"What are you talking about? I was vacuuming and then I'm going Christmas shopping with your sister."

His heart's manic beating did not slow; his breathing did not return to normal. The pulsing in his temples continued to throb. The fear that had choked him since the man's first phone call dissipated and was replaced with the growing and nauseating realization that he had been played.

*****

He sat on the edge of the couch, bent forward, and kneaded through his hair until it stood at wild angles. Annette was perched on the couch's arm next to him, sitting as close as she could get without sliding on his lap. Her hand alternated between massaging the back of his neck and his shoulder. He never wanted her to stop. Through the living room window, he could see police cars and television vans parked in his driveway and in front of his house; neighbors had gathered on the sidewalk, watching all the activity and occasionally pointing. Some raised cameras and snapped photos.

He rephrased what the detective sitting across from him had said. "Someone spliced the phone line?"

The detective nodded, his small notebook open and balanced on his thigh. "From the outside. They installed some type of connector and intercepted your call from the bank. The caller was never inside your house, Mr. Maibach."

"I was never in danger, Charles," Annette said, rubbing the back of his head, her nails tingling his scalp.

"Where was he?" he asked. "He said he was watching me."

"He could have been on the other side of the country for all we know."

"But you can trace the call, right?" Annette asked. "The police can do that type of thing, like on television and in the movies?"

"The phone company's working on it, but they're not optimistic. He had the call relayed all over the country."

"So, he's going to get away with it?" Charles asked. "All that money—I don't even know how much—gone?"

"We have officers canvassing the area, talking to neighbors to see if they saw anyone suspicious—a stranger on the street or a repairman working on the side of your house. We may turn up something."

He could hear the doubt in the detective's voice. He leaned back, pressing his head tighter against Annette's touch. "He got away with it."

"Maybe not. Can you think of anything about the caller's voice? Something distinctive, like an accent or a tic? A word or phrase that he repeated? That might help."

He thought before answering, replaying the conversations in his mind the best he could. "The calls were so short, so intense. It was all happening so fast."

"Anything at all," the detective said, his pencil—the kind used to record golf scores—poised above his small pad. "Maybe describe his voice or characterize it, if you can."

Annette's hand slid to the base of his neck and Charles closed his eyes. "He sounded calm, professional. Always in control. He never raised his voice."

The detective scribbled in his notebook.

"He sounded smart. Not like a thug. He didn't swear or talk poorly."

The small pencil made scratching sounds against the paper.

He opened his eyes and looked at the detective. A spasm of tension rippled through him and Annette's hand dropped to his shoulder. "There was something about the way he talked, though. Something behind the words…"

The detective stopped writing. "Like an accent he was covering up? A dialect, maybe?"

"No, it was more of a tone, an inflection. It sounded like he was having fun, that he was enjoying himself. He made little jokes. It sounded like..."

"Yes?" the detective prompted. "What did it sound like?"

His face collapsed as he searched for the right description. "It sounded like..."

"Take your time, sweetheart," Annette said, her voice gentle in his ear.

"It sounded like he was playing a game."

The detective stared at him for a moment before writing in his notebook.

"What kind of man does that?" Charles asked. "What kind of man robs a bank without ever setting foot inside?"

The detective shook his head. "I don't know, Mr. Maibach. We're going to try to find out," he said as two FBI agents entered the living room.

Charles saw the agents, and his body sagged. He knew he'd have to retell the story for them, answer the same questions, relive every terrifying moment and conversation he had with a man who could rob a bank without setting foot inside. The rehashing would conjure the horror he'd felt of almost losing Annette, and he never wanted to feel that way again. He leaned into her and she drew him close. Her lips pressed into his hair and she held him, slowly rocking him in her arms.

ROOK

*****

Lolly read about Charles Maibach and the bank robbery in the *Miami Herald*. The AP had picked up the story, and the article had run nationally. She read the account twice, processing the printed words as fast as she could the first time, and then she read more slowly during the second pass, being careful not to miss a single sentence or meaning. Since the annulment, she had received cards twice a year from Al: one at Christmas and another on her birthday. They were mailed first from Leavenworth, then from the Marion Correctional Facility in Illinois, and finally from Los Angeles where he'd lived since being paroled in 1976. He never included a note or news of what was going on in his life; he would just sign each card:

Always Yours,
Al

He had never remarried.

Alison, finishing her senior year in college and planning on law school in the fall, updated her mother on his accomplishments, bringing her copies of the magazines— *Alfred Hitchcock, Mike Shayne's Mystery Magazine, Ellery Queen*—that contained Al's latest short stories, or buying his most recent young adult novel published by Scholastic Books. She would feign indifference when Alison dropped them off and would wait until she was alone to read them. Alison would circle in red the *TV Guide* listing of the *Kojak* or *Baretta* episode that Al had written, and Lolly never missed a show. He wrote of bank robberies, escaped prisoners, and tortured ex-cons who tried hard to walk the straight line but always failed. She wished he would write a love story like the ones they had seen at the North Park Theater on Hertel Avenue when they were young and dating, holding hands in the dark and kissing during previews, but he never did. Instead he wrote about bank jobs and heists and never about the girl.

When Al won an award from *The Mystery Writers of America*, she read the article that Alison had given her and studied his picture. He was bald now and stockier, bulked by fourteen years of lifting prison weights. His beard was a mix of gray and black, and he kept it neat and close-trimmed. In his tuxedo, he looked like a magician who had made the award appear by flourishing a handkerchief. He stared unsmiling at the camera, but an eyebrow was arched and Lolly thought he looked amused, perhaps sharing a silent joke that only she would understand.

After she read the Peoria article, she rose from her chair, letting the newspaper fall to the living room carpet. She opened the sliding glass doors, stepped onto her balcony and looked out over the water; a boat's running lights could be seen bobbing in the distance, and the motor's hum—faint but audible—reached her. She hugged herself despite the warm Florida night and rubbed her arms. She couldn't explain it, but she knew, as sure as she knew a boat was passing her house, that the thirty-three thousand dollars stolen in Peoria, Illinois would never be recovered, and no arrest would ever be made. The job must have taken months, maybe years to plan, with every detail worked out and every contingency imagined, until there was no other outcome possible except for perfection. Something told her that the Peoria robbery was the swan's song, the final chess move, the last thumbed nose at the FBI, and she smiled.

About the Author

Stephen G. Eoannou holds an MFA from Queens University of Charlotte and an MA from Miami University. His short story collection, *Muscle Cars*, was published by the Santa Fe Writers Project. He has been awarded an Honor Certificate from The Society of Children's Book Writers and Illustrators, and won the Best Short Screenplay Award at the 36th Starz Denver Film Festival. He lives and writes in his hometown of Buffalo, New York, the setting and inspiration for much of his work. *Rook* is his first novel.

About the Press

Unsolicited Press was founded in 2012 and is based in Portland, Oregon. The press produces stellar fiction, nonfiction, and poetry from award-winning writers. Authors include John W. Bateman, T.K. Lee, Rosalia Scalia, and Brook Bhagat.

Find the press on Twitter and Instagram: @unsolicitedp

Learn more at www.unsolicitedpress.com.

CPSIA information can be obtained
at www.ICGtesting.com
Printed in the USA
LVHW042019220523
747702LV00002B/317

9 781956 692044